A CANDLE *for* CHRISTMAS
& *Other Stories*

Reginald Hill, who died in 2012, was a native of Cumbria and former resident of Yorkshire, the setting for his novels featuring Detective Superintendent Dalziel and Detective Chief Inspector Pascoe. Their appearances won him numerous awards including a CWA Gold Dagger, the Diamond Dagger for Lifetime Achievement and the Theakstons Old Peculier Outstanding Contribution to Crime Fiction Award. The Dalziel and Pascoe novels were also adapted into a hugely popular BBC TV series.

T0337776

Also by Reginald Hill

Reginald Hill

A CANDLE *for* CHRISTMAS

& Other Stories

FOREWORD BY MICK HERRON

HEMLOCK
PRESS

Hemlock Press,
An imprint of HarperCollins*Publishers*
1 London Bridge Street,
London SE1 9GF

www.harpercollins.co.uk

HarperCollins*Publishers*
Macken House, 39/40 Mayor Street Upper,
Dublin 1, D01 C9W8, Ireland

This paperback edition 2024

1

Published by HarperCollins*Publishers* Ltd 2023

A catalogue copy of this book is available from the British Library.

ISBN: 9780008430108 (PB)

Typeset in Sabon by Palimpsest Book Production Limited, Falkirk, Stirlingshire

Printed and bound in the UK using 100% renewable electricity at CPI Group (UK) Ltd

Contents

Foreword

First, let's run the numbers. Reginald Hill was the author of twenty-four novels in the Dalziel and Pascoe series, five Luton-based novels featuring former lathe operator turned private eye Joe Sixsmith, and twenty-one other novels of an extraordinarily high standard, their subjects ranging from British complicity in the murderous regime of Idi Amin to the hidden, sometimes heroic motives of French civilians accused of collaboration with the Nazis during the Second World War; from Masonic misdeeds involving the royal protection service to the trauma of discovering that one's spouse is a spy and a traitor. All this, and four collections of short stories. Such an abundant output that the writer adopted three pseudonyms to contain it – clearly, if Reginald Hill hadn't existed, we'd have had to invent him.

Such a task, however, would have required the collaboration of any number of talents, drawing on knowledge of a wide range of material whose sources recognized no boundaries, least of all those separating 'literature' from mere genre. As Hill wrote in 1986: 'I still recall with delight as a teenager making the earth-shaking discovery that many of the great "serious novelists", classical and modern, were as entertaining and interesting as the crime writers I already loved. But it took another decade of maturation to reverse the equation and understand that many of the crime writers I had decided to grow out of were still as interesting and entertaining as the "serious novelists" I now revered.'

It's clear, then, that Hill found sustenance and inspiration in both classical and popular fiction, and he delighted in constructing his fictions on foundations laid down by writers he admired. The partly epistolary *A Cure for All Diseases* was a continuation, of sorts, of Jane Austen's unfinished novel *Sanditon*, and when Hill co-opted Dorothy L. Sayers as a guiding light in *Under World*, it wasn't her detective stories he turned to but her translation of Dante's *Inferno*. That most bewilderingly prolific of creative artists, Anon., is also celebrated: *Bones and Silence* involves a cycle of that author's Mystery Plays in which Andy Dalziel gets to play God in a more literal manner than usual. At the same time, Hill's thematic preoccupations refused to fit genre tramlines. *On Beulah Height*, which many regard as his masterpiece, weaves a grim fairy tale entitled 'Nina and the Nix' into its essentially tragic plot; *Arms and the Women* includes Ellie Pascoe's retelling of the *Iliad* (or 'the *Elliad*' as it's dubbed), with Dalziel in the Odysseus role; while *The Wood Beyond* was essentially a novel about the First World War, but set in the 1990s in mid-Yorkshire.

There seemed, in fact, little Hill couldn't turn his playful pen to, or adapt into detective fiction. And without ever deliberately misinforming his readers, he took great delight in wrong-footing them, writing at least one novel in which he revealed the identity of the murderer in his opening words, though it would be an astute reader who picked up on this; at least one absorbing mystery novel in which no actual crime is committed; at least one in which the murderer gets away with it; and at least one in which his detectives fail to notice, let alone solve, a murder committed on their patch. At the same time, his novels provide a commentary on social change in Britain over the last quarter of the twentieth century and a little beyond, including, in *Under World*, what remains one of the finest novels yet penned about the 1980s miners' strike.

But imaginative as they are, these books would be much diminished if all they amounted to was a series of puzzles. It is, as every Hill reader knows, the characters who count, and his characters are bold and bright. At first glance, his leading pair are polar opposites. If Andy Dalziel's un-PC mindset provides plenty of belly laughs and some uncomfortable tittering to accompany his blunt-force brilliance, Peter Pascoe's more sensitive approach allows him to exercise compassion as well as deductive reasoning. Indeed, it's difficult to avoid the notion that, at least in his earliest incarnation, the university-educated, left-leaning, bleeding-heart-liberal Pascoe was intended as a mouthpiece for the author's own opinions, a notion that gathers strength when we consider his name. Hill never chose these at random, and once we reduce Pascoe to his initials, and set them alongside his author's own name, the idea that Pascoe is speaking on behalf of his creator becomes even more attractive:

Reginald Hill   p.p.   Peter Pascoe

But the older Pascoe is not as soft as he first appeared. His years on the job carve edges on to him instead of smoothing them off, his liberalism acquires a pragmatic sheen, and in one of the later novels he shows himself not above conniving at the simplification of a crime scene to ensure that justice is done. It's part of Hill's genius that Pascoe never realizes that in doing so he is in fact allowing a murderer to evade capture. Equally, it would be a mistake to write Dalziel off as a caricature: underneath that rough exterior lies a mind capable of human understanding and a heart capable of loyalty, even if his wallet rarely extends as far as the bar.

It was not only in Hill's novels that this couple flourished. In 1990 he published *One Small Step*, a *jeu d'esprit* celebrating his twentieth year as a published author. This novella, which later appeared in *Asking for the Moon*, imagined a Dalziel and Pascoe projected twenty years into the future, investigating a murder committed on the moon, a larky tale whose matching partner in the same volume, *The Last National Serviceman*, relates the pair's very first meeting. It was thus with the short form that Hill bookended the careers of his most beloved creations, and it is in short stories that we get to meet them again, long after most of us thought their curtain had been brought down for the final time. For here is another act, a further collection to augment last year's volume, *Dalziel and Pascoe Hunt the Christmas Killer*. Taken together, these include a generous handful of stories featuring his cop duo, a pairing that expanded into something of a rep company over the years, with the formidable Edgar Wield taking his place centre stage, and the reliable Shirley Novello – inevitably 'Ivor' to her boss – increasingly present in the wings.

When these characters come together, the reader knows there are riches in store. Indeed, as Val McDermid noted in her affectionate and insightful foreword to the previous collection, another writer might have been tempted to expand some of the stories into novels, as rich in possibility as they are. That's especially true here, I think, of 'A Candle for Christmas', which presents a more complex and satisfying puzzle than many of us manage in a full-length work, while at the same time giving generous glimpses into the home life of Peter and Ellie Pascoe and their rambunctious young daughter Rosie. Rosie – it's hard not to imagine – would have grown into an equally rambunctious adult had Hill lived to make her grow; as it is, her relationship with 'Uncle Andy' finds greater expression here than in the longer works, and the ways in which these two understand – and occasionally misread – each other adds yet another layer to those already enfolding Andrew Dalziel.

This complexity was no accident. Hill, as his regular readers know, wore his humanity on his sleeve, and nowhere is this more apparent than in his understanding of the ambiguities of character, whether that character leans towards the benign or the malicious. Those same regulars, as Hill was fond of pointing out, are an uncommonly literate cohort, happy to pick up on the subtle shading he applied to his dramatis personae, but readers unversed in nuance – a group seemingly on the increase – might well be puzzled by Dalziel, who is always cheerfully rude to those who deserve it, and frequently to those who don't; who has monstrous appetites unalloyed by any sense of shame; and whose pursuit of justice is rarely trammelled by the demands of his role as police officer. Hill himself, I think, would have welcomed such puzzlement, and seen in it the opportunity to educate as well as entertain. After all, he rarely let occasions for improvement slip by, always seeming, to borrow from Val McDermid again, 'to include at least one word in every novel that drove [the reader] to the dictionary'. In this collection, he merrily applies the epithet 'infundibular' to Dalziel's nostrils, which resulted in this reader not only expanding his vocabulary to include 'a funnel-shaped cavity or structure' but also reaffirming an awareness that Hill never reached for an unusual word that didn't perfectly suit his purpose. Showing off didn't come into it; it was, rather, a justifiable reaching for the exotic, the better to paint Andy Dalziel's portrait in ever richer oils. Sheer *joie de vivre*, in other words. Or *joie d'écrire*, perhaps, for which I'm sure Hill would forgive me, even if others won't.

I could write about the Dalziel and Pascoe series for as long as my laptop's battery allows, but there is more ground to cover. The stories collected here range across centuries and landscapes, and show Hill at home wherever he planted himself, always providing local knowledge, always delivering the necessary, killing detail. 'A Shameful Eating', one of several historical tales included, is a seafaring story with a pay-off as economical as it is brutal – though the brutality is left to the imagination: Hill wasn't a graphic writer, and the violent acts his imagination encompassed take place off the printed page. But while he was never a cosy writer in the sense that the term is employed within the crime genre, he was frequently a cosy writer in the way his beloved Jane Austen was, which is to say that he was capable of wreaking devastation without raising his voice. Another example of this can be found in 'The Italian Sherlock Holmes'. This, as the title suggests, is a Conan Doyle pastiche, and one with a genuine surprise in store – which, like other twists with which Hill peppered his work, might be unexpected but is the logical outcome of the facts he's already presented us with. Other stories take in contemporary publishing, Victorian London, and the always unfathomable depths of the human psyche, and scattered throughout are allusions – not for the first time in his work – to the football match played at Christmas 1914 on No Man's Land. This was, it's hard not to feel, one of Hill's touchstones, bearing witness as it did to the human ability to reach out to one another in companionship even in the midst of inhuman slaughter. His crime fiction, wherever it was set, remained rooted in the hearts and minds of people.

When Reginald Hill died in January 2012 I was one of many who felt his passing as a personal loss, for though I was never lucky enough to know him, he had been a companion for decades. It's therefore a delight to be introducing this volume – one last gift from a prodigious talent. With many writers, the appearance of a posthumous collection of stories, let alone two, might indicate the scraping of a barrel; the hasty sweeping together of previously unconsidered trifles. With Hill, nothing could be further from the truth. This collection, like its predecessor, rescues some jewels from oblivion, and adds lustre to a reputation that has continued to grow since his death. I am, as you might have gathered, something of a fan of Reginald Hill, and would actively seek out publications containing his stories. Even so, many of those here had not come to my attention before, and at least two are among his very best – which is to say, they are two of the most satisfying crime stories I've had the pleasure of reading. For the avoidance of spoilers, I won't reveal which they are. The joy of discovering them is now yours.

Mick Herron
Oxford
February 2023

A Candle for Christmas

1.

'December twenty-fourth, nineteen ninety-eight. Ten fifty-seven a.m. Interview of Mrs Angela Fraser. Present, Ms Juliet Dacre, solicitor; Detective Superintendent Andrew Dalziel; Woman Police Constable Deirdre Collingdale; and myself, Detective Chief Inspector Peter Pascoe.

'Mrs Fraser, I should remind you that you are under caution.'

He was seated directly opposite Mrs Fraser, with Dalziel facing the solicitor. WPC Collingwood was seated behind her colleagues and slightly to one side. Pascoe glanced around at her and gave her a reassuring smile. Poor kid, nineteen years old, eighteen months in the job, recently engaged, and probably looking forward to heading home at the end of her shift to a merry little Christmas with her fiancé and family. Then fate in the irresistible form of Andy Dalziel had volunteered her as token female presence at what promised to be a harrowing interview. No wonder she looked pale and unhappy.

But she was the picture of health compared with Angela Fraser, a small, plumping woman in her early forties, though with thirty years pared off her face by the cosmetic of stress, which had pallored her cheeks and darkened her eyes to a waiflike mask. Her fingers, patched with burn dressings like a flaking mummy, picked restlessly at the small gold crucifix around her neck.

Next to her Juliet Dacre was doodling with a pencil in a leather-bound notebook. She was in her late twenties, with the kind of bright bouffant hair, pneumatic figure, and vacuously pretty face which would have got her the role of dumb blonde in any of the old Hollywood comedies.

Pascoe was not fooled. He and Jools Dacre were long acquainted and he knew all her ways.

Opposite her, Andy Dalziel was scratching the furrow under one of his chins like a JCB excavating a drainage ditch, at the same time studying the contents of a box file with all the intensity of a medieval scholar. Pascoe could see that it contained a meat pie and a copy of the sports section of the local paper.

The silence had stretched long enough now for small and distant sounds to make their presence felt. The low hiss of the tape; the occasional bubble of the radiator; a door banging; a faraway laugh; a gusting wind hitting the one high window and bringing with it faint snatches of 'Once in Royal David's City'; the Sally Army Band playing in the shopping precinct a quarter of a mile away.

How sad the slug-horn's call, deep in the forest glades, thought Pascoe. And sadder still for this woman, bringing with it echoes of normal everyday life where last-minute shoppers scuttled around to lay down essential supplies against the long siege of Christmas.

The emergent noises only increased the tension in the room, like the last shufflings and coughings prefacing the moment when the conductor raises his baton. But Pascoe made no move. It

10

was Tubby the Tuba who signalled the kick-off in this particular ensemble, which since his last promotion did not perform together all that often. Supers and DCIs rarely teamed up for interviews. It took something special to conjure such a coruscation of brass.

Setting fire to a policeman was something special.

A strong blast of wind hit the window with what sounded like sleet in it. The band was into 'Angels from the Realms of Glory' now. He should have been out there shopping with Ellie. When he'd wangled both Christmas Eve and Christmas Day off, it had seemed like a seasonal miracle. But while only God in heaven has power to perform miracles, His agent in Mid-Yorkshire has authority to cancel them.

When the phone had rung, Ellie had glared at him with precognitive fury.

'Tell him to sod off,' she'd said. 'And if he tries to give you orders, tell him to stick them up his bum if he can reach round that far.'

But Dalziel had not been in commanding mood. Incredibly, he'd used the P-word.

'I'd appreciate your support in this one, Pete. *Please*.'

Which in itself would probably have been enough to ensure Pascoe's presence.

But there'd been something else. Ellie was not the only one who got these flashes of foresight. Last night Pascoe had gone to the Plods' Party, Uniformed Branch's seasonal thrash in the Police Social Club. Not really his kind of thing, but it didn't do to look standoffish, especially if you'd got a degree and still opened doors for ladies. So he'd put in a token appearance. Well, maybe a bit more than *token*, as every time he made a move for the exit, Fat Andy, like a punch-drunk bouncer with a limited grasp of his duties, was standing there smiling to prevent him from leaving.

Finally he'd called a taxi and used its imminent arrival as his escape clause. The Fat Man had followed him outside. As they stood there in the chill night air, a man of about forty with a cigarette dangling from his lips opened the door behind them. He was muscularly lean with black unruly hair and the kind of long craggy features Pascoe associated with sexily taciturn sheep drovers in Australian movies. He recognised him as Sergeant Joe Fraser, officer in charge of the Ridley substation about twenty miles away. Pascoe didn't know him all that well, but the Fat Man greeted him like an old friend.

'Smokey, what fettle? Don't see much of you since you got exiled out among the yokels.'

'Can still see a hell of a lot of you, Andy. You're looking well, or the whisky's looking well in you.'

'Fat' jokes. A real old friend.

Dalziel said, 'You're not shogging off too, are you, Smokey? By God, what's happening to the world? I can remember do's when you and me were the only ones left standing.'

'Aye, likely 'cos I were holding you up,' said the saturnine Fraser. 'But none of us have got any younger.'

'Hold on,' said Dalziel, stepping close and sniffing. 'Here, you've been drinking. You're not fit to drive. You'd best come back in and have another!'

Somehow when the Fat Man said things like this, they sounded almost rational.

Fraser shook his head, flicked his cigarette to the pavement and ground it out.

'Think I'll just walk a bit to clear me head, then I'll get a taxi. Have yourself a merry little Christmas, Andy.'

The man started to walk away.

Dalziel called after him, 'Not getting religion, are you, Joe? They say it's like malaria – once you've had it, you never get shut of it.'

Fraser paused and turned. Muzzily silhouetted against the light filtering out of one of the club windows, he presented a dark, menacing figure. He had, Pascoe now recalled, a bit of a reputation as a hard man: hard drinking, hard smoking, hard playing, and hard-headed in his attitude to crime and criminals. In fact, very much Andy Dalziel's kind of cop.

Fraser pulled another cigarette out of a battered gunmetal case and lit it with an old-fashioned petrol lighter made out of a cartridge case. The wavering flame ran light across his face like sunbreaks across an alien landscape. To Pascoe, his spiky hair seemed touched with a phosphorescent glow and his skin with a corpse's pallor.

'Careful what you say, Andy. Never know who's listening at this time of year. But don't worry, I'll light you a candle for Christmas.'

Then he snapped the lighter shut, extinguishing (or so it seemed to Pascoe) himself with the flame, and in that moment he knew with a certainty beyond reason that he would never see Sergeant Fraser in this life again.

Then Dalziel called rather plaintively, 'Need to make it a big one, Joe,' and the moment was past.

'Known each other a long time, have you, sir?' he asked.

'Aye. Me and Smokey Joe go way back. Golden days, lad, golden days.'

He spoke with such affection Pascoe was surprised by a pang of what he hoped wasn't jealousy. As he rode away in his taxi, it occurred to him that he could have invited Fraser to share it. The road out to Ridley passed through his suburb. He peered out of the window but couldn't spot the man. He felt rather relieved. It would have been too much like inviting a corpse to climb into its own hearse.

The macabre fancy had made him smile, a smile he'd recalled this morning when he got Dalziel's phone call.

'Superintendent. *Superintendent!* Don't you think it's time we made a start?'

Pascoe was jerked back to here and now by Jools Dacre's voice, edged with irritation.

Dalziel looked up, blinked, yawned, then said, 'Aye, what's the hold-up, Chief Inspector? Let's get on with it.'

Pascoe said, 'Of course. Mrs Fraser, for the record, would you confirm that you are Mrs Angela Fraser of twenty-four Latimer Grove, Ridley, Mid-Yorkshire?'

'Yes.'

Her voice was low and smoke-roughened, but the tape needle confirmed it was being picked up.

He went on, 'Mrs Fraser, a woman telephoned the emergency services at six eleven a.m. this morning to report a fire at twenty-four Latimer Grove. Can you confirm it was you?'

'Yes.'

'The call was recorded. Ms Dacre, you've had a chance to look at the transcript?'

Jools Dacre said, 'Yes, though I should like to hear the tape itself. Often there are considerations of stress and intonation which the written word cannot indicate.'

She accompanied the words with an apologetic smile. Pascoe's answering smile was mouth-deep. Letting Dacre's sweetness-and-light manner relax you was like binning your brolly just because you saw a bit of blue sky on an April morning.

He resumed, 'On the tape you say, "Please come quickly. There's been a dreadful accident. I think my husband's dead. It's all my fault." Do you remember this?'

'Yes.'

'The fire brigade arrived at six thirty-six a.m. and an ambulance shortly afterwards. You were given first-aid treatment but refused to leave the scene until the fire officers had recovered your husband's body. When he was brought out, you are reported by fire officers and paramedics as saying, "Is he dead? Oh my God. It's my fault. I killed him."'

Jools Dacre was at it with the apologetic smile again.

'Forgive me, Mr Pascoe, but Mrs Fraser is making no effort to deny her sense of responsibility for the tragic death of her husband. In view of which, do we need to plough through all this painful detail? Is it really germane?'

Dalziel's head came up from the file.

'Germaine?' he said. 'I thought her name were Angela.'

Pascoe winced and said, 'I think Ms Dacre means, germane to our inquiries.'

'Oh. *That* germane,' said Dalziel. And resumed his reading.

Pascoe had no objection to the Fat Man winding up lawyers, but he felt that this heavy-footed mockery was not only bad taste but bad technique.

No two ways about it, it was a mistake for Dalziel to be here. Last night Pascoe'd got a whiff of how close Dalziel and Fraser were, and when he'd arrived at the station that morning, he'd found a grieving Fat Man readier to lead a lynch mob than an investigation.

'Where's Mrs Fraser now?' Pascoe had asked.

'Cow's in hospital. Too ill to talk except to her brief. Know who it is? Bloody Dacre!'

'Jools Dacre? In that case, sir, we'd better go into this very softly, sir.'

'Softly?' Dalziel's face was working like a cauldron of porridge. 'After that murdering bitch put a torch to her man in his bed and burnt him to death?'

'We don't know what happened, sir. Not till we talk to Mrs Fraser.'

'We know what she said on the emergency tape and we know

her brief's that bitch from VIM, so I reckon I could write you a pretty fair script. *Domestic violence. Provocation.* Bitch!'

VIM stood for Violence in Marriage, a high-profile Yorkshire-based support group. Pascoe knew a lot about it. His wife was a founder member. And Juliet Dacre was its legal adviser.

Pascoe said, 'Have we got anything from the fire department yet?'

'No. The bedroom was so badly damaged, they're afraid the whole bungalow roof might collapse in, so they're messing around making it safe. But I'll bet your pension on what they'll find.'

'You may be right, sir,' said Pascoe gently. 'Look, I can see how much Sergeant Fraser meant to you, but I really think you should step away from this one. You know how easy it is to spook the CPS in cases like this.'

The argument seemed to work. Dalziel relaxed and said gloomily, 'Aye, bunch of girls' blouses! Why do you think I got you in to take over? With Pious Peter in the pulpit, no one's going to query the hymn sheet. Get to it, lad.'

So Pascoe had got to it. Inquiries at the hospital as to when Mrs Fraser would be fit to be interviewed had brought Jools Dacre to the phone.

'Peter, you're in charge? That's great. Listen, Angela's so keen to get this dreadful business sorted, she insists on discharging herself and coming down to the station to make a statement. We should be there in an hour. I'm sure you'll agree that in the circs we ought to keep it short and sweet. Is that all right?'

Pascoe, who knew that few people managed to insist on doing anything Jools Dacre didn't want them to do, said carefully, 'You are, of course, aware that in the light of Mrs Fraser's admissions, she will be undergoing a formal interview as a criminal suspect.'

'Yes, I know we've got to go through the formalities. Isn't it a bind? But best for all parties in the long run, of course. Ciao!'

When he'd told Dalziel, the Fat Man had rubbed his hands.

'Grand! Sticking her head into the lion's mouth, is she? Well, let's see if we can't bite it right off.'

'We? I'll be conducting the interview, sir,' said Pascoe coldly.

'Of course you will, lad. That's why you're here, isn't it? To make sure it's all done by the book. I'll just sit so quiet you'll think I've snuffed it.'

And I'm to be Queen of the May, Mother, thought Pascoe.

For the first time in his life he wished he was in a crowded department store, laden with bags, debating with Ellie whether they should get Rosie the Rollerblades she'd been dropping large hints about for weeks.

He said, 'We will, of course, show Mrs Fraser every consideration, but we have to get to the facts.'

Jools Dacre said, 'So long as we don't lose sight of the fact that she is here of her own volition, against medical advice, and still suffering from the shock of Sergeant Fraser's death and the injuries she sustained in her efforts to rescue him.'

There was a snort from the Fat Man which a deaf man in a storm might have mistaken for a repressed sneeze.

Pascoe said, 'Of course. Meanwhile, if you could give us your account of what actually happened, Mrs Fraser . . .'

Angela Fraser took a deep breath. One hand went to her throat, perhaps to touch the crucifix, perhaps in anticipation of pain. She took a long drink of water, then started speaking in a low, monotonous voice.

'Joe said he had to go into headquarters yesterday afternoon and he'd probably look in at the club later on as it was the Christmas party. I knew what that meant . . .'

'What, precisely?' urged Pascoe when she fell silent.

'It meant he'd be back heaven knows when with a bellyful of booze,' said the woman wearily. 'I said I hoped he'd not be driving, and he said he'd get a lift in and a taxi back. It was about two o'clock when he got home. I'd been watching the telly and must have fallen asleep. I always sit up when Joe's out late . . .'

'Like any concerned little wife, eh?' muttered Dalziel from the depths of his file.

'No!' lashed Angela Fraser with a sudden startling intensity. 'Like someone who's learned from long and hard experience not to be caught lying helpless when Joe Fraser comes home full of drink!'

Dalziel yawned so noisily it set the tape needle flickering.

Pascoe said quickly, 'Could you explain that, please?'

She glanced at her solicitor, who nodded encouragingly.

'He knocked me around. He didn't have to be drunk to do it, but when he was drunk, he didn't seem to be able to help it.'

'And was this how he behaved when he got home?' said Pascoe.

'Not to start with. When he came in, he was fairly quiet, subdued almost, like he'd got something on his mind. I thought it might be going to be all right and I made him some coffee, but when I gave it to him, he yelled, "You know I like it black, you stupid cow," and sent the cup flying across the room. I said, "Please, Joe, it's the best china," and he yelled it was him that paid for it and he could do what he liked with what was his. And then he started smashing things up.'

She paused. After a few seconds Pascoe said gently, 'And what did you do then, Mrs Fraser?'

'I sat quiet till he'd finished. Then I went to the kitchen to get a brush and pan to clear the mess. When I came back in he'd got a litre of Scotch out of the sideboard and he was drinking it straight out of the bottle.'

This was too much for Dalziel.

He said incredulously, 'Your husband's drunk and dangerous

and smashing up your home, and all you do is start clearing up the mess?'

Dacre said, 'Is that a question, Mr Dalziel?'

'No,' he said. 'It's a bloody mystery.'

Dacre smiled, glanced at the recording machine, and made a note. She's lapping this up, thought Pascoe. I've got to get the fat sod out of here. He said, 'What happened then?'

'He told me to stop the racket, so I put the pan down and sat opposite him. I hoped he would fall asleep but suddenly he said, "Come here." And I knew it was going to start.'

'What?'

'The pain. He grabbed my arm and forced it up my back till I nearly fainted. Then he started beating me.'

She was back to her level monotonous tone.

Dalziel said, 'Hang about. You say he's done this before?'

'Many times. Over many years. For as long as I can remember.'

'So you're married to a sadistic bastard who's been giving you hell for years and you just put up with it? Why not walk out? Why not make a complaint? Why not do *anything*?'

Jools Dacre said sharply, 'Please don't hector my client, Superintendent.'

'Hector? He's not involved, is he?'

Suddenly Angela Fraser broke out passionately, 'I didn't walk out because I'd nowhere to go, and I didn't make a complaint because I'd only the police to complain to, and he was always sorry after he'd done it and he always said it wouldn't happen again, and I always wanted to believe he meant it and I think he really did, I think he really loved me and he couldn't help it . . .'

She looked on the point of breaking into tears but when the sobbing started it came from the wrong direction.

Pascoe turned to see WPC Collingwood's face rubbery with emotion.

Mrs Fraser said, 'Oh, Deirdre, I'm sorry, love . . . I don't know why they had to have you in here . . .'

Tears streaming down her face, the young constable stood up and rushed out of the room.

Pascoe, amazed, said, 'Deirdre? You know PC Collingwood?'

'Oh yes. When she was attached to the substation as a probationer, she came round to the house a lot . . . she was like a daughter to us . . . we never had children . . . maybe if we had . . .'

And now she too was out of control. She collapsed across the table, her whole body racked with sobs.

Jools Dacre put her arms around her and cried angrily, 'What the hell's going on here?'

Dalziel said, 'Think it might be a good time to suspend the interview, lad.'

Ten minutes later, Mrs Fraser was on her way back to hospital with Dacre spitting Parthian threats of official complaint. Angrily, Pascoe went looking for the Fat Man and found him in his room feeding coffee and presumably comfort to Deirdre Collingwood. When he saw Pascoe, he made a sternly reproving face like a *Carry On* matron and came to the door.

'Show a bit of tact, lad. The girl's upset,' he whispered.

'I can believe it,' hissed Pascoe. 'You knew she was a friend of the family, didn't you? And you thought it would be clever to use her to put extra pressure on Mrs Fraser. Well, all you've done is compromise the whole investigation, that and your stupid interruptions.'

'Oh aye? And what am I interrupting? I've been at livelier prayer meetings. That bitch is laughing at you, lad. Laughing!'

'If you know something about Mrs Fraser I don't, shouldn't you be telling me, sir?'

'I know she messed Joe's head up. Sex every four years – she thought that's what leap year meant. No divorce 'cos she's a good Catholic. And if he tried to leave her, she'd top herself the day he went!'

'Really? In case you haven't noticed, it's Sergeant Fraser who's dead,' said Pascoe.

For a second he thought Dalziel was going to hit him.

Then the Fat Man said wearily, 'I think you'd best take the rest of the day off, lad, and try to get your head round where your loyalties lie. I'll let you know when you'll be needed again.'

And he closed the door in Pascoe's face.

Early that evening, Pascoe and Ellie were setting out presents under their Christmas tree. On the sofa, their daughter Rosie lay asleep, her resolution to stay awake all Christmas eroded by sheer fatigue.

'You decided against the Rollerblades then?' murmured Pascoe neutrally.

'Yes. I really don't think they're safe,' said Ellie defensively. 'I took a vote and as you weren't there, I won. Peter, he won't muck up Christmas Day as well, will he?'

'God knows. Mrs Fraser certainly looked like she'd be better off in a hospital bed.'

'That poor woman. I almost wish I was religious, then I could say a prayer for her.'

Pascoe smiled at her fondly. Sometimes her logic reminded him of Fat Andy's.

'I'll see she gets a fair crack. No harm in lighting a candle for her, though.'

'You reckon?'

Ellie struck a match and set its flame to the candles under a set of angel chimes. The circling angels gathered speed and sent up their gentle chiming. On the sofa, Rosie rubbed her eyes and said sleepily, 'Why do you light a candle for people?'

'You been earwigging?' said Pascoe. 'To keep them from harm, I think.'

'And does it really work?'

'Why wouldn't it?' He picked her up and swung her high as the star on the tree. Fat Andy and Jools Dacre and the sad tragic Frasers seemed light years away.

The phone rang.

He set his daughter down and picked up the receiver.

It was the Fat Man, gloatingly jolly.

'Pete, lad, over your sulk yet? Good. Listen, great news. I've got the fire report. Definite use of petrol. And there's better still. They found a jerrycan in the kitchen and it's got our Angela's prints all over it. So we've got the bitch! But don't worry. Hospital says they want to keep her in tomorrow so you can enjoy your turkey and stuffing. See you Boxing Day. Merry Christmas.'

Slowly Pascoe replaced the receiver. Alongside it the angel chimes spun faster and faster, filling the air with music. 'Merry Christmas,' he said.

2.

'December twenty-sixth, nineteen ninety-eight. Eleven thirty-five a.m. Interview of Mrs Angela Fraser resumes. Present, Ms Juliet Dacre, solicitor; Detective Sergeant Edgar Wield; WDC Shirley Novello; and myself, Detective Chief Inspector Peter Pascoe.

'Mrs Fraser, you are still under caution. I hope you're feeling better. If at any time you feel in need of a break for refreshment or for medical attention, please do not hesitate to say so.'

He stared Jools Dacre straight in the eye as he spoke. They

both knew he was trying to repair the damage of the last interview, and she nodded as if in approval of his effort, at the same time smiling faintly as if to indicate it was wasted.

At least this time he didn't have the ticking bomb of the Fat Man at his side.

Dalziel had been surprisingly conciliatory, as if the evidence of the fingerprints and fire report had settled him down. It had started the previous afternoon when the doorbell had rung just after the Queen's Speech.

'Probably Prince Charles doing an abdication poll,' said Ellie.

A moment later Pascoe heard her saying, 'Good Lord, it's never you,' and wondered if she'd been right.

Then a most unregal voice said, 'Nay, lass, I've not got me dates mixed. Supper on the twenty-eighth, right? But I just thought I'd drop in as I was passing.'

It had become a tradition that the Fat Man came around for a meal between Christmas and New Year, bringing with him a present for Rosie. 'Three kings more my style than Santa Claus,' he explained.

The little girl, who adored her Uncle Andy, ran to him now and insisted on taking him on a guided tour of her gifts, which had been plentiful enough to soothe her disappointment at the absence of the wished-for Rollerblades.

'Passing? To or from *where*?' whispered Ellie.

Pascoe, who thought he'd caught a whiff of ash, guessed Ridley, but he said nothing. He poured a Highland measure of Highland malt and waited for Dalziel to finish his avuncular duties.

'Cheers,' said the Fat Man. 'Pete, about yesterday, the interview, I just wanted to say I'm sorry. I were out of order.'

'Well, yes, I suppose maybe you were a bit,' said Pascoe, taken aback.

'No doubt about it. Thing is, Joe Fraser meant a lot to me.

Was a time way back when I were up for promotion to DI and something came up that could have got in the way. I'd made a few enemies upstairs who'd have been glad of an excuse to put a block in . . .'

He shook his great head as if finding this incomprehensible.

'Any road, Joe Fraser took it all on him. I got my promotion, Joe spent a year or so longer as a constable than he should have done. I owed him and never got round to paying, so you can see how this hit me.'

He sniffed, either in grief or to get the bouquet of his Scotch, which Pascoe wouldn't have been surprised to see vanish up those infundibular nostrils.

He said, 'I understand, sir. And I know you're as keen as I am to see that justice is done.'

'Aye, we're all on the same side, even your mate Ms Dacre, Ellie.'

Ellie said, 'Andy, if you're going to talk about this poor woman, let's get one thing clear. Anything Peter says to me about a case is confidential, but he's the only one I extend that privilege to, OK? Maybe I should head for the kitchen.'

'Nay, lass, no need for that. I'm not saying owt that's not for public consumption. I know you're a great supporter of VIM, and so am I. And I know how easy it is to be fooled by folk. No one knows what really goes on inside a marriage except them as are in there, slogging it out.'

He accompanied this with a glance at the Pascoes of such classical significance, Christie's would have needed an export licence to sell it to America.

'All right, I beat him up occasionally, but what the hell,' said Ellie. 'So you're willing to accept that your old oppo might have been a wife-basher after all?'

'Owt's possible,' said Dalziel with a sigh. 'But Smokey were my mate. If not wanting to think ill of your mates is a crime, then bang me up and throw away the key.'

The pathos was as rich as Christmas pudding.

'Why did you call him Smokey, Joe?' asked Ellie brightly.

'Thirty-a-day man. Always has been.'

'So, nothing to do with Joe Frazier, the boxer. Wasn't that his nickname?'

'*Smokin*', I think that was. But aye, that could have come into it. Did a bit of boxing, did Joe. Tidy light-middleweight way back.'

'Handy skill if you wanted to hit someone and leave no marks,' said Ellie, unable to remain unprovocative for long.

'Mebbe. What's certain is it came in useful training kids down the boys' clubs, helping keep them off the streets. Listen, Ellie. I know you'll be naturally all sympathetic towards Angela. Fair enough. Me, I just saw her through Joe's eyes. Strict Catholic, I gather.'

'Hardly a crime.'

'No? Thought you reckoned religion was the Prozac of the people? Never mind. Joe were a sort of Catholic too once, but it's hard to stay religious in our job. And there's no denying he were a hard man. He didn't believe in handling criminals with kid gloves, and they went after him a couple of times with complaints. You'll remember yon mad bugger Tommy Bingley, Peter? If ever a man needed thumping, it were Bingley! But nothing were ever proved against Joe, his sheet's as clean as mine.'

'That's really reassuring,' said Ellie.

Dalziel laughed, then said seriously, 'Any road, what you think or what I think doesn't matter, does it? I'm out of it, Pete's in charge. I reckon we can prove that she poured petrol all over him as he lay drunk in his pit. If Ms Dacre can persuade a court that she was wholly or even partially justified, I'll not quarrel with her. Either way, it won't bring Joe back. Now, I've interrupted your day long enough. See you on the twenty-eighth, luv. And you tomorrow, lad. Cheers!'

After he'd gone, Ellie said, 'I feel like Scrooge after the visitations. The fat Devil sounded almost human.'

'Be careful,' said Pascoe. 'He's a playground Napoleon. Never stops thinking tactics.'

'And you? Don't you play the same games?'

'Not me. I'm the school swot.'

But he too was puzzled.

Later the phone had rung. Ellie answered it, talking for some time. When she came back into the room, Pascoe said, 'Anyone interesting?'

'Only Jools, just ringing to say Merry Christmas.'

'Oh yes. You didn't talk about the case?'

'It was mentioned,' she said defensively. 'Andy did say I wasn't sworn to secrecy, you heard him. And she says to say she's looking forward to seeing you tomorrow.'

'I wish I could return the compliment,' said Pascoe.

Not that there was any argument but that Jools Dacre was a very pleasant sight for a man of lively fancy to rest his eyes upon. He moved his gaze firmly to Angela Fraser and said, 'Mrs Fraser, you were telling us that your husband assaulted you on the morning in question. I have here the report of the doctor who examined you in hospital. It mentions burns on your hands and forearms but no other visible injuries. How do you explain that?'

The woman looked at Dacre, who said, 'Go on. Tell them what you told me.'

Angela Fraser leaned forward and said almost apologetically, 'Joe used to say he knew ways of hitting a man and leaving no sign. He said he could put a man through hell and leave

26

nothing showing that he couldn't have got from sleeping on a hard mattress.'

Pascoe frowned and said, 'Why did he tell you this? Was it a threat?'

'No. More like a boast, really. He got into bother over some prisoner who accused him of beating him up. I got worried about it and Joe told me not to be daft, that there was no way anything could ever be proved.'

'So you have no witness to Sergeant Fraser making this statement?'

Jools Dacre said, 'Obviously not, Chief Inspector. But it's well known Sergeant Fraser was a trained boxer. And won't his records show that he was indeed accused of using undue force against Mr Thomas Bingley, a prisoner in his care?'

Edgar Wield's face was not constructed to give away feelings but Pascoe sensed his body tensing at his side.

Pascoe said, 'I think the record will also show no evidence was found to substantiate the charge.'

'And I think that's the point Mrs Fraser has just been making,' said Dacre sternly. 'While we're on the subject of Sergeant Fraser's violence, I should perhaps mention the corroboration afforded by her consultations with VIM.'

'Which have been going on how long?'

She looked at her papers.

'Since mid-November.'

Edgar Wield leaned forward and said, 'Just a few weeks then? Pity.'

Dacre stared at him as if amazed that a human voice could come out of a face that wouldn't have disgraced an iguana.

'Why so?' she said.

'If she'd gone to you earlier, you might have had time to give her some good advice.'

'Of course she was given good advice,' said Dacre indignantly. 'And offered a place in our refuge if things got too bad.'

'Oh aye? So she weren't advised to dispose of her husband then, just leave him? Pity she didn't listen.'

And now the third member of the interviewing team came in, WDC Novello.

'Come on, Sarge. Sometimes the cure's worse than the disease. Who wants to exchange the comforts of home for a grotty refuge full of whingeing women?'

They were turning into a nice double act, these two, thought Pascoe appreciatively.

'It wasn't like that,' cried Mrs Fraser. 'It sounds simple here and now. And when I was sitting talking to the advisers at the refuge, things seemed nice and clear too. But in the small hours of the morning, with everything quiet and cold and dark, I felt so alone, like there was just the two of us and only one of us could survive . . . I felt desperate . . . despairing . . . the sin against the Holy Ghost . . . I couldn't even pray . . . it wasn't my decision . . . sometimes you've got to leave it to the angels to choose . . .'

Her voice had risen close to a shriek and Jules Dacre put a protective arm around her.

'I think we'd like a break now, Peter,' she said urgently.

The Fat Man would have gone in with both boots, thought Pascoe as he suspended the interview and said, 'I'll send some coffee in.'

Outside he said, 'So what do you think?'

'Don't know,' said Novello. 'She looks so ill, it's hard to see deeper than the symptoms. Lot depends on how well this domestic violence stuff stands up. Is it true what Dacre says about Sergeant Fraser being investigated for assault on a prisoner?'

'Oh aye,' said Wield. 'Tommy Bingley. Don't know how Dacre got on to that seeing the complaint was thrown out.'

'Then they can't use it in court anyway.'

'I don't think anyone will object,' said Pascoe. 'Certainly not the super.'

Novello was puzzled.

'But I thought Joe Fraser was his special mate. Or am I missing something?'

Pascoe and Wield exchanged glances. Then the sergeant said, 'Tommy Bingley is a serial complainant. There's hardly an officer in Mid-Yorkshire he hasn't accused of beating him up. We've even got him on video inflicting injuries on himself to back up his story. He's been in Wakefield for the last five years, and I hear he accuses the prison officers by turn, alphabetically, once a month. If Ms Dacre tries to use Tommy to support her case that Fraser was violent, she'll look a real nana. Whoever leaked that to her wasn't doing her a favour.'

'Indeed,' said Pascoe. 'See they get some coffee in there, will you? I'm going to have a word with the super.'

He found Dalziel in the canteen. This was not an area much frequented by high-ranking officers, but the Fat Man avowed that they did the best bacon and bangers this side of paradise.

He was tucking into a plate packed with enough fat to see a polar bear through two hibernations.

'How do, Pete lad,' he said. 'Got that cow safely tethered yet?'

'Not quite,' said Pascoe. 'But you'll be pleased to hear your little game worked.'

'I'm not with you, lad.'

'You were with me yesterday, making sure Ellie heard about Tommy Bingley accusing Smokey Joe?'

'You're never saying your missus mentioned it to Ms Dacre? You ought to have words there, Peter,' said the Fat Man seriously.

'Oh, I shall. And I'll mention that everyone from the PM to the Queen Mother's being accused by Bingley too!'

'Aye, well, I'll give Her Royal Highness the benefit but I'm not so sure about Tommy. Nay, lad, don't take on so or you'll ruin them baby good looks. Heard something might interest you, though. Christmas Day Mass in the hospital. Our Angela didn't take communion.'

'So what? She's ill.'

'Or nursing a mortal sin.'

As he spoke, his gaze drifted behind Pascoe, and suddenly his face lit up with a smile like dawn on Ben Nevis.

'Hey there, young Deirdre, you pushing for plain-clothes transfer or wha'? You'll need to find summat a bit plainer than that. Doesn't she look a picture, Mr Pascoe?'

Pascoe turned to see that Deirdre Collingwood had come into the canteen with a group of uniformed constables. She was wearing a deep-blue silk blouse and tight-fitting burgundy jeans. It was the first time Pascoe had seen her out of uniform. She looked several years older than nineteen, and very attractive.

Breaking away from her friends, she came to the Fat Man's table.

'Hello, sir,' she said. 'I'm not back on duty till tomorrow but I was passing and thought I'd just look in . . .'

'Devotion to the job, that's what I like to see,' said Dalziel approvingly. 'Had a good Christmas so far, lass? That's a lovely necklet you've got there. Prezzie, was it?'

She had a heavy gold chain around her neck from which depended a single ruby to match the one shining in her engagement ring.

'Yes, sir. From my fiancé. Sir . . .'

'Aye, Deirdre's engaged to young Sandy Armstrong, Mr Pascoe. You'll know his dad, runs the Land Rover dealership down Millgate. You've done well there, lass. It'll be four-wheel drive all the way once you and Sandy get hitched. Hope you won't let it interfere with your career. But no need nowadays. Lass can enjoy a happy marriage and still make a good career.'

'Sir,' she said, 'I was wondering how Angela, Mrs Fraser, was . . .'

'As well as can be expected,' said Dalziel, very serious. 'I'm sorry you got mixed up in that t'other day. I didn't realize you were close. You did very well in the circumstances. Here, sit down and Mr Pascoe'll get you a cup of something.'

The girl's face was showing signs of strain again.

'No, I can't stay,' she said. 'Sandy's outside . . . I just said I had to pop in for a few moments. What's going to happen to Mrs Fraser? What really happened that morning? I read the papers but they don't seem to know much . . .'

'That's 'cos we don't know much ourselves,' said Dalziel. 'Mr Pascoe's still interviewing the poor woman. But if what she says about all that violence stands up, then there'll be plenty of sympathy for her in court. The DCI can pass on your regards. He's just going back up there now, aren't you, Mr Pascoe?'

'That's right,' said Pascoe. 'I'll finish talking to you later, sir.'

And if that sounded threatening, good! Back in the interview room, Angela Fraser was looking frail but composed.

'All right?' he said to Jools Dacre. She gave him a nod and without further ado he started the tape, spoke the ritual words, then went on, 'So let's cut to the chase. We've heard how your husband assaulted you, Mrs Fraser. What happened next?'

His new brusqueness of manner won him a warning glare from the solicitor but her client didn't seem to notice.

'Eventually he stopped,' said Mrs Fraser. 'I was lying on the floor. I didn't move. He sat there drinking the whisky. I think he must have got through the whole bottle. Then he said something like, "What are we going to do, Angel?" That's what he called me. Sometimes. And I said, "You mean, what are you going to do, Joe? It's you who're destroying everything we built together. Go on like this and you'll have destroyed it all." Then he sat quiet for a long while till at last he said, "Maybe that will be best then," and he got up and went out.'

'To the bedroom.'

'No. Into the kitchen. I thought I heard the door into the garage open and I hoped he wasn't going to get the car out and drive away. He wasn't fit, you see.' Her tone of concern was pathetic in every sense of the word.

'But he didn't?'

'No. He came back into the hallway. We've got cork tiles. You can hear every footstep. He stood there a moment like he was thinking of coming back into the lounge. Then I heard him going down the passage to our bedroom.'

'What did you do then?'

'I lay where I was for a long while. Finally I stood up. And I started clearing up again. Like I told you, that's what I do.'

Pascoe glanced at his two colleagues. They avoided his gaze. He said, 'How much time had passed?'

'An hour. Two. I've no idea. When I finished, I sat down on the sofa and waited. I thought he might come back in. I think I fell asleep. It's exhausting, this kind of thing, you know. Finally I went to the bedroom. I thought it should be safe by now, and I was right. He was lying across the bed, snoring. He didn't look as if he'd wake up for hours. You have to believe me. He really didn't.'

There was a sudden urgency in her voice which Pascoe couldn't understand. Perhaps she thought that setting fire to a man asleep was less reprehensible than if he were awake.

'So what did you do then, Mrs Fraser?' he said coldly.

'I just stood looking down at him and wondering what God meant by it all. Then I noticed the smell.'

'The smell?' he echoed, puzzled. 'What smell?'

'The petrol, of course,' she said impatiently. 'I touched the bedspread. It was sodden. The carpet, the furniture, everything. There was a petrol can on the floor. I picked it up. The top was off and it was empty. And then I realized what he'd meant by saying what he did about destroying everything.'

Pascoe closed his eyes briefly, partly to adjust to this unexpected turn, partly to say a little prayer of thanks that Dalziel wasn't in the room.

'You're saying it was your husband who poured the petrol?' he said, trying to sound neutral.

'Oh yes. But just because he was drunk, Mr Pascoe,' she said eagerly. 'He wouldn't really have meant any harm. And then because he was so very drunk, he must have fallen into a stupor before he could set it alight. I saw the hand of God in that.'

He felt like closing his eyes again, but didn't.

'But it was set alight, wasn't it, Mrs Fraser? Was that God's hand too? Or yourself?'

Now that was a turn of phrase the Fat Man would have been proud of!

All it provoked was an irritable shaking of the head, as if at a small child's lack of understanding.

'I took the petrol can into the kitchen to put it out of harm's way,' she said. 'It was like being in a dream. I thought I ought to move Joe, but he was too heavy for me by myself. Then I decided the best thing to do was ring for help.'

'Hold on,' commanded Pascoe, determined not to be side-tracked. 'By the time you rang for help, the fire had started. So who set it going, Mrs Fraser? Was it you who lit the petrol?'

She looked at him as if he were crazy.

'No. It was Joe. I should have known. It was my fault.'

This was getting worse.

'Known what, Mrs Fraser?'

'Known that if he woke up he'd do what he always did when he woke. Every morning as long as we'd been married. Doesn't . . . didn't even open his eyes. He just pulled out a cigarette and lit it. I saw him. Oh God.'

Pascoe looked at Jools Dacre in wild surmise. Did he imagine a small sympathetic smile?

He tried again.

'Mrs Fraser, it's quite clear that when you made your phone call for help, the fire had started. You say so yourself.'

'No, no. You're wrong. I was ringing to find out what I ought to do about Joe.'

'Then why did you say, I quote, "Please come quickly. There's been a dreadful accident. I think my husband's dead. It's all my fault?"'

The woman looked bewildered. Jools Dacre was delving into her briefcase.

'I think you're confused, Mr Pascoe,' she said. 'But perhaps understandably so. You are referring to Mrs Fraser's call of six eleven a.m. to the fire service. The call for help she is talking about was made nine minutes earlier, at six-oh-two a.m.'

He was beginning to feel more concussed than confused.

'An earlier call? Who to? What was said? Why haven't we been told about this?'

'I should have thought that a routine check with the telephone company would have given you this information,' said Dacre sweetly. 'Fortunately, I'm in a position to help you with the detail. You see, the call was to me. Or rather, to my answer machine. And I have a copy of the tape here and shall, of course, be happy to make the original available.'

From her case she produced a portable cassette player, set it on the table, and switched it on.

'*Hello . . . Miss Dacre . . . it's me, Angela Fraser . . . You're probably still in bed . . . I didn't know who else to ring . . . it's Joe . . . he came home drunk and he started beating me and he's poured petrol all over the bedroom and he's lying there drunk and I don't know what to do . . . oh God, he's moving . . . Joe, no! JOE!'*

The voice rose to a scream and the scream ran into a sound like a huge balloon being pricked. Then a bang as the phone fell, noises off, footsteps running, the voice shouting, and finally silence as the tape ran its allocated course.

Jools Dacre said, 'Mrs Fraser was standing in the hallway of her bungalow making the call. She could see down the passageway into the bedroom where her husband lay. But when he woke and she realized what he was going to do, she was too far away to do anything but scream. It's all on the tape. She did all she could to save her husband. As you can see, going through it all again has been a considerable ordeal for her, and I suggest this interview now ends.'

She was right. Mrs Fraser looked ready to drop. Her black-rimmed eyes, huge in her pale pinched face, fixed on Pascoe and she said earnestly, 'The angels took him, Mr Pascoe, not me. The angels . . .'

And with perfect timing as he switched off the tape, she fainted into her solicitor's arms.

3.

'December twenty-eighth, nineteen ninety-eight. Ten thirty-five a.m. Interview of Mrs Angela Fraser resumes. Present, Ms Juliet Dacre, solicitor; Detective Superintendent Andrew Dalziel; Woman Detective Constable Shirley Novello; and myself, Detective Chief Inspector Peter Pascoe.'

When Dalziel heard the outcome of the Boxing Day interview, he'd reacted with a strange calm, like the silence of the big guns after a long barrage. He'd played the answerphone tape twice, then shook his head sadly and said, 'So I got it wrong, did I? Well, well.'

He played the tape again.

'Hear anything else there, besides Angela's voice?' he asked.

'Apart from the explosion?' said Pascoe. 'No. And this came from Jools Dacre, remember.'

'Aye, I'm sure it's genuine. But I'll send the original down to the lab anyway. So, Peter, it were all an accident after all.'

'An act of God, according to Mrs Fraser. Or – how did she put it? – the angels took him.'

'Great one for angels, our Angela. One thing, but. This stuff about Joe pouring the petrol himself. You persuaded?'

'Not completely. But even if Angela did it herself, then got scared and changed her mind, it was still an accident. All right, we could charge her with reckless endangerment, but what are we going to get? A bad press and a suspended sentence.'

'We'll get the truth, lad,' said Dalziel ponderously. 'So get her back in. We'll need her to sign a statement anyway. No rush, though. Let's show some sensitivity, eh? Tomorrow . . . no, day after, twenty-eighth. I'd best be there to make my peace. When I get things wrong, I know how to take my bumps.'

And here he was, still all sweetness and light, in stark contrast to the boorishness he'd displayed on Christmas Eve.

So why don't I feel like a shepherd in the field abiding listening to the Christmas message? Pascoe asked himself.

After his initial charm offensive, Dalziel retired once more to the depths of his box file. This, at least, hadn't changed. It still contained what might have been the same meat pie plus a copy of the local paper's first post-Christmas edition, with what looked like a piece about the Ridley tragedy in it.

'Right,' said Pascoe. 'Mrs Fraser, I'm pleased to see you looking so much better.'

It wasn't flannel. She really did look a lot better. For the first time, Pascoe could see her as an adult woman, not a victimized waif, which made it easier to launch his last assault.

He said, 'Mrs Fraser, when you removed the petrol can from the bedroom, how did you carry it?'

'It's got a handle,' she said, surprised.

'Yes, I know. But if it was heavy you might have needed to take two hands to it.'

Dacre came in smoothly at sight of what she took to be a trap.

'Mrs Fraser has told you her husband had already emptied the can, so lifting it one-handed would have been no problem.'

'Of course,' said Pascoe. 'The thing is, while no definite prints from your husband's fingers can be found, yours are very clear. On the handle. And all four fingers of your left hand on the underside.'

He did a mime, making a tipping motion.

Jools Dacre demanded furiously, 'Just where is this leading us? It was a stressful situation. The exact details of how Mrs Fraser grasped the can are naturally vague in her mind.'

Andy Dalziel suddenly sat up straight, smiling and nodding his head as though the piece he'd been reading in the newspaper had come to a satisfactory conclusion. Then he shut his box file with a tremendous crash and said, 'I agree with Ms Dacre. This is all a bit insensitive, Chief Inspector. And not all that *germane*.'

It was like being stabbed by Brutus. But before he could offer a dying reproach, there was a tap at the door, which opened to reveal Edgar Wield.

'Sorry to interrupt, sir,' said the sergeant. 'But WDC Novello's needed urgently. Only take half an hour.'

'Damn,' said Dalziel. Then, smiling unctuously at Dacre, he said, 'Can you hang on another thirty minutes or so?'

'I can't for the life of me see why we should. Do we really need DC Novello?'

'CPS guidelines, female officer present when interviewing a female witness,' said Dalziel. 'Could you dig us up another lass, Sergeant?'

'Bit thin on the ground, sir. No one in CID. Did see WPC Collingwood in the canteen.'

Dalziel shook his great head reprovingly, smiled reassuringly at Mrs Fraser, and said, 'She'd never do . . .'

And suddenly the woman, faintly but definitely, was smiling back. Now she looked different again, thought Pascoe. Now she looked . . . in control?

'Please,' she said, 'don't worry on my account. If she doesn't mind, it would be nice to see a friendly face.'

Jools Dacre didn't look like she agreed, but Dalziel was saying, 'Grand. Wheel her in then, Sergeant. Tell her it'll only be for a few minutes.'

And then the charade was over, for Pascoe had no doubts that this was what it was. Wield had been put up to this; the box file banged on the table had been a signal; the stuff about CPS guidelines and shortage of women officers was mere verbiage.

He thought of suspending proceedings and demanding an explanation, but while he was still debating, the door opened.

'WPC Collingwood has entered the room,' said Dalziel. 'Take a seat, lass.'

Mrs Fraser was smiling again, this time to welcome the young constable, but Deirdre wasn't responding. She looked almost as bad as Angela on Boxing Day. Maybe she'd had a very heavy Christmas.

'Right, let's get on,' said the Fat Man, now very much the ringmaster. 'Mrs Fraser, Angela, shouldn't need to keep you much longer. What I've done is prepare a statement based on your own words. Perhaps you could read through it, then, if you agree with it, sign it and that'll be us done.'

He opened his box file again and took out a folder hidden beneath the newspaper. Apologetically blowing off a few pie crumbs, he handed it to Angela Fraser. With Jools Dacre peering over her shoulder, she began to read.

'If you could do it aloud, luv, for the tape, that would really speed things up,' said Dalziel.

'Superintendent, I don't see why—'

But the woman interrupted her solicitor.

'It's all right. I don't mind. In fact, it might help.'

Quietly, she began reading.

It was, Pascoe had to admit, a beautifully prepared statement: clear, balanced, and perfectly tailored to the woman's tongue. He felt moved as he listened. This was more than simple narrative, it was a requiem for a marriage. Mrs Fraser's tone was sad and serious. He felt sympathy for her as he listened, and admiration too. He glanced at the Fat Man to see how he was reacting and saw that his gaze was not directed at Angela Fraser.

He was watching Deirdre Collingwood.

And in that moment, Pascoe solved the charade. This was what it had all been about, a device to get this girl in this room listening to these words from Angela Fraser's own mouth.

She was weeping silently, tears tracking down her pale cheeks. This was the bubbling over of a grief her young will wasn't strong enough to contain. And he knew beyond doubt that it wasn't Angela Fraser she was grieving for; it was Smokey Joe Fraser; and it was herself.

Behind the blank of Dalziel's face he read something too. Anxiety. Somehow this was a last throw. Whatever game he was playing, if all he got out of Deirdre were silent tears, he'd lost.

'. . . I rang Juliet Dacre because I'd met her at VIM and she'd been very supportive and told me to contact her if ever I needed help. I got her answer machine and while I was talking, I looked along the passage into the bedroom through the open door, and I saw Joe move. He was still more than half-asleep but he was pulling his old cigarette case out of his pocket. I knew what he was going to do because every morning of his life, the very first thing he did was light a cigarette. I think I shouted, but it was too late. He flicked his lighter and everything went up in flames. I'll never forgive myself. Despite everything, I loved Joe, and I believe he loved me . . .'

And Dalziel had won.

Collingwood was on her feet, spilling her chair behind her.

'Bitch, bitch, lying bitch!' she screamed. 'Stinking, lying, murdering bitch. He hated you . . . he wanted to leave you and marry me . . . liar! liar! liar!'

She was leaning across the table, spitting the words into Mrs Fraser's face. Jools Dacre was on her feet too, her arms defensively around her client while Dalziel grappled the WPC from behind.

Only Angela Fraser looked unperturbed.

'Oh, you poor child,' she said with infinite compassion. 'You loved him, didn't you? I never knew. You poor child.'

Dalziel dragged the sobbing girl out of the room, leaving Pascoe to turn off the tape and pick up the pieces.

Jools Dacre was regarding him with cold fury.

'Did you know that Constable Collingwood had a relationship with Sergeant Fraser?' she demanded.

'I'd no idea,' said Pascoe.

She scrutinized him closely, then said, 'No. It's not your style, Peter. But that fat bastard . . . I'll see it's the last time he pulls a stroke like this.'

'Yes. I'm sorry. Please, will you just wait in here a moment?'

He went out. Once more, as on Christmas Eve, he saw the Fat Man in his office in close confabulation with Deirdre Collingwood. This time he didn't interrupt.

After several minutes, Dalziel came out into the corridor with the girl. She didn't look at Pascoe but headed straight into a cloakroom.

'Repairs,' said the Fat Man. 'So what can I do you for, lad?'

'You can tell me what's going on.'

'Simple, lad. Smokey Joe and Deirdre had a bit of a thing going while she was on attachment out at Ridley. Nothing surprising about that. Joe was famous for chancing his arm with any pretty plod who came his way. Hit or miss, it meant nowt. No comebacks, and usually they stayed friends. Real charmer, Joe.'

Pascoe said, 'And his wife, was she charmed?'

'In a way. Thought sex was for having kids, and when she found she couldn't, she gave it up. Turned a blind eye to Joe getting his exercise elsewhere, long as he didn't frighten the horses. Like I told you afore, divorce was out 'cos the Church said so, and separation was out 'cos she said so.'

'Why the hell didn't you tell me about Fraser's reputation?' demanded Pascoe.

'Thought everyone knew,' said Dalziel. 'You should spend more time in the canteen. Deirdre seemed the same as the rest. Enjoyed the exercise, then moved back to HQ and got down to the business of carving out a career, plus she got herself engaged. She kept young Sandy, her fiancé, well clear of the job. Didn't want him put off by seeing the plods at their play. But she really liked Joe, and when they ran into each other at the club, early in November, she didn't see any obstacle to a one-nighter. Trouble was, Joe began to get serious, which put her in a dilemma. If word got out, naturally it would put the kibosh on her engagement. And breaking up a cop's marriage could get her card marked in her career.'

'Why not just drop it?'

'Not so easy. Very persuasive guy, was Joe. Things drifted till they met at the Christmas thrash. When we saw Joe leaving, he was heading round the corner to meet up with Deirdre in her car.'

'You knew this at the time?'

'No. But I'd clocked him smooching with her at the party. When I went back in, I couldn't see her anywhere, and when I realized it had taken Joe over two hours to travel twenty miles . . .'

'Well spotted, sir, but I don't see where all this is leading.'

'It's leading to Smokey Joe getting home and telling his missus he's dumping her for Deirdre.'

'And what difference do you imagine that makes?'

'Come on, lad! For a start, it makes the difference between Smokey Joe beating up his wife, which is a crime, and wanting to leave her, which ain't.'

Pascoe shook his head and said urgently, 'Sir, it doesn't matter. OK, I can see how you'd prefer to think of your mate as a womanizer rather than a wife-beater, though I should point out the two aren't incompatible, and she did go to VIM. Anyway, all we're doing is arguing motives when there's been no crime. It was an accident. You've heard the tape. I suppose the lab's confirmed it's genuine . . .'

'Aye. Those tech lads are wonderful. Something I'd like you to hear, but.'

He drew Pascoe into his room. On his desk was a cassette

player. He switched it on. Angela's voice came out, very loud and distorted, then slowly it faded away, and in among the hiss and buzz Pascoe heard a sort of tinkling, chiming noise which had something familiar about it.

'Recognize that? No? How about this?'

From a drawer, the Fat Man took a set of angel chimes and lit the candles. Around and around went the angels, sending up their tinkling notes.

Puzzled, Pascoe said, 'Yes, could be that. So what?'

'So listen again.'

Dalziel blew out the candles, and played the tape once more.

'Notice how the chimes fade away, then suddenly there's that explosion as the petrol goes up? Now, imagine you're in the hallway of that bungalow, talking on the phone, leaving a timed message on your solicitor's answer machine. You've got the chime candles burning on the hall table which has got wheels on. OK?'

'With you so far.'

But beginning to wish he wasn't.

'Grand,' said Dalziel, going through an elaborate mime. 'Now, as you talk you give the table a firm push. The entrance hall's got corked tiles. The table runs straight and smooth down the hall, along the passage, through the bedroom door. WHOOSH! End of Smokey Joe, and you've got a tape to support your story.'

'And what exactly do you have to support yours?' enquired Pascoe sceptically.

'There's this,' said Dalziel. From the drawer he pulled an evidence bag containing a small twisted lump of brass.

'Found that in the bedroom ashes,' he said. 'Bit of wax on it, too. Also found what could be the wheels off a small table. There you are, lass. With you in a tick.'

Deirdre Collingwood had appeared in the doorway, looking wan but presentable. She moved away.

43

'In other words, you've got nothing,' said Pascoe. 'Which is why you're using that child. First time, you were just fishing. This time you knew exactly what you were doing, getting her back into the interview.'

'Child? Wash your mouth out, Chief Inspector. She's an adult woman and a trained cop. She wanted back in, and yon bitch wanted her back in too, so's she could see her suffer.'

'She'll get her wish then, won't she?' said Pascoe angrily. 'This could ruin Collingwood, professionally and personally. And for what? Even in the remote contingency you're right, you're never going to prove anything. Face it, sir. It's over.'

'Not till the fat lady sings, isn't that what the Yanks say? Watch this space, lad. I may be on the turn. Get back inside, I'll be along shortly.'

He went out of the room and walked away deep in conversation with the WPC.

Full of foreboding, Pascoe returned to the interview room.

Jools Dacre said, 'About time. Mrs Fraser, acting on my advice, is ready to sign the statement.'

'Excellent,' said Pascoe. 'If we can just wait for the superintendent.'

'Why? We only need one police witness, and after I'm finished with him, Mr Dalziel's signature will carry very little weight.'

Pascoe doubted it. To the Fat Man, solicitors' complaints were like flea bites to Tyrannosaurus rex. But it might be a good move to get the statement signed and the women on their way before the dinosaur returned.

He almost succeeded, but Dalziel re-entered the room just as the women stood up to leave.

'Sorry about that,' he said, beaming. 'Young lasses today, eh? I blame television.'

'Mrs Fraser has just signed her statement, sir,' said Pascoe.

'Grand. Then that's that. Poor Joe. Smoking killed him in the end. Sorry, luv, but I can imagine how you felt when you saw him drag out that old cigarette case and lighter. He inherited them from his granddad, you know.'

'Yes, I know.'

'Lighter never failed,' he said. 'More's the pity. It was definitely that lighter, was it, the one made from a bullet?'

'Oh yes.'

'And the old gunmetal case?'

'Superintendent, this is very insensitive,' said Jools Dacre.

'Sorry. Just anticipating questions the coroner might ask. He'll likely want to establish just how clearly Mrs Fraser could see from the hallway. It was still dark, after all.'

'The bedroom light was on and I could see quite clearly,' said Mrs Fraser firmly. 'It was definitely his old lighter and case.'

'So that's settled. Funny, but. The fire lads didn't find any trace of them anywhere near the body.'

Jools Dacre said, 'So? With a fire of such intensity they probably melted.'

'Still would have left some trace,' said Dalziel. 'And there's something else. WPC Collingwood claims she drove your husband home that night, Mrs Fraser. She says they parked in a lay-by. To have sex.'

No reaction.

Dalziel continued, 'Afterwards she says he swore he was going to get a divorce and marry her.'

This got a rueful shaking of the head and the woman said, 'Joe always told a good story. I'm sorry if Deirdre was taken in.'

'Actually, she wasn't. Also she'd got other fish to fry. Trying to let him down soft, she said she wouldn't dream of marrying a man who always stank of tobacco. And he said, "That's easy, I'll give it up."'

Now Angela Fraser laughed out loud.

'The silly child,' she said derisively. 'I'll tell you something, Mr Dalziel. There was more chance of Joe giving up breathing than smoking.'

'Given up both now, hasn't he?' said the Fat Man softly. 'But he must have been serious at the time 'cos the last thing he did before he got out of her car was put these into the glove compartment.'

And onto the table, with a crash that echoed around the room like gunfire, Dalziel tossed a metal cigarette case and a lighter made out of a bullet.

Her face waif-pale again, Angela Fraser sank back into her chair.

As she diminished, Dalziel seemed to swell.

The fat lady's going to sing, thought Pascoe.

'That's right, lass. Make thyself comfortable,' said Dalziel with terrifying solicitude.

'Mr Pascoe, why don't you switch the tape back on? Now this interview can really begin.'

That evening, as they prepared for Dalziel's visit, Pascoe told Ellie what had happened.

'So,' she said. 'One woman facing a murder charge, another with her career and engagement in tatters, and Jools Dacre looking an asshole. The Fat Controller should be bouncing tonight.'

'Ellie, he's our guest. So stay cool, please.'

'You know me. Miss Frigidaire. I can keep a truce.'

'Yeah? I sometimes think if you'd been playing football in No Man's Land back on Boxing Day nineteen fourteen, you'd have been sent off for fighting.'

But all had gone well, mainly because of Rosie's presence at the table. The Fat Man's fondness for the girl and her unambiguous love for her Uncle Andy created an atmosphere it was hard to resist.

At the end of the meal they headed into the lounge for coffee, but at the doorway Dalziel whispered something to Rosie, then retreated.

'What did Uncle Andy say?' asked Ellie suspiciously.

'Nothing,' said the girl, all innocence. 'Gone to the lavatory, I expect.'

They sat in a silence which somehow became expectant. Then there was a sound like a finger tapping on the French window, and immediately Rosie got up and drew the curtains as for a stage performance.

Nothing moved outside, but something had triggered the patio security light.

Seconds passed, and Pascoe was just about to break the silence when into the illuminated area moved a figure. It was Dalziel, hands behind his back, left leg in the air, gliding smoothly and elegantly across the stone flags on his right foot. He vanished into the shadows only to reappear a moment later, this time gliding backwards on the other foot.

'Oh God,' said Ellie. 'He's on Rollerblades.'

She tried to look furious but it was hard with Pascoe laughing out loud and Rosie clapping her hands in glee.

Now he was back, legs astride, doing a circle. And finally he performed a little pirouette in the middle of the patio, came right up to the window, and made a deep bow, at the same time moving slowly backwards.

'Andy,' called Pascoe. 'Andy, I shouldn't . . . watch out . . . oh hell!'

The Fat Man had reached the edge of the patio unawares. For a moment he teetered there, mouth agape, arms waving madly, then he tumbled backwards onto the shadowy lawn.

They rushed out, picked him up, and brought him in.

'I'm fine, bit of a bruise mebbe, nowt a gill or two of malt won't cure.'

'I didn't know skating was one of your talents,' said Pascoe, pouring the drink.

'Lots you don't know about me, lad. Used to be a bobby-dazzler on the ice. Nay, lass, they're no good for thy little plates of meat.'

Rosie had slipped her feet hopefully into the discarded blades.

Dalziel glanced at Ellie, who returned his gaze blankly, then he said to the girl, 'They can be grand fun, these things, like your dad says. But you saw me take a tumble out there, so you'll know they can be dangerous too, like your mum says. If you ever got a pair of your own, you'd need to be trained proper by someone who knew what they were doing.'

'Someone like you, Andy?' said Ellie.

'Aye, mebbe.'

'And this someone would take full responsibility for instilling safety rules, making sure she understands that she is never to use these things on a pavement or near a public highway?'

'I'd beat it into her with a rubber truncheon,' said Dalziel.

'I'll need that in writing . . . Rosie, what are you doing?'

Her daughter had struck a match and was setting it to the candles under the angel chimes.

'I'm just lighting a candle for me and Uncle Andy to make sure we come to no harm on our rollers,' she explained.

Ellie and Pascoe exchanged glances, then the Fat Man said, 'If you go outside to my car, you might find some sort of parcel on the front seat.'

Rosie looked at her mother, who nodded, then she rushed out of the room.

The candle flames were setting the brass vanes spinning faster and faster and gradually the soft golden sound of the chimes filled the room and their thoughts.

Suddenly Ellie said, 'Andy, I never said, I'm really sorry about your friend, for your loss, I mean.'

'Yeah. Well, thanks,' said Dalziel. 'Here's to you, Joe.'

He raised his glass. Pascoe and Ellie followed suit.

'To Joe.'

They heard Rosie open the front door. The through draught pulled open the French window, which had been left ajar, and for a second the candle flames burnt still brighter in the rush of cold air.

Then they all went out together, and the chimes fell silent, and nothing remained but a few thin skeins of grey smoke which rose slowly to the ceiling before they too faded away.

A Shameful Eating

A shameful eating is better than a shameful leaving, my dear old gramma used to say as she urged me into a second circuit of her groaning table. And I never saw any need to disagree with her, not until the start of my third week in that wallowing lifeboat.

The *Needle's Eye* had gone down fourteen days earlier, split apart by a squall so sudden that only the three of us on deck at the time had any hope of surviving. The youngest was Perkin Curtis, a fresh-faced lad on his very first voyage, with a fine tenor voice whose rendition of '*A poore soule sate sighing by a sicamore tree*' brought tears to the rheumy eyes of those same grizzled tars who lusted after his pink-and-white flesh. Three of them would have had him across the long cannon on the poop deck during the dog watch one night if I hadn't come up for a breath of air from the afterhold which I was using as a sickroom during an outbreak of Yellow Jack. I swear the boy was so innocent that he thought it no more than a bit of boisterous fun. I told him to pull his britches up, ordered two of the men below with a promise that they'd be up for captain's punishment in the morning, and kept their ringleader beside me. This was Josh Gall, the bosun's mate, a small plump man whose surface of placid amiability had scarce been touched by half a century of evil habits and riotous behaviour. But he was a fine seaman, none better for anticipating and dealing with a nautical emergency.

I should have remembered this as I savaged him with my tongue, promising him the extremities of the law for his assault on young Curtis. But I took no notice of a sudden change in his expression from abject contrition to active alarm, save to congratulate myself on having pierced his carapace with my threats.

'Sir,' he tried to interrupt, 'will you listen—'

'Too late for excuses now, Gall,' I shouted him down. 'This time it's the lash for you!'

Alas, it wasn't his excuses he wanted me to listen to, but that change in the wind's note which gave him warning of the fury that was almost upon us.

'For God's sake, bring her round!' he yelled suddenly, trying to spring by me towards the wheelhouse. Still deafened by my own rage, I caught his arm and held him fast.

Then in a trice the wind shifted from west to south, from light airs to a near-tornado, which hit us like a man-o'-war's broadside. The *Needle's Eye* went over till her masts lay parallel with the sea, then a wave like a giant's fist struck her amidships, and the poor old tub folded in two and turned submarine.

Somehow a lifeboat was ripped free, and somehow Josh Gall with his instinct for being in the right place at the right time came up alongside it and scrambled in. I surfaced half a furlong away and saw him quite clearly, for despite the fury of the wind there was not a cloud to be seen in the huge starry sky. I shouted, then went under again, so deep that I saw as in a dream the bow section of the ship with its figurehead of a full-breasted mermaid drifting downwards to its eternal rest.

Perhaps I did dream that I could see desperate hands clawing at the fo'c's'le ports, but the image gave me strength to kick upwards one last time, and when I broke the surface I saw the lifeboat bobbing past within a couple of feet. Gall lay sprawling over the gunwale. His eyes met mine. I called for help but he regarded me indifferently and made no move, and the boat would next moment have been beyond my reach had there not been a line trailing behind. This I seized and with my last strength hauled myself along it till I could grasp the stern and drag myself aboard.

I had no strength or breath to express my contempt for Gall, but lay there, giving God what proved premature thanks for my deliverance. Then I became aware Gall was standing upright in that rocking cockleshell with a sailor's ease, pointing and shouting.

'Over there,' he cried. 'Do you not see?'

I forced my head up and looked. About fifty yards away in the surging sea I glimpsed a wooden cask with a man clinging to it by one arm.

'Quick!' urged Gall. 'I can't manage on my lone!'

He was trying to paddle towards his shipmate, using a length of wood ripped from the shattered thwarts. I pulled free another piece and taking my place on the opposite side of the boat, joined my efforts to his. I confess I felt a little shame at my recent condemnation of Gall for his apparent failure to offer assistance to me. And my shame grew when I saw that it was no special crony of the man's we were trying to rescue, but young Perkin Curtis.

We would probably not have reached him had the storm not abated as suddenly as it came and the ocean rapidly deflated from Pennine peaks to Lincolnshire levels. But as we drew alongside Curtis, my new respect for Gall died like the wind.

He reached out, seized the boy's arm, prised it loose from the cask – then thrust the unhappy youth down into the sea!

For a second I believed he had merely lost his grip. Then I realized that what Gall was concerned to rescue was not the boy, but the cask he was clinging to!

'For God's sake, man!' I cried. 'Will you let a fellow human perish?'

'Without water, we all perish,' he snarled. 'Give us a hand to get this aboard.'

There was no point in cutting off my nose to spite my face, so I helped him drag the cask over the gunwale. Then as I stared sadly into the ocean which I thought had closed over the unfortunate youth for ever, to my joy and relief I saw Curtis's head break the surface only an arm's length away. He was clearly *in extremis*, perhaps even past relief, but I reached out my hand and grasped his shock of corn-blond hair.

'Help me!' I screamed at Gall, who regarded me with a sneering indifference for a moment. Then perhaps his cunning mind took into consideration that if we survived, my evidence to an inquiry might yet do him some harm, and he leaned out to take Curtis by the collar and between us we pulled him aboard. He collapsed in a heap in the bow, looking for all the world like a dead man, but I have had plenty of experience of dealing with men snatched from the deep and knew what to do. Rolling him on his back, I knelt beside him and pressed hard against his stomach. A great gush of water issued from his mouth but he did not start to breathe, so I used a technique I had learned from the savages of the Carolinas and, putting my mouth to his, filled his lungs with air from my own, then expelled it by pressure to his chest. This I repeated three or four times till of a sudden he retched, bringing up more water, and I turned him on his side, seeing that he could now breathe on his own.

I looked up to catch Gall's twisted smile.

'It's a strange world, Mr Teasdale,' he said. 'Less than thirty minutes ago you were threatening to have the skin off my back for little more than what you've just been doing.'

'You're a foul creature, Gall,' I said contemptuously. 'You sit there sneering when you should be giving gratitude to God for sparing this boy's life.'

'Oh, I'm grateful enough, Mr Teasdale, sir,' he said. 'God moves in mysterious ways, and the lad is certainly well fleshed.'

I thought his mind was simply dwelling on its usual vile carnal obsession, but perhaps already his undoubted seaman's nous was anticipating the trials ahead and providing his own unthinkable answer to them.

Now he turned his attention from me to the cask. The way it had floated told that it could be no more than half-full but if that half were water, then it was indeed a priceless discovery. Gall gently twisted the spigot till a thick liquid started to ooze out. He let it touch his fingers, sniffed, tasted, and laughed his grating laugh.

'God's good to patriots, it seems,' he said. 'We can drink the King's health afore we light our pipes tonight. This here's our late lamented skipper's best rum!'

I reached over and tasted. He was right. It was one of several casks which Captain Danby had insisted on taking on board in Jamaica despite my advice that we would do better to cram our limited storage space with fresh fruit and vegetables.

'At least we can wet our whistle and die merry,' said Gall.

'Die you will if you take too much of this, Gall,' I said sternly. 'Alcohol dries up the blood and redoubles a man's thirst. But yet it is a good restorative and may help this poor boy.'

So saying, I caught half a gill in the palm of my hand and gently poured it into Curtis's mouth. It set him coughing and spluttering once more, but when the fit was passed, he had some colour in his cheeks and was able to struggle upright. He looked all around him. The sea was smooth as his own unrazored cheeks and the moon lacquered it with light so that he could see for miles in all directions. Save for a few spars from the wrecked ship, we were the only thing to trouble that polished surface. I think it was only now that his desperate plight struck him, for the tinge of colour the rum had restored drained from his cheeks once more and he cried, 'Mr Teasdale, where are the others? Where is the *Needle's Eye?*'

'Sunk, lad,' I said. 'And all your shipmates with it, God rest their souls. But do not despair. The Almighty has seen fit in His infinite mercy to spare us the full measure of His wrath, and I cannot believe that He has preserved us from the deep but to watch us perish in plain air.'

My words of comfort had but little effect, I fear. Young Curtis collapsed to the bottom of the boat once more, sobbing and howling, and his eyes gushed forth as much water as his belly had after his submersion.

Gall meanwhile had settled himself comfortably against the tiller on the one unshattered thwart in the stern. I glared at him angrily. As the one surviving officer of the *Needle's Eye*, it was time to assert my authority.

'Gall,' I said coldly, 'will you be good enough to move? It is the captain's place, I believe, to be at the helm.'

For a second I thought he would defy me, then he grinned and said, 'Aye, aye, *Cap'n* Teasdale, sir,' and shifted down the boat.

I took his place on the stern thwart and grasped the tiller. It moved in my hand like a twig on a sapling, I peered over the stern and saw that the rod linking tiller and rudder had shattered.

'Shouldn't worry about that, Cap'n,' said Gall. 'No great loss not being able to steer when we've only the currents to carry us.'

He was right. There were no oars, no mast, no sail.

'We can paddle, with the broken thwarts,' I said with a show of authority. 'Come, best make a start before the sun comes up and the heat saps our strength.'

Gall grinned again, picked up the length of broken wood and said, 'Aye, aye, Cap'n Teasdale. What's your course, Cap'n?'

I saw his game. He knew well that, as ship's doctor, my expertise lay in charting the course of men's ailments, not the ways of the sea. But with the stars showing in their full refulgence, I at least had no problem in finding directions out.

'West,' I said, pointing. 'We will head west.'

'Back to the Americas?' he said. 'Well, 'tis certainly a large target, sir, and one that would be hard to miss. Trouble is in these waters, west's the direction the prevailing winds came from and also the great currents, and while I dare say two men paddling hard might hold their own for a while, yet I do not see how they could hope to make any progress.'

'You would have us go east, then?' I asked, swallowing my pride.

'East? Now certainly that would mean we had wind and water in our favour, but betwixt us and Africa there is nothing but the Azores, and they are such a tiny target I doubt that we could hit it even if our strength held out that long.'

'So what do you suggest, Mr Gall?' I demanded. 'Bob around here, doing nothing?'

'What point in doing anything else?' he asked. 'We are as like to meet with a ship here as anywhere else. We are close to the main lanes to and from the Indies. Here let us rest, and the Lord have mercy on our souls.'

*

And so our ordeal began. We pooled our resources. They were poor enough in all faith. All I could supply was a tinderbox which lived up to its claim to be waterproof, a clay pipe broken in three pieces, a pouch of sodden tobacco and, most useless of all, a few silver guineas in a wash-leather purse I kept hung around my neck. Gall had even less to offer: a piece of twine about four feet in length and a broad-bladed knife such as butchers use for the dressing of meat. Young Curtis's pockets provided the best trove. Clearly he had a boy's endless appetite and out came two apples, a block of treacle toffee, a wedge of cheese, and a hunk of bread turned by its immersion in the sea into a grey and glutinous putty which nevertheless I spread out to dry, foreseeing that a time would soon come when we would be ready to eat anything.

These, with the cask of rum, were our provisions. I took charge of the rum, doling it out in the smallest of measures, fearful of the effect it could have on our weakened frames and also eager to save some in case we had to signal a distant ship. I discovered that the strong fumes given off by the heavy treacly liquor were readily ignitable by the flint from my tinderbox, and though fire is a dangerous companion on a small boat, yet it would be worth the risk if it meant a chance of rescue.

Water we had none, but God soon sent the mixed blessing of rain, which slaked our thirst while drenching our skins again, for we had no means of shelter either from clouds or the sun.

Despite my utmost parsimony, our small store of rations did not last beyond a week. Some of the cheese we sacrificed on a hook made from a shoe buckle tied to the end of Gall's piece of twine, in an effort to catch fish, but without luck. Gall slashed wildly with his knife at the occasional seabird which curiosity brought near our craft and though he once disturbed a feather, he got no closer.

We passed the second week chewing salty tobacco, sipping minute quantities of rum, and moistening our lips with rainwater. I think that I possibly suffered the most. The other two were well fleshed but I was ever lean and bony, and while they fed on their own fat, I became skeletal. But it was young Curtis who suffered the worst in his morale. Despite all my efforts at comfort, he would weep for hours on end, raving of his mother and his sisters, till finally he had no strength to weep or talk, and would not even have roused himself for his ration of water and rum had I not forced it through his flaked and bloodless lips.

'It's a waste,' said Gall one day as he watched me.

'A waste,' I said. 'Why? Do you think if you took his share it would prolong your miserable life by more than a miserable minute?'

'No, I meant it's a waste that we starve when there is victuals aplenty before us,' said Gall.

It took me a long moment to get his meaning and when I did, I looked at him aghast.

'What new depth of foulness is this?' I cried in disbelief.

'Don't preach at me, you poxy quack,' he snarled. 'The lad's good as dead. Why strive to keep him alive just so that we can all die together? Let's make an end of him now and save ourselves. You're a surgeon, you should know best where the most nutrition lies in human meat!'

He had his knife in his hand and on his face was a look of madness which warned me I must be careful how I interfered.

I said, 'Let me have the knife, Gall. Come, you said I was the surgeon and thus best fitted to do the carving. The knife, if you please.'

He looked at me doubtingly, then slowly he handed over that dreadful weapon. I drove it into the thwart beside me.

'What? Do you betray me then? Will you not do it?' he cried.

'I am a doctor, Gall,' I answered. 'I have taken vows to preserve life, not to destroy it.'

'That's all I'm suggesting we do,' he answered with the cunning logic of insanity. 'Save two lives at the expense of one. Like you said to Curtis at the start, God won't have saved us from drowning at the bottom of the ocean just so's we can starve on top of it!'

'No,' I cried. 'Thou shalt not kill! God is just testing us. He will provide. He will show us another way.'

'Then He'd better show it quick, Cap'n Teasdale,' mocked that vile and villainous creature. 'Else, if He waits another few hours, He'll be able to tell us what we ought to have done face to face!'

I think my faith in a loving God died at that moment. I turned the spigot on the rum cask and filled the wooden cup which Gall had roughly fashioned from a piece of the useless tiller. When I handed it to him he looked at me speculatively, then downed the lot. I refilled the cup and poured the liquor down the unresisting Curtis's throat. Then I passed another brimming measure to Gall.

'Mr Teasdale, sir,' he said. 'I see you're a true gent after all. If a man must die, then let him die merry. Here's health.'

He downed the rum in a single draught. In his weakened state his old capacity for hard drinking was of no avail and I could already see the fiery liquor taking effect, while after a single draught the boy was almost unconscious.

I filled the cup again.

We were picked up ten days later by a Portuguese brigantine hauling copra from the Leeward Islands. She had sprung a seam and was making heavy weather to the Azores, and our new conditions were but little improvement on those we endured in that open boat. Yet the Promethean spark at the heart's core is most obstinate against extinction, and my two companions were carried ashore at Ponta Delgada on San Miguel with breath enough still to mist an eyeglass. We were taken to the town's infirmary, run by Father Boniface, a Catholic priest more skilled at steering his patients to the next world than keeping them in this. He expressed great amazement at our survival, especially as we were all three Protestant, but his admiration for me as a fellow doctor was unstinted.

'Gangrene, you say?'

'Aye, gangrene,' I replied indifferently.

'And with a carving knife?'

'Aye, a carving knife.'

'And how did you cauterize the arteries?' he asked eagerly.

'With the lees from a keg of rum which I then fired with my tinderbox,' I said wearily. 'Enough of these questions. They are in your care now, Father. My responsibility for them is done.'

'*Non nobis, Domine,*' he proclaimed. 'Not unto us, my friend. They are in God's care and always have been, for truly His hand must have guided thine.'

'Your care, God's care, take the credit who will,' I cried wildly. 'Only they are out of my care. And if they now die, as seems most likely, it cannot lie at my door!'

He put my outburst down to a hysterical fever and mixed me a filthy potion which I poured down the jakes after he had gone. It did not seem possible that my companions who had no such strength to resist could long survive such divine ministrations.

I slept well that night and felt stronger in the morn, and when I learned that the brig which had brought us here was now repaired and ready to resume its voyage to Lisbon, I announced that I purposed to sail with her. Some money from the purse I wore about my neck I gave to the good Father.

Perhaps it was the clink of the coins which penetrated Gall's ears, for he opened his eyes and spoke the first words he had uttered since our arrival.

'What? Are you leaving, Mr Teasdale? Nay, you are right not to delay on our account. God speed. And rest assured young Curtis and I will never forget what you have done for us.'

His voice was low but every word fell on my ears like a bell-note. Then he closed his eyes once more.

I made for the door, pausing only to shake hands with Boniface.

'You have two friends forever here, I think,' he said, smiling. 'Let us pray they survive.'

'I know you will do your best for them, Father,' I said. 'Be not sparing of your prayers. Nor your potions either.'

And with that I hastened down to the harbour where the brigantine was already hoisting her sails to catch the freshening western breeze.

I gave up the sea after that and went back north to my native Derbyshire, where I set up practice in the wild country of the Peak. Here distances were long, weather was wild, and payment was as like to be in eggs and vegetables as coin of the realm. Yet it was a comfort to me even as I laboured through the wildest storm to taste no tang of salt in the rain, and to know that the nearest sea was three days' hard riding to east or west. My patients apart, I saw little company for I proved far too abstemious for our hard-drinking, hard-eating, hard-hunting squire, and far too contentious for our prating parson. Once a week I would ride the seven miles to the Black Tor Inn which stood high on an edge overlooking the road from Buxton to Sheffield and learn what news the mail coach had brought in. Occasionally there might be some respectable company to talk to, but usually I made do with John Farley, the landlord, swapping local gossip over a pint of his sour ale. Then, after a plain repast of bread and cheese, with perhaps a bowl of vegetable broth if the weather were chill, I would take my leave. At my first coming to those parts, the landlord had tried to press me to a joint of meat or a bowlful of beef stew, convinced as such men are that flesh is necessary to human health. But my continual refusal, and I dare say my continual survival, persuaded him in the end that a man might live on cheese and vegetables alone, though he begged me not to recommend such a diet to my patients and his customers.

'There's little profit to be made in such plain fare,' he confided. 'For when a man can see exactly what he is eating, he can add up the cost of the parts and complain bitterly if he thinks a poor innkeeper is seeking too much profit. But once let there be meat in it and gravy and spices and herbs, though it be but in truth three parts vegetable water, then is he more willing to pay what I ask without quarrel!'

He spoke thus familiarly with me only after long acquaintance, and also because he was convinced by my frugal method of life that I lived up to the old reputation of my profession and loved gold as much as he did.

I smiled and thereafter joined him in long plaints about the rising cost of things and the parsimony of our shared customers, and on such plain fare for the stomach and for the mind, I existed quite happily for near on ten years.

Happily, I say. Well, it is a question of degree; and though I oft-times felt that I would be as well out of this world as in it, yet it is a brave surgeon who can practise on himself, and an unbroken pattern of life can come to be pleasant though no single part of it has much power to please.

So my life passed till this bleak November day. It was a wild dark morning with the promise of winter's first snow in the blast and I almost abandoned my customary ride to the Black Tor. Yet, perhaps because I knew such a break in the pattern of my existence would make me feel unsettled, I saddled my patient old mare and set out. The stage had been and gone when I reached the inn. Some passengers had alighted, I was told, but they were resting after their long bone-shaking ride and had left orders not to be disturbed till their dinner was ready, so I went and sat alone in the upstairs parlour till John Farley came to join me.

'It's blowing up a real hurricano out there,' he pronounced. 'Feel how it makes the old timbers shake. You'd almost think we were out at sea.'

I smiled thinly, thinking how little he knew of what it really felt like to be in a storm in the Atlantic's bubbling cauldron. But he was right about the rising wind for I could hear it singing in the chimney and around the shutters, and from time to time it did indeed seem as if the boards beneath my feet vibrated like a ship's deck.

'It will be good for trade, John,' I joked. 'Those who are here will not be able to leave for home.'

'Nay,' he said gloomily. 'You mean those who are at home will not set out to come here.'

So we talked of nothing in particular, and smoked a pipe, and supped our ale, till there came a knock at the door, or rather a thud low down, as if someone had kicked it.

'Who's there?' called Farley.

'Doctor's dinner,' came back a voice I recognized as belonging to Willie Bell, a slow-witted youth who worked in the kitchen.

'Well, fetch it in, you great lubbock!'

'Can't open the door, maister,' replied Willie.

With an exasperated groan, Farley rose and pulled the door open.

It was immediately apparent why Willie could not turn the handle himself.

Instead of the usual small tray with a loaf and a wedge of cheese, he was carrying a huge pewter salver with a great domed lid.

He staggered forward and deposited it on the table in front of me, then waved his hands in the air, saying, ''Tis hot.'

'Hot? What's hot?' cried Farley. 'What's this you've brought, you idiot?'

And so saying, he snatched the lid off the salver.

A great cloud of aromatic steam arose, obscuring what lay there for a moment. Then as the morning mist is sucked up the fellside by the reddening sun, it cleared to reveal two mountainous joints of roast meat, one a leg of pork, the other a shoulder of mutton.

My first thought was that this must be some monstrous joke of mine host's, and I leapt to my feet, ready to vent my indignation upon him. Then I looked into his face and saw that his amazement was as real as mine.

'Numbskull!' he yelled, raising his fist threateningly above the pot-boy's head. 'What stupidity is this? Have you not been working here long enough to know what manner of vittles his honour prefers?'

Willie cringed away, crying, 'Aye, maister, but the missus told me as he wanted this here today.'

'The missus?' Farley looked at me with wild surmise. 'Doctor, I'm sorry. Clearly this fool has got more muddled than he usually is, if that's possible. We'll have this sorted in a trice. Dora!'

His bellow shook the room almost as much as the storm without, which was increasing in intensity with each passing minute.

A few moments later Mrs Farley, a stout good-natured woman whose natural generosity when it came to loading plates brought her into frequent conflict with her husband, appeared in the doorway.

'This idiot says you gave him this as the doctor's dinner,' said Farley, pointing at the steaming salver.

'That's right,' said his wife. 'Is something wrong wi' it?'

'Wrong? A leg of pork and a shoulder of mutton, and you ask if something's wrong?' cried Farley. 'When did you know Dr Teasdale let a morsel of meat pass his lips? What are you thinking of, woman?'

'I'll thank you not to *woman* me,' said his wife with spirit. 'It was the doctor's friends as told me to send it up.'

A blast like a giant's hand struck the building so that it seemed that at the very least it must tear the chimneys off, and for about half a minute speech was impossible. Then the wind subsided to a steady roar, and I moistened my lips with beer and asked faintly, 'What friends, Mrs Farley?'

'The two gentlemen who got off the coach,' she replied. 'They ordered a roast leg and a roast shoulder as soon as they arrived and naturally I thought it was for them, though a lot it seemed for just the two of them. But when they came down just now they said, no, it weren't for them, it was for their friend, Dr Teasdale, and would I send it straight up? I hope I didn't do wrong.'

Farley was looking at me. What he saw in my face must have assured him that these men were no friends of mine, for he said, 'Right, wife. Let's you and I have a talk to these two gentlemen who make themselves so pleasant with decent folk.'

'Oh, it's too late for that,' said his wife. 'They've gone.'

'Gone?' said Farley, looking aghast at the loaded salver. 'Did they pay their reckoning?'

'Oh aye. They paid in full. For their room, the food, and the other things they bought. I asked 'em if they didn't want a word with the doctor, and they said no, they'd likely see him at home later.'

'Well, this beats cock-fighting,' said Farley with undisguisable relief at learning that this jape was not going to cost him money. 'What do you make of it, Doctor?'

'Mrs Farley,' I said with difficulty. 'What did they look like, these two men?'

'Oh, if it's a description you want for the constable, I'd know 'em again anywhere,' she cried. 'They were the oddest pair. Him, the older one who did the talking, he had one of them peg-legs and walked with a crutch. And the other, the younger one, who never opened his mouth, poor lad, he had his sleeve pinned across his chest like he had no arm to go in it.'

I could speak no further but Farley's curiosity was bubbling over.

'You said they bought some other things, wife. What manner of things did they buy to carry out into this terrible storm with them?'

'The oddest set of things you can imagine,' she replied, shaking her head in puzzlement. 'But they did not carry them off with them. No, they said they was sure the doctor, understanding their disabilities, would oblige them by fetching them along hisself. And they left them on the kitchen table.'

'Left *what*, for God's sake, woman?' cried Farley in desperation.

But I did not stay for her answer.

Rudely thrusting her aside, I clattered down the narrow stairway to the kitchen, and flung open the door.

There on the great oak table, in a miasma of smoke and steam and the reek of roasting meat, stood a cask of rum; a tinderbox; a carving knife.

Brother's Keeper

I hadn't seen my brother for seven years till I switched on *Crimewatch*.

A security camera film of a bank robbery is not unlike those old blue movies we used to hire for stag nights. Black-and-white, very grainy, lots of jerky movement, no sound, and all utterly unreal. That's a cock; that's a gun; that's a girl being screwed; that's a cashier being shot. None of it convincing enough to stimulate lust, or horror.

Then the silly bugger looked right up into the camera, and they froze the picture.

My first thought was – it's me!

My second, just as shocking – it's Jake!

Seven years it had been, and seven wasn't enough.

Having a petty crook in the family is bad; having an unsuccessful one is unbearable. Dad died when I was fourteen and Jake twelve. I became the man of the house and from that moment Jake was a constant charge on my purse, my time, and my nerves. Our mother could see no fault in him. He rifled her purse, pawned her rings, forged her signature on hire purchase agreements, but it made no difference. In Mum's eyes, these were all childish pranks. I caught him going through my wallet once and hit him with a cricket bat. Result: he got spoilt rotten in luxurious convalescence for three weeks while I got the silent reproach treatment for the same period.

As we grew older and he spread his criminal wings in the great world of South London, I had hopes he might give us a bit of respite by fluttering into jail, but the trouble was he was too useless at it to get nicked! I mean, what do they charge a man with who usually ends up as the victim?

He stole a car once. It had no tax disc, no number plates, and finally he had to borrow a tenner from me to get the Council to tow it away.

He set up as a fence, and every wide boy with a load of junk they couldn't sell down Peckham market dumped it on Jake with some cock-and-bull about a big motorway hijack up north.

Next he turned burglar. The first place he broke into was a battered wives' refuge. They didn't bother to call the police, just hospitalized him for a fortnight.

Now here he was robbing a bank in Battersea, wearing a leather jacket with a flaking skull, flared jeans, and a pair of trendy trainers which seemed to be hurting his feet. And, of course, nothing at all to hide his face.

If there'd been any doubt it was Jake, it would have vanished when the presenter said that the robber had only got away with a couple of hundred pounds, and most of that in small change. Nevertheless the police were very keen to get him. They don't like people wandering around banks, firing guns, even if they are loaded with blanks. This time the cashier had only fainted. But next time, the presenter forecast very seriously, it could be for real.

I doubted it. Jake was a criminal butterfly. The only crime he ever stuck at long enough to get even mediocre at was conning money out of me. I thanked God and my own wisdom that we were three hundred miles apart, he didn't have my address, and I'd changed my name.

I was no longer my brother's keeper.

I switched off the telly and poured myself a congratulatory Scotch.

I was just getting ready for bed that same night when the doorbell of my flat rang. Not the main door, but the inside bell. A neighbour perhaps, wanting to borrow a cup of sugar? Hardly. I didn't know many of my neighbours, and those I did know, I didn't get on with.

I peered through the peephole. Two men stood there. They didn't need to hold up their identity cards to tell me they were police.

As I invited them in, I heard a neighbouring door close very quietly. In a flash I knew what had happened. Mr Mallick, retired tax inspector, with whom I had a running feud about milk bottles, mail delivery, and the incessant jabbering of his pet macaw, must have been watching *Crimewatch* too and had mistaken Jake for me.

With what delight he must have rung the police.

With what delight I would bid them a loud goodnight as I ushered them out, graciously accepting their embarrassed apologies.

It didn't quite work out like that.

The trouble started with the date, May the fifth, three weeks earlier. The police had sat on the film till forced to admit they were getting nowhere. Of course, if they'd ever bothered to nick the most incompetent criminal ever born, Jake's face would have been on the record and they'd have had him safely under wraps by now.

As it was, they'd got me, courtesy of old Mallick, and I could see my vague reaction to May the fifth gave them great joy.

'Let me think,' I said. 'I was probably here. Yes, I'm certain I was here. I'm a freelance writer, you see, and I work at home. Often I don't go out for days on end, specially if the weather's bad, which it usually is up here in Newcastle.'

I laughed at my little joke and they smiled too. But not at my joke.

'Weather was fine and sunny that week,' said the elder of the two, a totem pole of a man called Inspector Edgerley. 'Also one of your neighbours seems to think you were away for a few days about this time.'

'Mr Mallick, you mean?' I said negligently. 'He'd say anything to do me down. We're old adversaries. I guessed it was him that rang you.'

They exchanged glances and the younger man, a dog-faced sergeant with a high Geordie lilt, said, 'And what makes you think someone rang us then?'

It was a slip, of course, but having made it, I saw no alternative but to go boldly on.

'I presume this is about that *Crimewatch* programme?' I said. 'I had it on earlier and when I saw that fellow robbing that bank, I thought, good Lord, he's not a million miles away from me! But I never dreamt that anyone could be so stupid as to ring the police. I'd forgotten about Mallick. I am right, I take it?'

Edgerley said, 'We've had a word with Mr Mallick, it's true. And he's very insistent you were away from home at the beginning of May. He recollects that your milk delivery was suspended and also that the postman asked if he would take in a parcel for you, which he refused to do. Presumably you had to pick it up yourself at the post office, so a check with their records, also with the milkman, should settle the issue.'

Now this set me racking my brain. If a doddering geriatric like Mallick appeared to have a better idea of my movements than I did, it would be hard to blame the police for being suspicious.

Finally I got things sorted in my mind and smiled with relief.

'Look,' I said. 'In fact, I doubt if I can tell you positively where I was on that precise day, but one thing's certain – I was nowhere near London. In fact, quite the reverse. Like I said, I'm a writer and I'm currently researching a piece on the commercial spolia-tion of the Scottish Highlands. I was up there, touring around, for several days at the start of the month, so that's where I certainly was on the fifth.'

'Presumably you slept somewhere that night, sir,' said Edgerley.

'Of course I did, but don't ask me where. I was doing bed and breakfast, somewhere north of Inverness I should think. But it was all cash-in-hand, no-register, no-VAT stuff. I doubt even if you went round with my photo, you'd get very far. They've got selective memories, these Scots, where the taxman's concerned! And there's something else . . .'

I paused, thinking I had a clincher.

'Yes, sir?'

'At the start of the month I had a beard. Big black job. I didn't shave it off till I got back from my trip, so there's no way I could be that chap in the bank, is there?'

'Not if what you say is true, sir,' said Edgerley. 'Why did you shave it off, as a matter of interest?'

'Why not?' I said surprised. 'It was a winter-weight job, and with summer coming on, I didn't fancy getting overheated.'

Edgerley glanced at the sergeant who went out. Then he said to me, 'Mind if I take a look around your flat, sir?'

I could have stood on my rights, I suppose, but as I wouldn't be seen dead in the kind of clothes Jake had been wearing, and all the small change I possessed was in my trouser pocket, I said, 'Be my guest.'

He started in the living room, searching in a desultory fashion as if he were merely going through the motions. When we heard the sergeant re-entering the flat, Edgerley went out into the hall to meet him. He returned looking grave.

'Mr Mallick, your neighbour, confirms you did have a beard at the start of May, sir. But according to him when you returned from your trip, you'd already shaved it off.'

'Well, he's either mistaken or he's lying,' I said indignantly. 'Look, Inspector, I'm getting rather tired of this . . .'

But my excursion into the attractive terrain of righteous indignation was cut short by the entrance of the sergeant carrying a gun.

It may sound hard to believe that I'd forgotten I had a gun, but that's the truth. My mind had been full of leather jackets, flared jeans and tight trainers, which I knew I didn't have. Of course I was able to produce the licence and explain I was a member of an authorized gun club, but I could see that from being a nice each-way bet, I had suddenly become hot favourite.

Now why didn't I simply tell them about Jake?

I owed him nothing and he owed me plenty. He'd even robbed me of my chance of happiness with the one girl I ever loved by vomiting over a priceless Persian rug at our engagement party before vanishing into the night with her mother's jewellery stuffed into his pockets.

Well, we got the jewels back, and there was no prosecution. But there was no wedding either.

It wasn't even as if I'd made some kind of deathbed promise to our mum to take care of him, though I don't doubt she'd have exacted one if death hadn't come suddenly in the form of a florist's delivery van in Peckham High Street.

Jake said he'd take care of the funeral arrangements, and he seemed so genuinely cut up that I was stupid enough to give him Mum's insurance cheque to cover expenses.

He assured me everything was taken care of and to do him justice, the funeral was a real treat, everything of the very best. I should have anticipated that in Jake's world view, taking care of things wouldn't actually extend to handing over hard cash.

First came the undertaker's bill, then the caterer's and the Red Lion's where we had the booze-up. I decided to check the florist before he came chasing me. It turned out it was the same firm whose van had knocked Mum down. The manager was surprised I should be expecting a bill. Not only had he agreed to supply all our floral requirements free of charge, he'd also given Jake an ex-gratia payment in return for a guarantee there'd be no compensation claims arising from the accident.

It was this that sickened me most of all.

Naturally Jake had vanished after the ceremony, but I knew he'd be back once the money ran out, in search of the shelter and support he regarded as his natural due.

I also knew there was no way of getting free of him if I stayed in London. Threats to his person or appeals to his better nature were alike useless. A couple of days would pass and he'd be up to his old tricks as if nothing had been said. My business, social and personal life would be under continual threat.

Only a fool doesn't run when running's the only option.

I headed north. I changed my name. And I finished up in Newcastle Upon Tyne where the wind might be cold, the language unintelligible, and the beer unbelievable, but there was no chance of being accosted by Jake.

After seven years, I'd become hardened to the wind, fluent in the dialect, and addicted to the ale.

Now, indirectly and unbeknowingly, Jake had tracked me down.

So why didn't I just tell the police the truth?

Many reasons, the simplest being I thought I could handle things without mentioning Jake. By the time I realized my error, the cops had me so firmly in the frame they'd have probably bust a gut laughing if I'd suddenly said, 'Look, I should've mentioned this before, but it weren't me, it was my kid brother.'

And anyway, suppose they *had* tracked down Jake, it was going to be his word against mine, and one thing Jake was good at was telling lies. The tabloid shit-diggers would have a field day, and whichever of us ended in court, both of us would have our dirty linen flapping out across the front pages.

So I stayed shtum.

I suppose I still believed they wouldn't be able to put together any real case against me. I mean, how strong was the true resemblance between us after all these years? Black-and-white security film was one thing, but in the flesh, there must be a hundred differences.

They put me in an identity parade and every employee of the bank plus half a dozen customers identified me.

After that it was all downhill.

By this time I was back in the Smoke and my gentle Geordies had been replaced by a dog-faced DCI from Dagenham. I tried to convince him of my innocence but he shook his head and said, 'Forget it, John –' which happened to be my name, but he called everybody John, so it wouldn't have mattered – 'innocent, guilty, we've got you by the goolies and we ain't letting go. You're looking at five years, maybe more. Is that what you want?'

'Show me an alternative,' I said, alerted by his tone to the possibility of a bit of illicit plea-bargaining.

'How about three years, two suspended? With remission you could be out for Christmas.'

'What do I have to do?' I said. 'Marry into the Royal Family?'

'No. Just plead guilty. Full cooperation, reformed character, positive psycho report. I'll stand you up in court and make you sound like Saul of fucking Tarsus!'

'Just for pleading guilty?' I said incredulously.

'That's right. Also you might like to clear your slate by asking for a few other offences to be taken into account.'

'What other offences?' I asked, feeling alarmed.

'These,' he said, pushing a sheet of paper across to me. I looked at the list and laughed.

'They'll put me away for ever if I cough this lot,' I said.

'No, they won't,' he assured me. 'You're easily led, fell into bad company, it'll be mascara-running time all round. Besides, to show you're truly repentant, you'll be pointing the finger at all the real villains.'

He gave me another list, this time of names.

'But I don't know any of these men!' I declared indignantly.

'In that case, it won't bother you grassing them up, will it?' he said.

I couldn't fault his logic. So we shook hands on the deal.

He was good as his word, I'll give him that, except that I only got eighteen months of my sentence suspended, so I'll miss Christmas. Good riddance. After a childhood spent watching Jake opening the best presents, I never did like it much.

So now, after a few token nights in the Scrubs, I'm settling in very nicely at this gleaming new Open Prison in rural Essex.

Today was my first visiting day. I wasn't expecting anybody, but my name was called and off I went.

I stopped dead in my tracks when I saw who was waiting for me.

It was me, myself, exactly as I had been when I wore a big black beard!

Except for the godawful clothes. They were the giveaway.

'Hello, Jake,' I said. 'Nice of you to come.'

'Hello, Jonty,' he said. 'Look, I'm really sorry about this.'

'Sorry?' I said. 'If you're so bloody sorry, what am I doing eating your porridge?'

'I didn't realize what was going off, did I? I mean, when I read they'd caught some geezer for the job, I just thought I'd fallen lucky. I didn't recognize the name, how could I? You'd changed it, hadn't you? Why'd you do that, Jonty?'

He spoke accusingly. Here was I, doing his time, and he was taking offence!

I said, 'Never mind that. When did you realize it was me?'

'I popped into court for the verdict,' he said. 'I'd been growing the whiskers ever since the job and I reckoned no one would spot me. I was really knocked flat when I saw it was you. Did you realize it was me that done the bank?'

'Yes, Jake,' I said. 'I realized it was you.'

'And you never let on? That was really nice of you, Jonty.'

Really nice! That was it, my thanks for saving his skin at the expense of my own. He sounded like I'd given him a birthday present, pleased but not ecstatic. I mean, you expect birthday presents, don't you? Your nearest and dearest have got to cough up, haven't they? This was Jake's attitude to all the gifts of goods and protection he'd received from childhood on. He expected to be taken care of, and my gift of several years of freedom was just like all the other non-returnable loans he'd received from me over the years.

I began to rise.

He said, 'No, hang about, please, Jonty. Don't rush off. I really wanted to talk to you.'

I sat down again, wondering if for once I'd misjudged him, and after all he was about to express his heartfelt gratitude, perhaps even offer to set the record straight.

He said, 'The thing is, Jonty, I thought I might go away for a while, keep my head down, you know. To tell the truth, there's a lot of people I owe money to, I've had a run of bad luck, and I thought, maybe a trip abroad would be a clever move. Only I'm a bit short at the moment . . .'

I began to laugh.

I said, 'You mean, you've come to visit me here in jail, doing bird for a crime you committed, and all you really want is to touch me for some cash for a foreign holiday?'

'I'd not put it quite like that,' he said, looking hurt again.

I said, 'Jake, you're priceless.'

He said, 'I know I've not always been as straight with you as I'd have liked, Jonty, and I'm sorry. But I've got no one else to turn to, and if you could see your way . . . one last time . . . for our mum's sake . . .'

That was the button which broke my resistance. I regarded him with weary resignation and said, 'All right, Jake. Why change the habits of a lifetime? Here's what you do. You go along to see my brief. I'll let him know you're coming. He'll give you a tin box. He won't give you a key, because he don't have a key. I trust him but not that much! So you'll have to open it yourself. I presume over the years you've at least learned how to open a tin box?'

'Yes, I can manage that,' he said eagerly.

'Don't use a blowtorch,' I advised. 'There's a lot of highly inflammable paper money in that box, some sterling, but mostly Italian lira. Take as much as you think you'll need and keep the rest for me, OK?'

I could see his eyes lighting up, like a kid who has asked Santa for a pedal car and gets a beach buggy instead.

'Yeah, I'll do that for you, Jonty. Just as much as I'll need, I promise.'

'And have a good time. Decided where to go yet?'

'I thought maybe Spain.'

I frowned and said, 'Full of Anglo crooks, Spain. If you've offended someone serious, they can easily get to you there. Why not try Italy? Save you changing those lira. Sicily's the spot I'd recommend. Smashing island, lovely beaches, gorgeous girls. You'll love it. Got a passport, have you?'

His face fell. That's my Jake! Fleeing the country, and he hasn't even thought about a passport.

I said, 'No sweat. You'll find a passport in the box. It's in my old name, our name. I had a beard then too. With your face fungus, we don't look a million miles apart. Use it. All you'll have to do is remember you're John not Jake.'

'I don't know what to say,' he said, looking genuinely moved. 'You must be the best brother in the world. I'm going to pay you back for everything one day, I promise. I'll really do it.'

'Yes, I know you will,' I said, standing up. 'Now push off and enjoy yourself. Drop me a postcard.'

He reached out and took my hand. I swear there were tears in his eyes.

I almost felt guilty as I watched him go.

Almost.

I mean, he had alternatives, didn't he?

He could get an honest job. He could go to the police and tell them the truth. He could . . .

All right, I know it's most probable he'll break open the box, spend the sterling on some more godawful gear, stuff the lira notes down his Y-fronts, and head off to Sicily, waving my old passport.

But even then, he might spend his time tanning on the beach without ever being spotted as the black-bearded Englishman who on May fifth last, during a heated negotiation over some drugs which in fact he didn't have, shot and killed the manager of a Mafia-run bank in Palermo before decamping with a large sum of Mafioso money.

If he does get picked up, I hope he has more sense than to say it couldn't have been him because he was robbing another bank at the time!

Who's going to believe a stupid alibi like that?

Especially when the best brother in the world has been authorized by a High Court judge and twelve good men and true to use it already.

Silent Night

It was Christmas Eve.

Needing the stimulus of sunrise to get him out of bed, Tommy Atkinson, seventeen and not yet employed, felt he'd really done rather well to be only fifteen minutes late ringing the bell of the Scotts' that evening.

'I've come for Pauline,' he said. 'We're going to the carol singing.'

'She's gone on,' said Mrs Scott. 'She's not best pleased with you, Tommy. She said you promised faithfully.'

'Oh heck,' said Tommy with the rushed grin of one whose seventeen years were littered with the wreckage of faithful promises. 'It's this weather. It never got properly light today, did it? I've not known where I'm at.'

Despite herself, Mrs Scott returned his smile. Clad in basket-ball boots, bleached jeans and an old khaki overcoat, with tufts of blue-tinted hair escaping from beneath a heavily darned bala-clava, Tommy was definitely not son-in-law material, but it was hard not to like him.

Encouraged, Tommy said, 'I've got Pauline's Christmas prezzie here. I'd best leave it, or I'll just lose it. I'll put it in her room, shall I?'

Without waiting for an answer, he clattered up the stairs two at a time. A second later, there was a crash, and when Mrs Scott followed him, she found him stooping to pick up an old-fashioned photo frame.

'Oh heck,' he said again as he retrieved the pair of hinged ovals and saw the glass was cracked in both of them. There were two of them in matching oval frames. A moment earlier they had been hinged together. Now, from Tommy's right hand, a young man in uniform smiled through splintered glass at the strong-featured young woman to his left. The latter was Pauline's great-aunt whose name she'd inherited, as well as her strong, handsome features. Pauline had told him that the young man was her great-aunt's beau, who had got himself killed in the Great War. Her great-aunt had since been drowned, perhaps accidentally, in Bluewater Beck. Tommy thought history (which for him began at the day before the current football season opened), was really boring. And this wasn't the only difference between them. She was serious, orderly, reliable, forward-looking, and had a job. He was careless, chaotic, feckless, and out of work. He sometimes wondered what she saw in him, but as he also sometimes wondered what he saw in her, it hardly mattered.

What did matter was that he'd cracked the glass of one of her most treasured possessions and, coupled with his failure to pick her up for the village's annual carol round tonight, this could really mess things up for the holiday. There was no chance of fixing the glass, so he'd just have to try to repair the damage caused by his lateness.

He went down the stairs four at a time.

Pauline's mother came out of the kitchen.

'Here,' she said, giving him a hug. 'I bet you've not had any tea. There's a fresh-baked pasty and a couple of apples in there.'

'Great!' he said stuffing them into the pocket of the shabby old army greatcoat he'd bought at a jumble sale. 'See you. Merry Christmas!'

She closed the door after him, smiling.

The rendezvous for the carollers was the war memorial by the church. There was no one there but he'd expected that. They'd be on the road to the Hall where they always started. With his usual optimism, he assured himself that if he cut across the fields he could probably overtake them.

Putting one foot on the knee of the crouching bronze soldier who symbolized Hartlow's dead in two world wars, he jumped over the church wall and strode through the lank grass between the old headstones. One of them he used as a stepladder at the other end of the churchyard, and very conveniently there was another smaller one to aid his descent on the far side. There were three or four of these miniature headstones along the outside of the wall. The graves of those who committed suicide, the villagers said. The family liked to get them as close to consecrated ground as possible.

It was very dark here, but he strode out confidently. Straight across old Stride's pasture and through Brockley Wood would bring him out into the Hall's formal gardens, no sweat. This terrain was as familiar as his own back garden.

Now, though, he stumbled and nearly fell. It was the darkness of course. Even the flattest field had unevenness. He wished he'd thought to bring a torch, but he'd been so rushed. Christ, that was a big hole! What was old Strides up to? Digging for coal? Thank heaven there was the outline of the wood ahead.

'Bloody hell!' Tommy swore aloud.

He'd almost walked right into a high fence of barbed wire!

What was that silly old fool thinking of? There'd never before been anything but a straggly and easily penetrated hedge between the pasture and the wood. It took him a good ten minutes and some minor damage to his hands and trousers to climb through the wire. By now he had stopped feeling guilty and started feeling furious. This was all bloody Pauline's fault! She was always going on at him about being selfish, but if this was what worrying about other people did for you, well, sod it!

He had half a mind to go back but that would mean climbing that fence again. Besides, looking back across the field he realized he could no longer see the outline of the church. A mist had risen and was creeping slowly across the grass towards him. He didn't care for mist, and he turned quickly and set off through the woods, but within two paces the whiteness was all around him. Nothing to worry about though. Didn't he know most of these trees like his own bleeding hand? All their odd-shaped knots and hollows, all the initials and the messages carved into their mossy bark?

But when he looked for these familiar marks he found to his surprise that he could see none. What was more, a lot of the trees had been reduced to charred stumps. There must have been a fire here during that last hot summer. Now, standing uncertain among these ruined trees, their dead limbs ahead all wreathed with strands of smoky mist, he felt not merely lost, but adrift in a totally alien landscape. Nor was it a silent landscape. He thought he heard something piping like a bird. Fearfully then hopefully he strained his ears, and finally he laughed aloud in glee. It was singing! It was carollers! And now, as he hurried forward, he could even make out the tune. *Silent night, holy night* . . .

It was only as the singing grew louder that it occurred to him that he couldn't hear the little brass ensemble from the Grammar

School's orchestra which usually accompanied the carols. Perhaps he wasn't alone in being late!

But now something else struck him too.

They were singing the old carol in the original German.

Stille Nacht, heilige Nacht . . .

He slowed to a halt, uncertain again. Surely there couldn't be two parties of carollers out in the district tonight? Just how lost was he?

Then once again all fears were blown away as a man's voice called, 'Hey, Tommy! Come on, Tommy! Over here.'

Obediently he advanced, and within a few paces he began to make out figures. There were about a dozen of them, all men as far as he could see, dressed in long grey topcoats with woollen hats pulled down over their ears. He didn't recognize any of them. They certainly weren't the village party.

But how did they know his name?

He paused again and one of them came forward with his hand outstretched, saying, 'Welcome, Tommy! Merry Christmas to you.'

He was tall and spoke with a distinct foreign accent. Tommy took the outstretched hand and, feeling the chill of the night in the ungloved hand and the chill of the night in his ungloved fingers, suddenly shivered. The man spotted them and said, 'You're cold, my friend. Here, have a drink. This will warm you up.'

Someone turned a long thin bottle to the speaker, who pulled out the cork and passed it on to Tommy. He drank. It was some fiery spirit, raw and sudden. He coughed violently and the men all laughed.

'Not used to schnapps, Tommy?' said the tall man. 'Don't worry. We will teach you.'

'I'm sorry,' said Tommy. 'I was looking for the singers, I mean from the church—'

But before he could explain he was interrupted.

'So you think we cannot be the singers, is that it?' cried the tall man in mock indignation. 'Such beautiful sounds from such dreadful creatures! Well, listen, Tommy. Drink some more and listen.'

They began to sing, still in German, but this time a much jollier, livelier tune. Tommy didn't understand the words, but he caught the feeling of happiness. He took several more pulls from the bottle as he listened. Whoever these fellows were, it was a lot more interesting here than with the church lot!

As the carol died away, he realized there were other listeners too, ten or a dozen of them, emerging quietly from the mist like shy animals attracted by a fire. The few quiet words said as they stood there, though dressed not like himself, were clearly native English. One, at least, he thought he recognized without being able to put a name to him, but even this half-recognition was comforting.

The last notes died away and the tall man looked at him and said, smiling, 'Now it's your turn, Tommy!'

Why he should be singled out, Tommy did not know. But the heat of the schnapps was in his body and its fumes were in his head, so he stepped forward boldly and began to sing 'The First Nowell'. Reluctantly at first, but by the time he got to the second chorus, all hesitation had gone and there was even a fine Welsh descant on the first 'nowell'!

'Bravo!' cried the tall man and his companions all applauded, and sang in their turn. Then Tommy and the others replied, and bottles circulated, and soon all barriers of suspicion and diffidence had been broken down. Food was produced; dark bread and spicy sausage from the foreigners, tins of stew and blocks of chocolate from the locals. Tommy was aware, and rather ashamed, that he had nothing to contribute but no one seemed to mind. One of the Englishmen said, 'Good grub this, mates. We don't get sausage like this back home.'

Everyone laughed, but for some reason the mention of home seemed to throw a pall over proceedings till the young lad Tommy had recognized said, 'Hang on,' disappeared into the darkness and returned a few moments later with a football.

'Hey! A football match!' cried the tall man. 'International! The only contest worth fighting!'

They divided into their teams. Tommy found himself in goal between two piles of coats. The game wasn't easy to follow. Though the atmosphere had brightened, the mist persisted, and for much of the time the players were only vague shapes milling around on the rough and pitted terrain; cries of protest, exhilaration and applause came drifting through the swirl of grey like the calling of seabirds.

Then suddenly solid figures came thundering out of the mist and Tommy had to fling himself sideways to catch the hard-driven ball.

'Bravo!' cried the tall man.

'Good save, mate,' grinned the youngster who'd brought the ball. Who was winning, who was losing Tommy didn't know, but he knew it didn't matter. This was like one of those spontaneous games which sometimes sprang up on the village green, with lads joining in as the fancy took them, older men showing off to their kids if the ball came near them, younger ones trying to impress their girls with their virtuosity. And afterwards as dusk fell, they would all drift away, some home to the family and supper in front of the telly, some to the pub for a couple of pints, some hand in hand down the narrow path winding alongside Bluewater Beck.

Suddenly his heart was aching, as if home and pub and the tumbling stream were all a million miles away instead of just beyond the wood across the Common.

It was growing dark again. In the distance he heard the golden
trill of a brass instrument with that curious otherworldliness a
frost-laced mist gives to sound. It must be the Grammar School
band, and the melancholy notes sobered him up, reminding him
of his promise to Pauline and of her probable wrath. Others too
seemed to be taking the brass as a summons. Men were dropping
out to pick up their coats, then drifting off into the darkness,
left and right.

The ball came hurtling out of the growing darkness and he
caught it. He could hear the tall man's voice saying, 'Let's not
go so soon, friends. A little longer, stay a little longer.'

The young Englishman appeared before him now and reached
out for his ball.

'Good game,' said Tommy. 'Pity it's got to finish. Here, mate,
don't I know you? You're not going to the carol singing up at
the Hall, are you? Maybe you're a friend of the Scotts?'

For a second the boy's frost-vapoured breath seemed to
condense before his face so that it was like looking at him through
a shattered pane of glass. Then he took the ball and turned away
without a word.

Tommy started to follow him, but a cold hand caught his
wrist. It was the tall man.

'Won't you stay a little longer, Tommy?' he urged. 'Don't you
see, if we all stay here, nothing can happen to us. Then it must
stop. Perhaps if only one from each side stays, only one . . .'

His voice was pleading and there was nothing of menace in
his person or his words, but a terrible fear was growing in
Tommy's gut, sharper even than the sour aftertaste of the
schnapps.

'No!' he cried. 'I've got to go with the others!'

And thrusting the man's hand roughly from his sleeve, he set
off after the young man with the football. He ran swiftly through

the trees, persuading himself that his haste was nothing to do with fear, merely with a desire to catch up with the church carollers. How much time had he wasted in the woods? They must surely have long since moved on from the Hall, but he kept on catching sounds of brass in the chilly air.

And at last he could see lights – a shifting pattern of torches and lanterns as their bearers arranged themselves in order – and there, beyond them, the solid bulk of the old Hall!

He found he was sobbing with relief and paused to collect himself. A noise to his left made him start nervously. He turned, fearful of what he might see. Quite close by stood a woman in a long dark dress, her face shadowed by a headscarf, but still familiar.

'Pauline?' he said uncertainly. 'Is that you?'

Her response astounded him.

'Why did you come away?' she cried passionately. 'Why?'

'I don't know! What do you mean? And why are you dressed up like that?'

'You should have stayed,' she said accusingly. 'Out there, there was hope. It could have ended if you'd stayed out there. You'd have been safe, everyone would have been safe! Why didn't you stay?'

His mind was still trying to pretend she was angry with him for being late, but his heart knew that this had nothing to do with it. He heard his voice saying, 'I was afraid . . . everyone was afraid . . . too afraid . . .'

'Too afraid?' she said piteously. 'Too afraid to live. Oh, but you should have stayed!'

He reached his hand to her. For a second he thought she was going to take it. Then something soft and white as a feather fluttered down into his palm, and she turned and was gone.

He stepped after her, calling, 'Pauline! Pauline!' From the

group of lights bobbing around the Hall, a single point detached itself and moved across the lawn.

'Tommy, is that you?' called a voice.

He turned and stared till the torch was close enough to illuminate the bearer. He saw without surprise or understanding that it was Pauline, dressed in jeans and a duffel coat.

'Where've you been?' she said sharply. 'I thought you weren't coming?'

'I should have stayed,' he said unhappily. 'I was needed.'

'Stayed where?' she demanded. 'You're needed here!'

Then suddenly she laughed and the scolding tone left her voice.

'I don't just mean the choir either,' she said softly. 'I need you. Happy Christmas, Tommy. I'm glad you've come.'

She embraced him and he hugged her tight with one arm, looking over her shoulder into the dark and listening woods.

'What've you got there that's so precious?' asked Pauline, indicating the tightly clenched fist of his free hand.

Slowly he opened his fingers. There was nothing in his palm but a few drops of water and a smear of white. He noticed that his fingers had stopped bleeding.

Pauline laughed and said, 'I don't think you need hoard that. There's plenty more where that came from, look.'

Now Tommy turned towards the Hall.

Everyone was still; the choir at last were ready to sing, the band to play, and all the cups of light around the lanterns and torches were slowly filling with feathers of snow. Breaking away from Pauline, Tommy stepped forward out of the sheltering trees and as the mellow brass sounded the opening bars of 'Silent Night', he raised his face to the skies and felt the gently falling flakes melt on his cheeks like tears.

The Boy and Man Booker

Boy Ansell awoke, had no idea where he was except that it wasn't his flat and for a moment felt afraid.

Then he remembered and joy washed away his fear.

Cautiously he raised his head from the soft bank of pillows. A slight muzziness, nothing more. It was true what they said, the best champagne leaves little trace of its passage and last night he had drunk nothing but the best.

He slipped his hand under the pillow. Another moment of panic, then his fingers touched paper. It was there, but he needed to see it. He groped for an unfamiliar light switch. A golden glow touched his surroundings like sunlight. A hotel room. But what a room! You could fit all of his Brighton flat in here. Furnished in the stately home neoclassical style with a sky-blue ceiling from whose lofty rococo cornice gilded cherubim looked down on acres of thick white carpet, it was probably costing his publishers more for one night here than a whole week at the kind of dump they used to put him in.

But they could do better.

They *would* do better now that he had this to wave at them.

He read the magic words on the piece of paper.

Pay David Boyd Ansell the sum of fifty thousand pounds . . . for and on behalf of MAN BOOKER . . .

Fifty thousand. With the kind of sales now in prospect, he could afford to smile at this paltry sum. It would, after all, buy him only five or six months in a room like this. He might even never bother to cash the cheque but keep it framed on his study wall.

Or better still, cash it but keep a convincing photocopy framed.

He swung his legs to the floor and viewed himself in a heavy gilt mirror nicely placed to catch the wide expanse of the king-sized bed. No sign that he'd had company last night. Not that it hadn't been there for the asking, he told himself complacently as he turned his face slowly from left to right profile. Boy David they called him, and even in his mid-thirties his face and figure still retained enough of the youthful perfection of Michelangelo's statue to justify the sobriquet. So pussy galore on offer. But at some point during all the back-slapping, cheek-pecking, body-hugging, champagne-swilling celebration, he had decided that this was a triumph he wanted to snuggle up with alone.

Molly had seen him safely back, he dimly recalled. Molly who was so sensitive to all his needs. Molly who, his sensual sensors told him, would not herself be averse to adding the remaining ninety per cent to the ten per cent of him she already had. But *never sleep with your agent* was the only useful bit of literary advice he'd ever been given.

Happily no one had ever said anything against sleeping with your agent's secretary.

If Toni had been around last night, now that might have been different. Timid little Toni, a real country mouse, still wide-eyed and tremulous at finding herself in the big city, might have seemed an impossible challenge to some. But the Boy's motto, as he boasted to his intimates, was *Vidi, vici, veni*. I saw, I conquered, I came. And as soon as he set eyes on this fresh young thing, a mouse in manner but a shapely pussycat in form, he'd known he had to have her.

It had taken him a mere ninety minutes from the first time he got her alone. Molly had sent her down to Brighton with a bunch of contracts for him to sign. She claimed she'd posted the originals to him weeks back. Well, she might have done. He wasn't responsible for the vagaries of the postal service. Now his signature was a matter of urgency, so shy little Toni got a day trip to Brighton. Tense at first, she soon relaxed under the glow of his famous charm. He could see she was ripe for plucking. It was in the stars, written there as reliably as a Fascist train timetable, a judgement confirmed when the phone rang and it turned out to be Molly with the news that her Booker mole had just given her the nod that Boy was on the shortlist. Pop! went the bubbly, and not long after, pop! went everything else, and as he put her onto the London train a couple of hours later, he was already looking forward to the next time.

But there hadn't been a next time. Enquiring after Toni when he turned up at Molly's office a couple of days later, he was told that family illness required her presence at home in the Midlands. Then, in the weeks that followed, he'd been swept up in a whirl of pre-Booker publicity, cashing in on being on the shortlist. You had to do it, Molly explained. Literary prizes were a lottery. Being odds-on favourite was no guarantee of success. Indeed, given the self-regarding vanity of some of the plonkers who did the judging, it could be counter-productive!

But this time they had been unable to resist the overwhelming evidence. In his mind he savoured the chairman's words once more.

'This was a shortlist of the highest standard. Each of these novels deserves superlative praise. Yet in the end we had no difficulty in choosing our winner. *The Accelerant* is a profound and moving modern fable. Superficially the story of a sexual predator who claims he never sleeps with any woman unless certain she wants to sleep with him, and who uses that certainty to justify all the shortcuts both moral and chemical which he takes, at a deeper level this is a powerful parable of political degeneration, mapping the path from idealistic, altruistic beginnings to ruthless and bloody dictatorship, both in its blatant forms in Africa, the Middle East and South America, and in its subtler manifestations in our own Corridors of Power. Covering four continents and two decades, this is not easy material to deal with. But David Boyd Ansell has such a sharp eye for detail, such a keen ear for nuance, such a fine sense of balance and proportion that he keeps everything under perfect control. Truly, here is a writer we can rely on to keep his head while all around are losing theirs . . .'

And so on, and so on. He'd stifled a small yawn at this point, ironically underlining on all the TV close-ups his indifference to such paeans. But oh! how the memory of them warmed his being like the memory of good sex.

He stood up, made the long journey to the window and drew the heavy damask curtains. Autumn sunlight streamed in, strong enough to make him blink. The view it lit up was undistinguished, anonymous rooftops mainly. But at least he could see a fair chunk of sky. London hotels charged for sky by the square inch.

A telephone rang. He found it, said, 'Yes?'

It was Molly.

'Good morning, Boy,' she said breezily. 'Just checking you're conscious and mobile.'

Sometimes her breeziness irritated him.

'Why shouldn't I be?' he said. 'I've been up for ages.'

'Excitement kept you awake, eh? That's good. We need to be bright-eyed and bushy-tailed for the press call.'

'The what?

'Come on, Boy, wake up, do! At last we're an overnight success and that means we've got a busy day. Conference suite, second floor, eleven a.m. Pics and a few questions from the mob, then an hour for *The Times* supplement piece. One o'clock we lunch with the Japs. This afternoon, there's a couple of telly things, then this evening *Front Row*. I'll give you a knock at quarter to. Don't wear that houndstooth shirt, by the way. You may not have time to change after lunch and it can look funny on the box. And dump that grotty leather jacket. We need to show the world that being a successful author doesn't have to mean dressing like Worzel Gummidge. Bye.'

She really did go too far sometimes. And what was all this *we* stuff? OK, in the five years since he'd used her, his sales had risen steadily, but what real part had she played in his success other than fielding the bids for his books? By rights, all this media crap should be the responsibility of those nice young publicists from his publishers, sexy young Emma, for instance, whom he'd teased to distraction on the last tour. Or roly-poly Clare with the huge knockers from the tour before. Molly needed to be reminded exactly who she was. It wasn't just a question of responsibilities, it was also a question of manners. He didn't expect deference, just a modicum of respect. But his appearance on the Man Booker shortlist, far from screwing him up a notch or two in Molly's estimation, seemed to have been the signal for a marked increase in that offhand deprecatory familiarity which she liked to think of as her trademark. In the past he'd heard her refer to her distinguished client list as *my performing fleas*. Up till now, like the other fleas, so long as she did the job, he'd opted to grit his teeth and affect amusement. Now, though, he was past all that. Yes, it was time for a serious talk. Or perhaps more than just a talk. There was that flash Yank who'd assured him he could get double his American advance no sweat, and that was before he'd joined the Booker pantheon. Maybe it was time to part company completely. He pictured doing it over a candlelit dinner in a room like this. Good food, fine wine, soft music. Then, just as she was relaxing into the certainty of at last enjoying that part of him she'd clearly so long desired, he'd reveal that the only hard and pointed bit of his anatomy she was about to get was the elbow!

He was brought out of this pleasing fantasy by a gentle tap at the door.

He went to open it.

A large trolley stood there. It bore an elegant coffee pot, two plates covered with silver domes, a selection of breakfast cereals, a fresh grapefruit, a basket of croissants, a jug of orange juice, a bottle of champagne in an ice bucket and a vase of orchids. Pushing it was a dark-haired young woman in a fetching black shirt and bolero jacket.

'Good morning, Mr Ansell,' she said with a smile. 'Your breakfast.'

'Thank you,' he said. 'Did I order this?'

He couldn't recall filling in a breakfast card last night. Such trivialities had not been on the agenda.

'Compliments of the management, sir. And may I add my personal congratulations?'

She pushed the trolley into the room alongside the table in the window bay.

Then, running what looked like an appreciative eye over his classical features and an even more appreciative one over his pyjamaed torso, she said, 'Don't let it get cold, sir. Enjoy your breakfast.'

And left.

Nice arse. Reminded him of Toni. Or perhaps it was just association of ideas. They all had nice arses.

Missed chance there, old son, he told himself. Should have asked her if she'd like to stay and serve me.

Still, there were other appetites which the smell of the fresh croissants had awoken.

He seized the handle of one of the silver domes and lifted it.

To his surprise, instead of the expected bacon, eggs, etc., he found himself looking at a white envelope with his name typed on it.

He picked it up and tore it open.

It contained a single sheet of paper.

He began to read what was typed upon it. After a few moments, he sat down on an elegant chaise longue and began to read again.

And so at last the Boy Wonder has scrambled to the top of the dung-heap!

Or to change my metaphor, the croaking frogs have gathered to cast their vote and once again come up with King Log. What interests me is, as we listened to that etiolated idiot singing your praises last night – 'such a sharp eye for detail, such a keen ear for nuance, such a fine sense of balance and proportion. Truly here is a writer we can rely on to keep his head while all around are losing theirs' – how much of this crap did you believe? One per cent? Ten per cent? Fifty per cent?

Not all of it?

Surely even you cannot believe all of it?

Or if you allowed the intoxication of the occasion to delude you into believing it last night, surely now in the cold light of morning you blush with embarrassment as the words come back to you? Or perhaps laugh with manic glee at the thought of how much wool you have pulled over all those stupid sheep eyes?

I should like to think so. I should like to believe that you are completely aware that you have done an emperor's-new-clothes job on the baa-ing classes, and that your sharp eye for detail and keen ear for nuance have left you gently amused at the yawning emptiness of it all.

But somehow I doubt it. I think it would take a very loud explosion indeed to blast such self-awareness into that classical head of yours which resembles Michelangelo's statue in one respect at least – it's as hard and dense as marble.

Talking of large explosions, I assume if you're reading this, you lifted the larger of the two plate covers first.

Enjoy your breakfast, Boy.

For a few seconds indignation overcame all other emotions. Then his gaze went to the breakfast trolley and fastened on the second silver dome.

'Oh shit!' he said.

Five seconds later he was running down the corridor. He didn't stop till he'd put several other rooms and a right angle between himself and his own door. None of the few people he met showed much interest in the rapid passage of a man in pyjamas which said something for the class of guest you still got at an old-fashioned five-star hotel. He came across a cleaner talking into a telephone. He took it off her without apology and barked into it, 'Security. Get Security to the fifth floor.' From the look on the woman's face, he saw that she thought this was a good idea too.

Half an hour later he was sitting in the manager's office, wrapped in one of the luxurious bathrobes which you would be billed for if you 'accidentally' removed it, drinking coffee laced with whisky, when Molly came in, looking anxious. 'Boy, are you all right? I went up to your room but it's like a war zone up there. What's going on?'

He told her the tale and her thin intelligent face was expressing just the right mixture of concern for his safety and admiration for his sangfroid, which was becoming *plus froid* with each telling, when the door opened to admit a small man wearing a grey suit and an expression that said *I may be tiny but I'm important.*

In his hand he held a transparent plastic bag.

'Mr Ansell,' he said. 'Commander Hewlitt, Special Branch. The bomb squad chaps found this.'

He held up the bag. It contained a white envelope and a sheet of typewritten paper.

Boy peered close and said, 'Yes, that's it. The letter I told your people about.'

'No, sir,' said Hewlitt. 'The bomb squad passed that letter straight out to us in case things went wrong and it got destroyed. It's on its way to the lab now for examination. This letter they found on a plate under the other lid.'

'I don't understand,' said Boy, peering once more at the plastic bag. 'Are you sure there hasn't been a mistake? It looks like the same letter.'

'It is, sir. Except for one word in the penultimate sentence. *Large* has become *small*.'

Molly got there before he did. 'You mean, whichever lid Boy lifted first, he was going to find a letter making him think there could be a bomb under the other one?'

'Exactly, madam. The bomb people are checking the rest of the room but I don't think they'll find anything. So, a silly time-wasting jape.'

'It didn't feel like a jape to me!' said Boy indignantly.

'No, sir. Which is why we take such things seriously. Do you

98

have any idea who might have perpetrated it? I gather from the letter that you won some kind of award last night?'

'Yes, the Man Booker.'

'Man Booker? That would be for a book, then? You are a writer?'

Molly tried unconvincingly to turn an involuntary guffaw into a fit of coughing.

He glowered at her and snapped, 'Yes, I'm a writer.'

'There would be other contestants for this award?' said Hewlitt. 'Good losers, would you say? Or might one of them have been disappointed enough to seek a stupid revenge?'

'I shouldn't imagine so . . .'

Then he hesitated. Why wouldn't he imagine so?

'Yes, sir?' prompted Hewlitt.

'Look, I'm not accusing anyone, you understand. But one of the writers on the shortlist's an Irishman and you know what they're like with bombs. Then there's that gay Australian, I wouldn't put anything past him. And that little shit from up north, I expect this kind of thing passes for sophisticated humour up in Heckmondwike.'

'You could be right, sir. I must enquire next time I visit my mother. Perhaps you could give me their names. And were there any other contestants?'

'Nominees,' corrected Ansell. 'It wasn't a game show. Yes, two more, but they are both women.'

'And that puts them out of the running, does it, sir?'

'Well, yes, I think it does, in most cases anyway. Though I say it myself, I get on rather well with women, which is perhaps another reason why some men might feel threatened enough to play a stupid practical joke. Can I go back to my room now?'

'Yes, sir. I'm sure they'll be finished up there now. We'll need a formal statement at some point . . .'

'But later, please, Commander,' said Molly. 'Mr Ansell has a press conference in a few minutes. Boy, can you make it? In the circs, I don't think they'll mind hanging around a little while.'

'If they do mind, they can sod off,' said Boy, finishing his coffee and rising.

As he went through the door, Molly shouted after him, 'And remember. Not the houndstooth!'

She'd definitely have to go.

The press conference went very well. All the papers were represented, even the grotties. WRITER WINS MAN BOOKER was a yawn to most tabloids, but PRIZEWINNER IN BOMB SCARE was worth a couple of paras. The revelation that in fact there wasn't any bomb rather took the gilt off the gingerbread, but Boy's relaxed, self-deprecating narrative plus his undeniably striking profile gave them the chance to present him as a uniquely British hero of a type not very common in these Americanized days.

He played up the image, interrupting some tabloid chick to protest that he was here to talk about his book, not about something as trivial as a threat to his life.

'OK.' The hack yawned. 'So where did you get the idea for *The Accelerant* from?'

He winced for the benefit of the broadsheets, then gave his usual bland answer and saw her eyes glaze. The truth would have woken her up. He imagined telling it.

'It was this old varsity chum of mine, Piers, actually. He was a med student and with his help, we were into all kinds of shit back in those days. But most of it was targeted on keeping you going, whether it was doing exams or disco dancing till you dropped. As far as seduction juice went, never really got much beyond slipping in an extra finger of gin with the old orange. I ran into Piers again a year or so back. Consultant at one of the big teaching hospitals. Like old friends often do on meeting, we quickly regressed to our early relationship, and one night after a few jars, he told me about this stuff he sometimes used just to help things along a bit, as he put it. When I realized what he was talking about, I was shocked. More than shocked. Horrified. When he saw this, he justified himself by asking what was the difference between getting a girl legless so you could screw her and slipping her a few drops of some harmless drug which left her without a hangover and next to no memory of what had taken place? I said the difference was about ten years in clink, and quite right too. He got quite heated, assuring me he never used it except when convinced the girl was as eager as he was.

'"You know how they can be," he said. "Positively gagging for it, but that doesn't mean they're not going to keep you waiting till you've gone through all the usual run-up rituals. Now, I don't mind that normally, but sometimes you just don't have the time. That's when an accelerant comes in useful. That's how I look on it, you see. Just an accelerant."

'And that's where I got the idea from. I'd been planning this political novel whose theme was the old one of ends justifying means and the consequent corruption. What I needed to make it fresh and immediate was an in-your-face analogy which would provide the page-turning dynamic to draw in the mass market. And here it was. My theme and my title. *The Accelerant*. I used it. It worked. And that's why I'm here, answering your stupid questions, with the Booker prize in my pocket.'

One day he might talk to them like that. One day when his bank balance was bigger than his life expectancy. But not yet.

So he gave them the usual line and when the bomb threat questions started up again, he reverted to modest hero mode with only token resistance.

*

'You knocked 'em in the aisle,' said Molly afterwards. 'Hold back on the personal details with *The Times*. They've got an exclusive on the literary career, but I think we can do a hot deal with one of the tabs for the childhood trauma stuff. You did have childhood trauma, didn't you, Boy?'

'By the bucketload,' he said.

'Good. I'll bring him up to you soon as he arrives. By the way, you should find a few hundred books in your room waiting to be signed. Why don't you make a start on them?'

Signing books was a pain even though he'd reduced his official signature to a single undulating scrawl. And it was worse when you didn't have a skivvy at hand to open the volumes at the title page and stack them to one side as they were done. But it was a necessary evil and he set to with a will, determined to get as many as possible out of the way.

As many as possible turned out to be five.

When he opened the sixth, he found the title page had already been written on.

Still with us, Boy? Not to worry. Just another couple of signatures, then you won't have to worry about signing any more. Ever.

He looked at the tower of books and was tempted to kick it over. But why risk losing your leg for a gesture?

He left the room and went in search of a telephone.

Commander Hewlitt arrived just as the bomb people gave the all-clear. They seemed pretty phlegmatic but the commander sounded definitely pissed off. 'False alarms like this tying up large numbers of highly trained personnel are a serious offence, sir. Up to seven years' imprisonment.'

'Is that all? I'd cut his balls off, whoever's responsible,' said Boy.

'Yes, sir. Now a few more questions, then a formal statement . . .'

Once more Molly protested that the pressure on her client's time was too intense to allow diversion, but this time Hewlitt was adamant.

When Molly continued arguing, Boy snapped, 'For God's sake, cancel the *Times* guy. Cancel the Jap lunch too. In fact, cancel everything. God knows what other little surprises this joker has got ready for me. If he's for real, I don't want to be about. And if it's just a pathetic game, soon the sympathy will start running out and I'll just look a laughing stock, which is probably what he wants anyway.'

'So what will you do, sir?' asked Hewlitt.

'I'll go home to Brighton and get on with my work, Commander, in the hope that you will get on with yours and catch the idiot behind these pranks.'

'Probably a good idea, sir,' said Hewlitt. 'But if we could just have that statement first . . .'

Two hours later Ansell climbed out of the elegant Mercedes his publishers had provided, said a curt thank-you to the driver and went into his flat. Four years ago, when he bought it, the price had seemed exorbitant even though he'd picked it up at the bottom of a slump. Sea here was like sky in London, you paid through the nose for the privilege of viewing what God had provided free. Now it was worth possibly double the money. Before Booker, he'd played with the notion that if he won, he might sell up and use some of his new earning power to buy something in town. But to get what he had in Brighton in any reasonably central location was going to cost an arm and a leg, and after today's experience, he was no longer sure he wanted to be so near the rotten heart of things, particularly if arms and legs were literally what he might have to pay.

He glanced at his answer machine, which formed the base of a four-foot-high resin copy of Michelangelo's *David* with a telephone as a *cache-sexe*. Some slight adjustment to the face made the personal resemblance even stronger, but the phone made it a joke instead of a vanity.

Some adjustment had been necessary to the crotch too, but that was for the lucky ones to find out.

The answer machine registered lots of messages, which was only to be expected. Everybody loves a winner, he told himself with that cynicism only winners can afford. But it would be nice to relax with a large G and T and let this torrent of praise wash away the day's less pleasant memories.

First things first, though, especially in matters of relaxation. He headed to the bathroom. When the bullets start flying, keep a tight ass, was a piece of veterans' lore he recalled reading somewhere. Perhaps Mailer in *The Naked and the Dead*. Or Kate Adie anywhere. He seemed to have been keeping a tight ass all day. No smart-alec reporter was going to be able to remark slyly that Boy Ansell reacted to threats against him by spending an unconscionable time on the loo. But now it was time to let go.

It was worth waiting for, till on the sixth sheet of toilet paper he found the message.

What a lucky Boy it is, then! One sheet the less and what worlds away. By such delicate chains do our lives hang.

He read it again. Unnecessarily. He'd got the message first time. This was an exercise in humiliation. He was meant to go scuttling off to summon the bomb squad once more, this time to work over an unflushed lavatory.

He looked up at the old-fashioned high-level tank from which a thin golden chain ran down to a metal ball, enamelled to look like planet earth (another of his jokes).

'Sod you!' he said.

And not giving himself time to reflect, he stood up, took the world in his hand, and pulled.

Water rushed and bubbled, the pan emptied. He stood there defiantly till the roar of the tank refilling died to a trickle then a drip. Finally, silence.

'Sod you,' he said again, this time in triumph.

He went back into his living room. The phone rang.

He sat down, unhooking the receiver from the Boy David's crotch.

'Ansell.'

'Boy, it's Molly. Just checking you got home safely.'

He thought of telling her about the latest incident, decided the absurdity outweighed the heroics, and said, 'No problem.'

'Oh good. I'm sorry it turned into such a trying day for you when you should have been simply enjoying your astounding triumph.'

His famous ear for nuance had always been able to spot a putdown at twenty paces. 'Astounding?' he said. 'To whom?'

'To you, I mean. Not to me, of course. But I can't believe that you in your heart of hearts really expected it. Did you?'

'Well, yes, in a way, I always hoped – look, what are you trying to say? That I didn't deserve it?'

He heard her laugh. 'I'm happy to debate *expected* with you, Boy. But I'm sure neither of us has any delusions about *deserved*.'

He opened his mouth, closed it again. He had misheard, he thought. Or was misinterpreting what he'd heard. Don't rush in with a hasty response. Keep control. Don't lose your head. Wasn't that one of the things he was famous for in his writing?

He said, 'You know me, Molly. No vanity. I never went around saying I thought I ought to win the Booker, but now that I have done, I'm certainly not about to quarrel with the verdict of such a distinguished panel of experts.'

'Experts?' She laughed again. 'If your claim to fame rests on being chosen by that bunch of self-regarding prancers, better forget it, darling.'

What had got into her? Not him, perhaps that was the trouble. Or could it be that, pissed off at having to cancel all that carefully organized publicity stuff today, she'd dived into a bottle and was now letting her resentment show? Whatever, it gave him the perfect cue for cutting the cord. And without the expense of a good dinner.

He said mildly, 'If you think so poorly of my books, perhaps it would be better for us both if you no longer had the disagreeable task of trying to sell them.'

See if that shocked her into sobriety.

It didn't.

'Oh, come on, Boy,' she said long-sufferingly. 'What I think about your books is neither here nor there. But surely even you won't grudge me a share of your success, after all the hard work I've put in.'

'All the hard work . . .?' he echoed in genuine puzzlement. 'You mean selling them to publishers who were gagging for them? Or ferrying me around to media events which, incidentally, is a task perhaps better left to my publisher's PR professionals who know how to treat a star.'

That set her laughing again. God, she must be really rat-arsed!

'Jesus, Boy, haven't you caught on yet that when you've got a tour coming up, the girls in the publicity department start going sick in droves? Given a choice between you and King Kong, they'd all be packing their jungle kit. That's why I took over myself, to preserve the peace. So I reckon that the time I spend on that, plus the work I've had to put in on your scripts, makes earning my ten per cent the hardest graft I've ever done.'

'On my scripts? My editor never has to do a thing with them. He says they're among the cleanest scripts he's ever seen. And I've heard you say so yourself.'

'Yeah, yeah, that's for Big Ears and Noddy out there, Boy, that's for the image. Come on, surely it must occur to you to wonder sometimes how your four hundred pages of waffly rambling turn into two-fifty of crisp prose? With the spelling correct and the punctuation in the right place? Or perhaps you never read the finished product? Probably wise.'

Suspicions were swirling in his mind like storm clouds, but he wasn't ready yet to admit the tempest blast while he still had some shred of vanity to shelter behind. 'I don't get you. You said . . . you seemed to be saying that you expected me to win last night. That must mean . . .'

'It means that I'd called in more favours than you'd find at a gypsy's wedding, not to mention rattling a whole catacomb of skeletons in judges' cupboards. But that won't keep me awake nights, that's par for the course in the glitzy world of awards. What really bothers me, Boy, is one of the judges said to me afterwards, "You needn't have bothered with all the pressure, darling, we all actually thought it was by far the best book." You see what this means? I've created a monster and no one else seems able to spot the stitching!'

Now the tempest broke.

'You bitch!' yelled Boy. 'It was you, wasn't it? These stupid jokes. It was you, trying to humiliate me.'

'Well done, Boy. I wondered how long that famous eye for detail and ear for nuance were going to take to get you there. Yes, indeed. And I actually got to the hotel early enough to see you sprinting down the corridor in your jimjams. *A writer we can rely on to keep his head* . . . yes, even if it means running around half-naked in public! God, you looked terrified!'

'Not so terrified I didn't pull the loo chain just now,' he snarled, defensive despite himself.

'Well done. On the other hand, sometimes a bit of real humili ating fear's not a bad thing, you know. Being brave kills more people than terror, I'd say. Though terror can leave permanent scars on the vulnerable and sensitive.'

'Well, it's not going to leave any scars on me,' he said. The famous control was back. For all he knew she was getting all this down on tape. He mustn't lose his head. 'You're the only one who's going to suffer damage here. We're finished, Molly. And by the time my lawyers are through, I doubt if you'll see a penny of my future earnings. I can't imagine what you thought you were playing at. Such silly pranks. A woman of your age!'

'What's my age got to do with it?'

'I understand strange changes often take place with the meno-pause. I advise you to see a doctor. Or a psychologist. There's been some good work done on sexual frustration, they tell me.'

'Frustration . . .? You mean I'm not getting enough generally? Or not getting enough of you?'

'You said it,' he replied equably. 'And it's too late now. I'm not in the therapy business.'

'Oh, Boy, Boy.' She sighed. 'That sharp eye, that keen ear, and you never caught on during our years together that I'm gay? And here's me thinking it must be that which was protecting me. But now I think about it, you'd probably have regarded it as a challenge, wouldn't you? Get me up to your flat, bucketfuls of boyish charm, rather less of cheap bubbly, then an irresistible offer to let me find out what I'd been missing. You like a chal-lenge, don't you? Toni must have seemed a challenge.'

'Toni?' He laughed triumphantly. 'Is that what this is really about? Young Toni? Now I begin to see things clearly. You found out. It wasn't me you were jealous of, it was her! Grooming her as a little bit on the side, were you? And then you found out she preferred the real thing. So you sacked her and thought you'd play your stupid pranks on me. And I used to think you were a sophisticated woman. I hope you had the decency to give her a good reference. I certainly would! Where is she now?'

'She's safe,' said Molly calmly. 'Recovering. It's going to take a long time, they say. Oh, I warned her that you'd probably have a go at her some time, told her to take no notice and eventually your vanity would make you give up on the grounds that if you hadn't tried anything, you couldn't have been rejected. I never dreamt you'd sink so low, Boy. What did you spike her drink with? Rohypnol, like the guy in your lousy book? Write about what you know, isn't that the advice they dish out on creative writing courses?'

Boy was genuinely horrified. Who the hell did this ancient dyke think she was, taking the moral high line with him? What did she know about good old-fashioned straight sex between a man and a woman? He could look back over a long line of willing and enthusiastic partners, most of whom came back for more, hence his initial revulsion at Piers's confession. OK, he'd repressed his true feelings in the interests of research but that was the price an artist sometimes had to pay. Practical experience was important and eventually he'd got a sample of the stuff from Piers who, like his victims, was in no position to resist. First of all he tried it out on himself. Result, irresistible drowsiness and when he recovered, a memory gap whose edges were as fuzzy as candyfloss. Next had been a woman he was in an intermittent sleeping arrangement with. When she woke up, she'd been apologetic, putting her retreat from full consciousness down to not counting the vodka Martinis. After that he'd only used it a couple of times, certainly not more than three or four, and always in the kind of situation described by Piers where it was merely accelerating the inevitable.

And that's how it had been with Toni. He'd soon seen that a couple of glasses of celebratory champagne weren't going to be enough. She was naive, she was nervous, but beneath it all, she was ready, he was certain of that. A light lunch in his flat – one of his famous aphrodisiac salads – another bottle of bubbly, a shot of Armagnac, and by two o'clock, two-thirty at the latest, they'd have been in bed.

The problem was there was this Yankee journalist, nine-out-of-ten attractive and desperate for an interview, who was lunching him at the Grand at one. He contemplated standing her up, but with news of the Booker nomination to drop casually into the conversation, this was too good an opportunity to be missed.

But so was Toni.

It was a situation tailor-made for the Accelerant. So tailor-made that he'd genuinely forgotten that he'd used it and when he did remember, the only regret he felt was that she might not be able to share completely his own delightful memories. He'd kissed her on the forehead as he put her on her train, still apologizing for her silliness in letting a little champagne turn her so woozy, and promised himself that next time he would make sure there wasn't any need to rush.

'You still there, Boy? Guilt got your tongue?'

There was a strong temptation to justify himself, but with this bitch, that could be hugely dangerous. Just keep your head, he told himself. Be very careful what you say.

'Yes, I'm still here,' he said. 'It's simple incomprehension that's reduced me to silence.'

'Come on, Boy! Give it up! OK, you probably told yourself all you were doing was speeding up the inevitable, you weren't

110

giving her anything she didn't really want. Just like your cardboard hero. And she wouldn't remember anyway. But she really didn't want it, Boy. And she does remember. In nightmares, in panic attacks. Oh yes, she remembers. It's going to take her a long time to forget.'

'I've no idea what you're talking about,' he said calmly. 'What I do know is, if you repeat any of these monstrous calumnies in public, I shall be obliged, albeit reluctantly, to seek protection from the Law.'

'Ah yes. The Law. That was my first reaction. Call in the police. But Toni got hysterical when I suggested it and Maggie, her sister, said no, it wasn't the way. Interesting woman, Toni's sister. Member of a club I go to. It was her got me to take on Toni in the first place, so we both feel responsible. Now Maggie, she's quite different from Toni. None of her hang-ups. Action woman, looks at life straight on, bags of self-confidence and common sense. Well, imagine you need all that when you're an officer in the Ordnance Corps. And like a lot of soldiers, she doesn't have much faith in civil justice.'

'No, she wouldn't,' sneered Boy. 'Even in this enlightened age, military dykes can't have very good career prospects. I can see why she'd want to steer clear of the cops.'

'Now I'd never have thought of that, Boy. Must be that famous artistic sensitivity of yours. But don't misunderstand me, just because she's a military dyke, as you put it, doesn't mean she can't pass for normal in the dusk with the light behind her. Or even at dawn. In fact, you can judge for yourself. It was her who served your breakfast this morning. Anyway, we both agreed, no police, unless of course you agreed to plead guilty at the trial and save Toni the trauma of giving evidence?'

'Trial?' He laughed. 'Molly, don't be ridiculous. We both know there isn't going to be a trial. My conscience is clear. I have done nothing wrong except spend a pleasant hour in bed with a willing and enthusiastic young woman.'

Put that on your tape and play it! he told himself gleefully.

'Willing and enthusiastic? Yes, I can see you smiling at the jury and urging them to ask themselves, why would someone as attractive as I am need to resort to foul play to get my end away? You really do think of yourself as the Boy David, don't you? One whirl of your slingshot and the whole world's at your feet. And if they're not worshipping, unconscious will do.'

'Molly, I think you've had some kind of breakdown,' he said with avuncular concern. 'I think you need help. I'm sorry I can't give it, but I advise you to look for someone who can in the near future. No more pranks, please, or I definitely will call in the Law. My solicitor will be in touch anyway about terminating our agreement. I'll instruct him to be generous. Despite everything. I'm grateful for what you've done for my career.'

That would sound well on the tape, if there was a tape.

'That's kind of you, Boy. And don't think I don't recognize your good qualities too. For instance, it was brave of you to pull the loo chain. And you often said things that made me laugh. OK, they were usually a bit sour and cynical, but they genuinely amused me. Which is why I'm putting in this effort to get you to see reason and face up to things like a man. A grown man, I mean. OK, it'll be painful and when it's over, you won't be the famous Boy Ansell any more. But you can't stay like that for the rest of your life anyway. You've got to grow up some time. Might even help your writing. So let's talk a bit longer and see if we can't come to some resolution which makes sense to all of us.'

She sounded so genuinely concerned that despite himself he felt touched. But the crack about his writing was the last straw. Who the hell did she think she was, a stringy middle-aged literary leech talking like this to a man with a Booker cheque in his wallet?

He said, 'Molly, there's nothing left to say. I'm going to ring off now.'

She said, 'Boy, don't hang up. I'm warning you, don't hang up. Please.'

But of course he did.

Though perhaps, as he did so, because he was after all a good if somewhat overrated writer and deserving of at least a third of the praise heaped upon him, perhaps his keen ear for nuance detected that there was more of appeal than threat in Molly's words.

Then perhaps his sharp eye for detail reminded him that Toni's sister was an officer in the Ordnance Corps.

And perhaps there was even time for his fine sense of balance and proportion to register that there was something not quite right about the set of the shoulders on Michelangelo's statue, as if someone had been mucking about with the resin.

But there was no way even his brilliant mind could put all these things together in time to abort replacing the phone on the statue's crotch.

Which was when both Boy Davids lost their heads together.

The Italian Sherlock Holmes

'Halloa! What's this,' said Sherlock Holmes, studying the sheet of paper he had just removed from a thick white envelope heavily embossed with a crest I did not recognize. 'I don't suppose you have ever attended an execution, Watson?'

'Indeed I have,' I replied, not displeased to be able for once to surprise my friend. 'As duty medical officer at a hanging in Afghanistan. Not my happiest memory of army life. Why do you ask?'

He tossed the sheet of paper to me.

'These Italians are an original race,' he said. 'This is surely the rarest Christmas entertainment a man was ever invited to!'

The news that Sherlock Holmes was wintering in Rome had spread through the British community like wildfire, almost eclipsing the rumour that the Prince of Wales, incognito, was dallying with an opera singer at Ostia. Had we so desired, we could have dined at the best tables in the city every night of Advent. But it was not for the social round that we had paused in Rome on our way north from Naples. I have met with few men capable of greater physical and mental exertion than my

114

friend Holmes, but frequently once the occasion of such exertions has passed, a period of deep lassitude ensues in which that most brilliant of minds fades to the merest glimmer of consciousness in an all but moribund shell. For a few days after the conclusion of the affair of Ricoletti of the club foot and his abominable wife, which had taken us from the foetid cellars of the Camorra's Neapolitan stronghold to the smoking rim of Mount Vesuvius, I had hoped that the surge of energy success always brings would carry him safe across Europe to the healing solace of Mrs Hudson's traditional Yuletide cheer in Baker Street. But as we entered Rome he had suffered an almost complete nervous collapse and there had been nothing for it but to take rooms in a respectable *pensione* and bide our time till a quiet atmosphere and healthy diet should have worked their repairs.

Alas, in Italy the one is almost as hard to find as the other, and once the news of his presence had spread, I was hard pressed for at least ten hours of each day turning visitors from our door.

The written invitations, however, I admitted in the hope that something in them might spark an interest. But up till now they had all fluttered from his hand after the most cursory of glances. So to see him react with something of his old alertness to this latest invitation at first made my spirits rise. When however I reread the elegantly penned missive, my pleasure diminished somewhat.

My dear Holmes,

My delight at hearing from my good friend the British ambassador that you are presently in Rome was naturally tempered by learning of the reasons for your stay. May I join with all the honest men of Europe in wishing you a speedy return to health?

But even out of evil may come good, and though you may set it down to mere Romish superstition, forgive me if I see the hand of God in this (I hope) temporary indisposition of yours. How else am I to interpret your unforseeable presence in my city on the very day which sees the culmination of my first poor efforts to emulate your unique methods? I refer of course to the tragic case of the murder of my beloved uncle, Count Leonardo Montesecco. Tomorrow morning at nine-thirty, the foul assassin, Giuseppe Strepponi, will meet his richly deserved fate on the scaffold in the Piazza San Cassiano. I and a few interested friends will be gathering to witness this triumphant vindication of the laws of God and man, and I would be honoured if, health permitting, you and your companion, Dr Watson, would care to join us. If so, my carriage will collect you at eight of the clock.

With deepest respect from one who is honoured to inscribe himself your disciple and colleague,

The signature was a hieroglyph too elegant to be called a scrawl but too ornate for legibility.

'So what do you make of it, Watson?' asked Holmes.

'To invite us to watch some poor devil being put to death on the Eve of our Saviour's birth is such a monstrous piece of impiety,' I replied indignantly, 'that I can only hope the missive is a fraud.'

'No fraud,' he replied with a lively smile which cheered my heart. 'I know the coat of arms of the Montesecco family, and from what I recall of the hand and signature of Bruno Montesecco, the present count, the letter bears none of the inevitable telltales of forgery.'

'In that case,' I replied, 'it is an impudence as well as an impiety. I am sorry that such an ancient family has finally forgotten its manners. Will you dictate our refusal or shall I pen it myself?'

Now Holmes threw back his head and let out that characteristic cackle of laughter which I had not heard for many days and, despite my indignation, my heart grew lighter still.

'I think, dear fellow, in your present state of mind,' he said, 'that any reply from you is likely to be read as an invitation to pistols at dawn, or more probably a stiletto at night in view of your plebeian origins. No, I shall write myself and what is more, I shall accept the invitation with pleasure. When in Rome, Watson! But first ring the bell and summon up Signora Grillo to order some luncheon. Also I have some telegrams I would like to send.'

As he spoke he leapt to his feet in search of his neglected pipe, and the heavy shawls in which his narrow frame had been swathed, even though a roaring sea-coal fire turned the room into an oven, fell away. And with them fell the greater part of my resentment at Count Montesecco's invitation.

'Tell me, Holmes,' I said as we sat over luncheon, which I was pleased to note he wolfed down, 'how is it you became acquainted with this Count Montesecco? And why should he think the fate of this poor devil Strepponi should be of interest to you? And is it the custom of this country to treat executions as an occasion of social festivity? And does—?'

'Stay, stay, my dear Watson,' he cried. 'Let me finish this excellent cutlet and I shall gladly try to answer your questions.'

Later as we sat before the fire, adding the sweet smoke of my Arcadia mixture to that of the coals, he began his explanation.

'I have never met the count in person, but he began writing to me early this year, before he had succeeded to his murdered uncle's title. From the style and manner of his writing, I put him down as the kind of young aristocrat who is rich enough to be idle but a little too intelligent to be satisfied with the customary recreations of his class. His restless enquiring mind, in search of some pastime which might satisfy his desire for activity without demeaning his self-esteem, chanced upon some of those infernal scribblings of yours about my cases, and having made his first deduction, which was that in England where we still set the standards for such things, it is possible to be a consultant detective without ceasing to be a gentleman, he decided to follow my example.'

'He must have a pretty large conceit of himself,' I observed.

'I think there can be little doubt of that,' replied my friend drily. 'I think that in his very first letter he pointed out a couple of apparent deficiencies in my deductive processes which he very handsomely laid at the door of my inefficient chronicler rather than my inefficient technique.'

'The impudent puppy!' I snorted.

'Youth must be given its head, Watson,' said Holmes. 'I replied politely but coolly, not so much because of anything I found offensive in his manner, though I was always left aware, despite the flattering tone of his letters, that he was an aristocrat and I was not, but rather because I am sensible that my methods misapplied are as capable of causing serious damage as a surgeon's scalpel in the hands of a schoolboy.'

'But he persisted in the correspondence?'

'Indeed. A snub must be very blatant to penetrate the complacence of such an innate conviction of social superiority,' said Holmes. 'And I saw no reason to descend to rudeness. Then late in the summer I received a letter which was so full of the sheer excitement of investigation that it almost forgot to patronize! After bemoaning in previous letters the lack of such challenging crimes as seemed to be the commonplace of my life, he found himself actually present at the scene, indeed almost the occasion, of one of Rome's most sensational murders. The fact that the victim was his uncle, the head of his own noble family, seemed almost inconsequential when set against the opportunity afforded him to investigate. Or perhaps he did not think it seemly to share a private grief with a stranger.'

'But from the sound of it, his investigation of the crime has met with some success?'

'So it would appear. His first letter on the subject, written the day after the murder, told me of a few preliminary deductions he had made and forecast complete success within twenty-four hours. I must confess I found his confidence smacked somewhat of arrogance.'

I concealed a smile. When it comes to an arrogant assumption of his own infallibility, Holmes can on occasion make the Holy Father *ex cathedra* sound like a bashful tyro.

'The next letter came hot on the heels of the first and proclaimed absolute triumph. The murderer was caught and all on account of Montesecco's insights. By now rather than asking advice, I felt he was with difficulty restraining himself from giving it. I sent a polite letter of congratulation. Since coming to Italy I have twice noted his name in the papers in connection with other investigations. They are calling him the Italian Sherlock Holmes! But as you know I have been too busy for more than a cursory interest. Now, however, fate has brought us close and I find I have a fancy to meet this prodigy. Who knows, Watson, he may be able to teach this old dog some new tricks, hey?'

'He would need to get up very early in the morning to do that,' I said loyally.

'From the sound of his invitation, that is one trick he has learned already,' said Holmes so merrily that I went to bed that night feeling more comfortable in my mood than for many a day.

Precisely on the stroke of eight on the morning of Christmas Eve the bell of our *pensione* was rung with a most imperious hand and a moment later Signora Grillo, our *padrona*, appeared to me in a state of great excitement to announce the presence of the Count Montesecco's coach. I summoned Holmes and was a little taken aback when on seeing me he burst into laughter and said, 'I hope the kernel is a little more fashionably shaped than the husk, Watson.'

Uncertain what local custom decreed was the acceptable garb for an execution, I had opted for comfort and was wearing my heavy Abercrombie with my long plaid scarf wound three times around my neck, my ear-flapped travelling hat pulled firmly on my head, and my legs cased in my stoutest boots. Holmes by contrast was clad in a light jacket and silk shirt, with a thin cloak thrown over his shoulders.

I said sternly, 'I may not know much about fashion, Holmes, but I have stood on more parade grounds than you and I think this wind which has rattled our panes all night will strike as cold in a Roman piazza as it would on Horse Guards. I would advise you at the very least to change into your twill trousers.'

He looked a touch disconcerted and replied, 'You may be right, but it is too late to change now. Punctuality is the courtesy of kings. Hurry, or else we shall be late!'

I told him rather testily as we bowled along that as the execution was fixed for nine-thirty and nothing in this country ever seemed to start on time anyway, there was little need for haste.

'Indeed,' I concluded, 'I cannot imagine why Montesecco should request our presence so far in advance of his main entertainment.'

'Come now, Watson,' he said. 'Surely you know that it is not the execution but our presence which *is* the main entertainment.'

I brooded on this till, as we neared the Piazza San Cassiano, our progress became noticeably slower. Looking from the window, I became aware that we were not the only people drawn out on a raw Christmas Eve by the prospect of witnessing a man's death. There were many other carriages and also men on horseback, but the greater part of those flocking to the square were pedestrians with every conceivable variety of citizen represented, from sober, suited businessmen to the rag, tag and bobtail. The chill winter wind was pulling at hats and tousling hair and I said to Holmes, 'Now you may see why our presence was required so early. From the look of it, no latecomer will get to see more than the top of the scaffold.'

He did not reply but I saw him shiver and, reproaching myself for my triumphant tone, I started to remove my coat, saying, 'Here, Holmes, take this. You've only just risen from your sickbed and your lungs could easily take an infection from this raw, dank air.'

He smiled at me with real affection and said, 'Watson, you are more good-hearted than I deserve. Thank you, dear fellow, but I do not think that after all your sacrifice will be necessary.'

I looked out of the window and saw that we had passed the narrow entrance to the Piazza San Cassiano and were coming to a halt outside a haberdashery before which a liveried flunkey was waiting to bow us out of the coach, after which he bowed us through the shop doorway, down a passageway, across a mean and shadowy courtyard, through another door, up several flights of stairs, and finally, with his deepest bow of all, ushered us into a spacious room across which advanced a tall, handsome, moustachioed man in his mid-twenties, showing dazzling white teeth in a wide smile.

'Mr Holmes!' he cried. 'Welcome. After so many letters between us, I am delighted at last to make your acquaintance in the flesh.'

'And I yours, Count,' said Holmes, taking his hand. 'May I present my dear friend and colleague, Dr John Watson.'

'Delighted,' I said gruffly. To tell the truth I was feeling distinctly uncomfortable. There were many other people in the room, of both sexes, all dressed most elegantly. The room was heated by a large stove and already I was beginning to feel overwarm, but my main discomfiture rose from my knowledge that I had seen no reason to wear beneath my topcoat anything other than a pair of balding moleskin trousers and the leather-patched Norfolk jacket which has accompanied me on so many outdoor expeditions.

'Dr Watson, the Boswell of the great detective!' cried Montesecco, wringing my hand warmly. 'It was through your writings that I first became acquainted with Mr Holmes's talents. You are the Vergil who has led me safe through the labyrinths of his mind.'

I cannot say I cared much for the flowery style of the Italian Sherlock Holmes and thought of pointing out that Vergil did most of his ciceroning in the circles of Hell. But Holmes, alert to both my mental distaste and my physical discomfort, took my arm and urged me towards a window which opened onto a broad metal balcony, saying, 'I see we must brave the elements after all, Watson. Once again you have demonstrated that while I may lay some claim to superiority of insight, in matters of foresight, you are the master. The rest of us must shiver while you stay snug and warm.'

'I have provided cloaks for everybody,' said the count petulantly.

'Then we shall all be comfortable together,' said Holmes, stepping out onto the balcony.

All concern about my comfort or discomfort vanished as I took in the scene spread out below.

The house we were in stood at one end of the long and

narrow Piazza San Cassiano, directly opposite the church of San Cassiano at the other end, some six hundred feet away. Already the square was full of people though not yet so crowded that they could not move freely about. It was a scene that an artist with our vantage point might have used as a model for a panorama of Bartholomew Fair. Hawkers hawked, tumblers tumbled, beggars begged, and the citizens of Rome strolled around in topcoats and tailcoats and long cloaks and short cloaks and some in no cloaks at all, wearing barely sufficient rags to cover their modesty. But all had that complacent air which says as clearly now as it must have done in Caesar's time, 'We are true Romans and may not be touched by any law but our own.'

At the very centre of the square stood the instrument of that law. Over the trough of a dry fountain had been erected the scaffold, a ramshackle jerry-built platform of uneven, unpainted planks some eight feet high, with a rickety ladder leaning against it, the ascent of which looked perilous enough to dispatch a condemned man without troubling the waiting axe, which gleamed sinisterly, high in its towering frame. The polished and, I hoped, finely honed blade contrasted powerfully with the ponderous rusting mass of metal attached above to provide the motivating force necessary to drive the cutting edge through the bone and sinew of a man's neck.

The scaffold was ringed with foot soldiers, and a double line of them showed the route from the church by which the condemned man would be brought to his doom. The soldiers were stood at ease, which command is taken much more literally here than it would be by a similar escort from a British regiment. The men slouched, scratched, chatted with their neighbours, and even laid their weapons on the ground to stretch their arms in huge weary yawns, while their officers strolled around, smoking cigarillos and occasionally exchanging banter with some of the ladies of the town.

'Tell me, Mr Holmes,' said the count, who had followed us onto the balcony, 'have you ever had the pleasure of following one of your cases to this last extremity?'

'No, Count,' said Holmes. 'I am glad to say that in my country we have abandoned the practice of turning some poor devil's death into a sideshow.'

'You are indeed a people of great restraint,' murmured the count, not making it sound like a compliment. 'But there is a certain completeness, a roundness if you like, in seeing a matter out to the bitter end, particularly when, as in this case, the investigator was present from the very beginning.'

'Ah, you actually witnessed Strepponi committing the murder, then?' said Holmes. 'I should have thought that would have rendered my deductive methods somewhat redundant.'

Someone laughed behind us. The count turned and the laughter stopped. This was clearly a man who did not care for contradiction.

'I forget my manners,' he said. 'Come and meet my other guests.'

He and Holmes stepped back inside. I remained on the balcony, partly for comfort, partly because from this vantage I could take close note of the room and its inmates without my being noted.

It did not need my friend's sharp perception to remark that, though the room was elegantly furnished and made gay by the beribboned icons and silk-draped religious pictures with which these Papists mark the season of Christmas, its basic fabric was in an advanced state of dilapidation. I guessed that the count had hired the apartment purely as a vantage point for the execution and commanded his people to make it temporarily fit for fashionable society.

The first guest in line was in something of the same condition as the room. In his sixties, cadaverous of face and skeletal of frame, he was clothed in colourful silk and mohair and his long bony fingers were banded with diamonds and gold.

'No need for introduction,' said Holmes, offering his hand. 'Who could work within the law and not be acquainted with the famous Judge Pinelli? I trust Your Honour's respiration has improved from your recent voyage to the Holy Land on Count Montesecco's yacht?'

The man's jaw dropped like Marley's when he unwound his scarf in the famous Christmas story. Recovering, he said in fair English, 'I see the count has given you my curriculum vitae, Mr Holmes.'

'Not in the least,' replied my friend, smiling. 'As the principal trial judge, your likeness was in the newspaper cuttings which the count was kind enough to send me. As for the rest, your lip and jaw are slightly paler than the rest of your face, suggesting that you recently grew a moustache and beard during a period of exposure to wind and warm weather. From this I deduced a long voyage on a private rather than a public vessel, permitting you to indulge in not shaving without provoking the interest of other travellers. The count's evident gratitude to you for your conduct of the trial provoked me to guess that the vessel was his private yacht. And the enamelled medal you are wearing of Our Lady of the Rocks looks new enough to suggest a recent visit to that particular shrine.'

'And the respiratory problem, Mr Holmes?' asked a handsome blonde woman of about forty, clad in the kind of loose flowing garment ladies are wont to wear when they become self-conscious about their spreading figures.

'Elementary, my dear Signora Masina,' said Holmes. 'I have heard the learned judge cough drily several times since I entered the room. My good friend Dr Watson could have diagnosed much more precisely. But your pain at losing such a very dear friend is beyond mere medical remedy, and I think you are wise to have decided to go and live with your sister in America.'

As he spoke, he bowed in the direction of another woman, dark and slim and wearing a long grey dress of rather old-fashioned cut.

For a second Signora Masina looked disconcerted. Then she rallied and said, 'Now this is first rate, Mr Holmes. I daresay my likeness too appeared in the papers, but as for my sister and my debate about joining her in the United States, only a wizard could know of that. And don't tell me there's a family resemblance. As your proverb puts it, we are chalk and cheese!'

'The dark and the bright, two different kinds of beauty,' said Holmes with greater gallantry than I had suspected he possessed. 'The accent of your English suggests a period already spent in America. This lady's dress is of a style more popular just now in New York than in Rome. She wears a brooch and you a ring which look to have been set by the same hand perhaps fifty years ago. It could be that you have a common jeweller, but it's more likely that these are part of a set of jewellery divided on inheritance, and a mother is the most likely source of such a bequest. What would be more probable than that a sister should rush to your side at your time of grief and offer you a permanent home in the bosom of her family.'

'In other words, these deductions of yours are mere guesses, and your fame depends largely on folk tending to recall the few instances when you hit the mark and forget the many where you are wide.'

This came from the lady in grey who spoke English with a very pronounced Yankee drawl and had a cynical eye to match.

I waited to see how my friend's gallantry would survive this attack but the count came smoothly in.

'I think, Mrs Jardine, that the occasion of our meeting here today shows that there is rather more to our methods than mere guesswork,' he murmured. 'Mr Holmes, would you like to make a further display of your powers with regard to any other of my guests?'

This was clever, I thought. *Our methods* implied an equality of standing with Holmes while *a further display of your powers* suggested that such vulgar exhibitionism was Holmes's alone.

Holmes glanced at me ruefully. Perhaps the count had hit a nerve. Or perhaps he had recollected the solemnity of the occasion.

The introductions continued, confirming my impression that most of those present had some close connection with the murder of the last Count Montesecco. As well as Signora Masina and her sister, Mrs Jardine, there were present the family lawyer, Signor Randone; Captain Zardi, who had been in charge of the official investigation; Dr Provenzale, the attending medical officer; and a very beautiful young woman called Claudia Medioli, who stood in an ambiguous relationship to the count.

Even the trio of servants who were constantly on hand with hot chocolate, cold champagne and a variety of little sweetmeats, turned out to have been in the employ of the dead man and present in his house at the time of his murder. There were two maids, Violetta and Susi, and in charge of them Serge Rosi, who had been the old count's and was now the new count's major-domo.

Finally there was a group of some half-dozen men standing a little apart who turned out to be representatives of the Italian press. Just as the introductions were completed, the door burst open and a young man of about the count's age entered. From his long unkempt hair, tied back in the peasant style, and his rather shabby suit, which stood out against the general elegance of the assemblage, I at first took him for another servant. But he came forward boldly, seizing a glass of champagne en route, letting his bright brown eyes run lightly over the other guests with a faintly mocking smile as he said in Italian, 'Sorry to be late, Montesecco, on such an illustrious occasion.' Then, switching to an accented but very correct English, he went on, 'And this must be the famous *British* Sherlock Holmes. How proud you must be that your influence now helps men to die in countries other than your own!'

Even allowing for the fact that he spoke a foreign language, this came close to being offensive, but Holmes merely held out his hand and said, 'I find no man's death an occasion for pride, Signor Chiari. Like yours, my interest is solely in *la verità*, the truth.'

For a moment the young man looked disconcerted, then the mocking smile returned and he said, 'So the count has warned you I am coming! Or are you going to claim it is the printers' ink on my fingers or the paper dust in my hair that helped you to make your conclusion?'

'I could hardly warn Mr Holmes of your arrival, as you were not invited,' said Montesecco coldly. 'But now you are here I will not deprive you of this chance to see how real justice works.'

Chiari bowed satirically. Holmes said nothing, but for once I needed no elucidation. It has long been his habit to study not only the English newspapers but also those of the main European capitals. 'The train and the steamship have made crime international, Watson,' he would tell me. 'It is no longer enough to know only what is going on in your own parish.' *La Verità* was an Italian weekly journal which I had often noticed lying around our chambers in Baker Street. All I knew of it was that its politics were radical, its style sensational, and its proprietor and principal reporter was Endo Chiari. I presume the magazine had at some time printed a picture of him, and of course Holmes never forgot a face.

Chiari now turned away from the circle that had formed around Holmes and the count and began a flirtatious conversation with Susi, the prettier of the two maids, till Rosi, the major-domo, sternly commanded her to go and fetch more refreshment. Outside in the square there was a sudden blare of a trumpet and everyone hurried out onto the balcony in case this signalled that events were going to start early. How anyone could spend a day in this country, let alone be a native of it, and still believe this was possible, I do not know! The trumpeter turned out to be some enterprising showman eager to attract customers to enter and view what he claimed to be the mummified and pickled remains of previous executed felons. The chill wind soon drove the others back indoors, but when they had retreated I found that Chiari remained. Perhaps his shabby suit was made of sturdier cloth than their finery, but he showed no sign of feeling the cold and leaned on the rail of the balcony, looking down at the growing crowd below with a mixture of sorrow and disgust.

'So, Dr Watson,' he said, 'and how shall you write of this spectacle you are to see here today?'

'I do not know that I shall write of it, sir,' I said shortly.

He turned his mocking gaze on me and said, 'But surely you are the chronicler of all Mr Holmes's triumphs?'

'Whether this be a triumph or no, sir, is not for me to say. But it is certainly not one of Mr Holmes's.'

'You say so? The count certainly gives him a portion of credit. The name Montesecco does not yet have quite the same power to make the virtuous bow and the criminal tremble, and though it must irk him, for the time being at least he is content to pull in the same yoke as your master and let himself be called the Italian Holmes.'

I drew myself up and replied, 'Sir, you may say what you like about your fellow countryman, though as he is your host and it is his champagne you are drinking, I should have thought common decency demanded some restraint. But I would have you know that Mr Sherlock Holmes is not my master, he is my close and trusted friend, and I will greatly resent any further slurs on his character.'

He frowned and said, 'Is the truth then a slur in England?'

'On the contrary, sir. It is our lodestone,' I declared.

'Then let us without quarrelling about slurs accept this truth,' he said. 'The count has used your friend's reputation to help secure his own, and by his presence here today, Mr Holmes seems to confirm the close connection.'

I naturally resented the implication but when I peered back into the room and saw how Holmes, like all the others, seemed to be hanging on every word the count said as he described the course of his investigation, I began to wonder whether my friend's recent nervous debility had temporarily impaired his fine judgement.

This was the tale that we heard.

The murder had been committed early on the last day of August in the Montesecco *palazzo* on the Via di Monserrato. At eleven o'clock in the morning a terrible scream ('like the sound of a pig being butchered,' averred the maid, Susi, who came from country stock) was heard throughout the palace, bringing all who heard it rushing towards its apparent source on the first floor. Here they found Giuseppe Strepponi struggling to force open the door of Count Leonardo's study, which seemed to be locked on the inside. Rosi, the major-domo, was one of the first on the scene. He quickly produced his set of household keys, unlocked the door and he and Strepponi burst in to discover the count lying across his desk with his throat cut from ear to ear.

The weapon, still lying on the desk, appeared to be an ornamental dagger honed to a razor edge, which the count used as a paper knife. Strepponi attempted to administer first aid, but it was far too late and the only significant result of his efforts was to cover himself with blood. Dr Provenzale was summoned and he confirmed what was evident to all present, that the old count was dead. The authorities were informed and Captain Zardi began his investigation.

Zardi, a laconic man with an upright military bearing, here took up the story. The key to the study was found on a marble plinth supporting a statue of Marcus Aurelius just inside the door. The central of the three windows was wide open and on the sill was the print of a bloody hand. The window opened on to the inner court of the palace, which was laid out as a formal garden. Up the wall grew an ancient vine, its thick, gnarled branches easily capable of bearing a man's weight.

From the courtyard garden there were many doorways and passages providing a wide choice of exits. Zardi immediately ordered a thorough search of the palace, but no fugitive was found, nor could any of the inmates recall seeing any stranger on the premises that morning.

Zardi now questioned Strepponi, who told him that the count had sent him away when he reported for duty at his usual time of ten a.m., saying that he would not require his services for another hour at least, as he was expecting his lawyer, Randone. Strepponi retired to his room on the upper floor. At five to eleven he came down and was just approaching the study door when he heard the scream from within. He rushed forward and tried to enter but found the door locked. He could hear sounds of movement from within but of course by the time Rosi arrived and unlocked the door, the room was empty, save for the dying old man.

Now Zardi applied all his energy to discovering who the visitor might have been. Everyone in the household had to account for his or her movements and very few of them, even among the servants, could produce witnesses to their movements in the half-hour before the death. Only the young count, who had been with Signorina Medioli in the chamber immediately below his uncle's study, had a real alibi. On hearing the scream, he had rushed upstairs just in time to see his uncle dying in Strepponi's arms.

'I was naturally too stricken with grief for rational thought in the first hours after this tragic loss,' he said gravely. 'But once the flood tide of emotion had begun to ebb and I started to examine my new responsibilities as head of an ancient family, I knew that first and most urgent among them was to track down and deliver to punishment this foul assassin. I put myself, my wealth and my little store of wisdom at Captain Zardi's disposal. Naturally as a professional officer of the law, he received my offer of help courteously but coldly.'

He smiled at the captain, who gave a somewhat ambiguous shrug.

'But when I told him that I was a student of and in close correspondence with the famous Sherlock Holmes, whose services the experts of Scotland Yard are not ashamed to call upon, he showed the other side of his professionalism and immediately admitted me to the penetralia of his thought.'

'No fool, is he?' murmured Chiari in my ear. 'He learned quickly from your friend's experience that there is little advantage to be gained from making the police look like idiots!'

'You assume a great knowledge of Mr Holmes's mind,' I said frostily.

'Only what I have learned from your books,' he retorted. 'Listen and you will see how the count can triumph without appearing triumphant.'

'Captain Zardi had done all the groundwork,' said Montesecco modestly. 'All I was able to bring to the investigation were the reflections of a quiet mind and a burning personal desire to see my dear uncle avenged. First I examined closely what it was that the captain had found outside and beneath the study window. This was most significant.'

He paused and right on cue, reminding me of myself, Holmes said, 'And what did these findings consist of?'

Montesecco paused for a perfectly judged beat of time, then, with a casual drama worthy of Holmes himself, said, 'Nothing. Absolutely nothing.'

Holmes nodded in approval.

'And of course you asked yourself, could a bloodstained man have climbed down the vine without leaving some traces on the leaves?'

'Precisely.'

'Perhaps he jumped,' said Holmes.

'There was no sign of anyone having landed on the ground with the kind of force such a leap would have entailed,' said the count. 'Also you will recall that I myself was in the room below with la Signorina Medioli. I am sure that one or both of us would have noticed the sudden descent of a human form past our window.'

'A fair deduction,' admitted Holmes. 'So where did your reasoning take you next, Count?'

'When you have eliminated the impossible, whatever remains, however improbable, must be the truth,' said this young pup with a nod in Holmes's direction which acknowledged the source of the maxim to those who already knew it without admitting it wasn't his own coining to those who didn't. 'If the murderer cannot have escaped via the window, then he must still have been in the room.'

'But the room was empty save for the murdered man.'

'On the contrary. From their own testimony, Rosi here and Strepponi did not pause on the threshold and take a quiet stock of what they saw. No, they rushed straight into the study. My uncle was dying but not yet dead. Rosi reached him first – is that not so, Serge?'

'Yes, Count,' said the major-domo. 'I flung open the door and for a moment we stood frozen on the threshold. There, silhouetted in the bright beam of sunlight which poured through the open window sat your uncle, the old count, his lifeblood streaming from his throat. Now I rushed forward with Strepponi close behind, and as I stood over your uncle, debating how best to proceed, the monstrous assassin pushed by me and took his victim in his arms, cradling his head on his chest and calling to me to summon the physician.'

It was clearly a speech he had made many times. I could imagine how very boring his friends and family probably found it after such frequent repetition!

Montesecco smiled at him approvingly and said, 'So you see, Mr Holmes, given that a man is not murdered until he is dead, there were two others in the study with the murdered man.'

This seemed to me so much chop-logic but Holmes appeared rapt.

'Continue, Count,' he said. 'This is quite fascinating.'

'See how the good teacher shares in his pupil's progress,' murmured Chiari.

'I suggest you wait a little,' I said with more confidence than I felt. 'The jails of England are filled with men who believed they could read the direction of Holmes's thought.'

'So. A miracle worker. And when he says, "That is the man!" are there any who quarrel?'

'It would take a very foolish or a very brilliant man to

dispute the reasoning of Sherlock Holmes,' I said with some fervour.

'Such a reputation is like the Gorgon's gaze. You must be careful where you turn it,' he said enigmatically.

There was no time to examine his point. Montesecco was reaching the climax of his tale.

'I spoke to the doctor now and asked him if a man would scream after he had his throat cut. The doctor said he thought it unlikely that in such a circumstance a man would be able to produce the kind of noise that was heard throughout the household. I then examined the handle of the door on the outside and found traces of blood there. My suspicions were now thoroughly roused. I examined the key found by the statue of Marcus Aurelius and sure enough there were dried flakes of blood on it also. I asked myself if a man who had just committed a murder in the course of which his victim had screamed so loud that the alarm must have been raised would have been so composed that he would rush to the door, lock it, and place the key carefully where it was found, before escaping. Surely, even if he did have the presence of mind to lock the door, he would have left the key in the lock?'

'Perhaps,' objected Holmes, 'the door was locked before rather than after the murder.'

Montesecco looked at Holmes with just the expression of long-suffering exasperation I have seen on my friend's face when some plodding policeman is slow to take a point.

'Then why should there be blood on the key?' he said. 'No, everything was leading to the sole explanation which took account of all the facts. Question: why was there blood on the key? Answer: because the murderer had touched it after the murder. Question: why was there blood on the outer door handle? Answer: the same, because the murderer had touched it after the murder. Question: who had let out the terrible scream which roused the house? Answer: the murderer! You see his ingenuity. Strepponi, having slain my uncle, sees that his hands and cuffs are covered with blood. He rushes to the window, leaving a print there, then realizing that it is going to be almost impossible to escape by that route undetected, he goes instead to the door, unlocks it, checks to be sure there is no one close outside, steps out, locks the door behind him, lets out that terrible scream, and starts rattling the door handle as if he is desperate to get in. Rosi appears, unlocks the door and rushes in. Behind him, Strepponi places the key by the statue, then rushes to his victim and takes him in his arms, partly to give himself a reason for being covered in blood, partly to prevent anyone else administering any aid which might have delayed my uncle's death. I immediately placed my findings in the hands of Captain Zardi, who then performed his duties with the vigour for which he is renowned.'

'Again, the sop to Cerberus,' murmured Chiari.

The captain nodded his appreciation and said in his bluff military manner, 'I meanwhile had interviewed all present in the palace, including Signor Randone, who told me he had just arrived for his appointment with the old count.'

'And I could not see how Strepponi should have imagined my appointment was earlier in view of the fact that it was arranged by himself in conjunction with my clerk,' interposed the lawyer.

'With this in mind, and after due consideration of the Count Montesecco's investigations,' resumed Zardi, 'I took the suspected man, Strepponi, into custody and searched his room. There I found correspondence of a threatening nature from Giulio Tebaldo, a well-known usurer, requiring immediate repayment of a large loan. When confronted, Strepponi admitted he had gone deeply into debt in order to purchase gifts for a certain lady with whom he had become deeply infatuated but without his feelings being reciprocated. Tebaldo, when interviewed, admitted that the evening prior to the murder he had sent a messenger around to talk to Strepponi. By messenger I understood him to mean thug. The messenger had returned with some items of jewellery on account, and a promise that Strepponi would be in a position to repay the balance within twenty-four hours.'

'And do we know the name of this lady?' enquired Holmes.

There was a silence. Then Claudia Medioli said, 'It was I. At first it was amusing, then he became a nuisance. Of course I returned his gifts but he kept sending more.'

'And did you tell your friend, the count?'

'No,' she said, her fine brown eyes downcast. 'His sense of honour would have required that he secured Strepponi's dismissal from his uncle's service. I was weak, and wished the young man no ill. How I wish now that I had spoken earlier!'

She wiped away a tear. Beside me, Chiari snorted derisively.

The count touched her arm comfortingly, then said, 'So now we had a motive. Strepponi approached my uncle for money. My uncle was a kind man, but he despised any weakling who let himself fall into the hands of the usurers.'

'Can't have had much time for his nephew, then,' muttered Chiari.

'But if my uncle could not help him living, Strepponi knew he could help him dead. In his will there was a generous legacy, token of my uncle's misplaced regard and more than enough to help him from his present troubles. Strepponi denied knowing of this, but Signor Randone was able to confirm that a copy of the will lay among my uncle's papers to which Strepponi as secretary had ready access. Perhaps my uncle in his disgust now threatened to remove him from his will.'

'This is possible,' said Randone. 'It was on a matter of his will that the old count had summoned me to see him.'

Montesecco frowned a little at this interruption, then resumed, 'So this egregious villain, finding himself in a desperate situation, did not hesitate to put his own security above the life of his noble benefactor, and slew him like a dog.'

There was a moment's pause, during which all the company save Holmes, myself and Endo Chiari showed signs of deep emotion. In some cases it looked likely to have burst out in the kind of loud lamentation these Latins are prone to, had it not been interrupted by a huge cry, half-welcoming, half-contumelious, from the mob in the square. Instantly all the guests crowded out onto the balcony, which creaked and groaned so much that I felt there was a real risk that we would all be precipitated to join the crowd below.

The cause of the uproar was the approach to the scaffold of a tightly bunched squad of foot soldiers, bayonets flashing in the wintry sunlight. In their midst, crouched low as if to conceal himself from the noisy mob, was a thin, shaven-headed man with a furtive, frightened expression whom at first I took to be the condemned prisoner.

'Why is he not manacled?' I enquired of Chiari.

The journalist laughed and said, 'You are mistaken, my friend. This is not Strepponi. This is the executioner who is held in such low esteem by the common people that they would subject him to his own foul craft if he dared appear without his armed guard.'

I glanced at my pocket watch. It gave ten minutes to the appointed hour. Could it be that in this matter alone, the Italians were untypically punctual?

Someone coughed. A small sound against the chatter of the guests and the tumult from the mob below as the executioner ascended his deadly machine. But it reduced all those on the balcony to silence as I had seen it reduce many other assemblages to silence during our long association, and every eye turned towards Sherlock Holmes.

'My dear count,' he said. 'My felicitations. To solve any murder requires the keenest of intellects, the finest of judgements. To solve a case with which you personally are so closely and painfully involved requires a dedication and a will almost superhuman.'

There was another huge roar from the crowd, mingled with a fanfare of trumpets. In the square the officers mounted their horses and unsheathed their sabres. The hundred or so foot soldiers lounging around seized their arms, fixed bayonets and cleared the corridor from the church, which in the relaxed atmosphere of the previous hour had been encroached upon by strolling pedestrians and pedlars of sweetmeats and cigar merchants. Then the bay of the mob suddenly declined to a single mighty gasp of superstitious awe, and many of them sank on one knee as out of the church emerged a macabre procession of priest and monks, some carrying banners, others, reliquaries, with at their centre two who bore above their cowled heads a huge, brightly painted crucifix on which hung an effigy of Christ, all draped in black hessian.

Holmes continued as if there had been no disturbance.

'Our art, Count, as you so clearly understand, is to select the single truth out of a wide array of erroneous possibilities, to refine what might be into what is. Above all we must not let ourselves be diverted from our purpose. A lesser man might for instance have wondered why, if Strepponi knew the lawyer's appointment was for eleven, he chose to include that particular lie in his story. Or why, having had all of his expensive gifts returned from the *signorina*, he did not return them whence they came, getting the most part of his money refunded and thus clearing his debts. A lesser man, needing to confirm to himself that the death cry could not have emanated from the dying man, might have wasted his and the doctor's time by checking whether in cutting the jugular vein, the killer had struck so deep as to sever the vocal cords also . . .'

He glanced interrogatively at Dr Provenzale, who looked confused.

'I presume also,' continued Holmes, 'that it was possible to tell from the direction of the death stroke whether the murderer was right- or left-handed . . .'

Another glance at Provenzale, another look of confusion.

'. . . and of course this information will no doubt have been cross-checked with the handedness of any suspected person.'

Outside there was another huge roar and all the kneeling spectators were back on their feet, craning to glimpse the last and most important player to arrive on this ghastly stage. As Holmes's long-time companion it has been my fate to see many murderers, so I know better than most that there is no distinguishing mark. But the pale-faced, slim, handsome young man who walked with his head held high at the centre of a squad of armed soldiers looked as little like one of the breed as any I have seen.

Chiari spoke, sounding puzzled.

'It seems to me, Mr Holmes, you are suggesting that perhaps the murderer might indeed have been in the locked room and made his escape through the open window as we all thought in the beginning.'

'Good Lord, no,' said Holmes indignantly. 'How could I suggest such a thing when the count has proved it impossible? To climb down the vine without leaving traces of blood on the foliage defies belief. And while it might be argued that a man could leap down onto the hard-baked earth without leaving an impression, fortunately the count himself, and Signorina Medioli, were in the room below. And still more fortunately, despite the fact that the full blast of the sun's heat must have been on their window (for was it not pouring directly into the study above?), they had broken with the custom of the country and had the protective shutters wide open.'

I saw several of the journalists exchange speculative glances at this juncture. What was Holmes up to? I wondered.

'And the blood on the key? And on the outer door handle?' said Chiari eagerly. 'Are you equally well persuaded of the accuracy of your pupil's deductions?'

'Naturally. That any other of the people entering the room in the hustle and bustle of those dreadful minutes after the discovery might have unknowingly become stained with the old count's blood and inadvertently transferred it to either the key or the handle is a possibility incapable of proof and therefore to be discounted.'

'That it is incapable of proof surely means it is also incapable of disproof,' said Chiari.

'Come, come, Signor Chiari, one pupil among your countrymen is quite enough for me to take on at a time,' murmured Holmes.

Below, a huge cheer signalled that the condemned man had successfully negotiated the perilous ladder to the scaffold platform. The black-draped Christ had been brought to a halt directly before him and his eyes were steadfastly fixed on the effigy. To a non-Papist it seems a tasteless pantomime, but I found myself praying it brought the young man some comfort.

'So you have no doubt that this poor fellow about to lose his head is guilty?' demanded Chiari.

'His guilt is between his judge on earth, who is here with us, and his judge in heaven, who I also believe is here with us,' said Holmes solemnly. 'All we can know for certain is that a good man on the brink of a new life with the lady of his choice has suffered a most terrible wrong which not only deprived him of his future happiness but also robbed the son he perhaps hoped to have of a name and a role, perhaps even of a country.'

Suddenly everyone was looking at Signora Masina, who was flushing tremendously while her sister was staring at Holmes with pale anger.

'But happily no act however foul is without good as well as evil consequences, and this particular deed has brought earlier than was dreamt possible a new, young heir to his title and fortune with many years ahead in which to prove how much he merits them.'

He bowed towards the count, who looked uncertain how he should react to this somewhat ambiguous compliment. But he was saved the trouble of reply by a deathly silence falling on the square, which drew all our attention as much as the previous noise.

Strepponi was kneeling beneath the knife. His head rested in a hole in a cross plank. Another plank with a matching half-circle removed from it was fitted over his neck. A priest made the sign of the cross over him. The executioner bent to a lever. And the next moment with a rattle like the passage of a metal-rimmed wheel over a cobbled street, the knife descended and the severed head fell forward into a leather basket. From this the executioner plucked it and, holding it by the hair, displayed it to the mob, prior to fixing it on a pole to be left as a target for the crows and a warning to the criminals of this great city. ·

It was all over in a few seconds and immediately the crowd began to disperse, save for some morbid souls eager to take a closer look at the headless body.

Our party all streamed back from the balcony to the room where fresh bottles of champagne awaited. Signora Masina and her sister did not pause but left immediately. I saw the judge and Zardi and Falcone and the doctor in a close group, deep in conversation. The count and Signorina Medioli stood close together but exchanged no words. And all the journalists were crowding around Sherlock Holmes, who raised his hand to command silence and said, 'Gentlemen, please. You have your own Italian Sherlock Holmes to question. And in Signor Chiari I believe you may have your own Italian Dr Watson to chronicle his exploits.'

He smiled at Chiari, who glanced at me with an expression eloquent of apology, then turned back to Holmes, who pulled on his cloak and said, 'As for me, I am too fatigued to talk. And besides, my good friend Watson and I have a train to catch.'

This was the first I had heard of this and at first I took it for a mere excuse to make a rapid departure. But half an hour later, with scarcely time to draw a breath let alone use one in idle conversation, I found myself seated in plush comfort in one of the most ornately decorated railway coaches I had ever seen, rattling northwards out of Rome.

'But our luggage, Holmes!' I had gasped as I was hurried aboard.

'All taken care of,' he said with that air of knowing far more of things than I do which I find so insufferable. I determined not to feed his complacence by asking questions about our travel plans. Instead as we relaxed and lit our pipes, I turned back to our morning's adventure, about which I was still greatly curious.

'Holmes, what you implied, most ungallantly I may observe, about the Signora Masina, that she was . . . *enceinte*, do you believe it true?'

'I should have thought a medical man could tell at a glance,' he replied. 'Sixteen to twenty weeks, I should have said.'

'And you believe this to have been the old count's child?'

'I would hope so. But no need to worry about her. She is going to America, where no doubt she will be presented as a grieving widow. And I do not doubt the new count has been most generous in making a settlement to take care of the upbringing of his bastard nephew.'

'Who would, if the old count had lived to marry, have been the legitimate heir,' I said slowly.

'Indeed,' said Holmes.

'And it is almost entirely as a result of young Montesecco's investigation including the evidence of his own *inamorata* that Giuseppe Strepponi was condemned?'

'Evidently.'

'Holmes,' I said, horrified. 'What have we done?'

'Explain yourself, my dear chap,' he said, affecting puzzlement.

'Everything you said towards the end of our visit seemed to me to imply a possible refutation of the count's logic. Now you seem to be suggesting that he more than anyone had an excellent motive for killing his uncle.'

'I cannot argue with you there,' said Holmes complacently.

'Then how can it not trouble you that even as you made your comments, that poor young fellow, Strepponi, was being hauled up onto a scaffold and executed within your very sight?'

Now Holmes threw back his head and laughed, a sound which would have struck me as callous had it been emitted by any other man.

'My dear Watson, rest easy. I cannot say how much the unfortunate secretary may have been egged on to the murder by his connection with Claudia Medioli. That is for Zardi and perhaps the Roman press to discover. But I can assure you that Strepponi was guilty, and probably committed the crime very much as the count worked out.'

'But how can you be sure after the way you undermined his deductions?'

'Oh, never doubt it, his *deductions* deserved to be undermined, but his *conclusion* was I believe correct. Partly because, a) he probably knew that Strepponi was the killer from the start, and b) if it had not been correct, he would not have dared involve me. But principally because the execution took place on time.'

'I'm sorry, I don't understand. I know these Latins are sadly deficient in their timekeeping, but I do not see how you draw such a remarkable conclusion from a single instance of punctuality!'

'Then you must learn to understand as well as pity and patronize these poor benighted foreigners, Watson. To these Romans, death by execution for no matter how foul a crime does not mean eternal punishment for the criminal. No, even the vilest creature may, after serving his time in Purgatory, be admitted to the grace of God, which passeth all understanding, even mine. But not if he goes to his death unconfessed and unshriven. Wherefore the young man Strepponi was taken into the church of San Cassiano on his way to the scaffold. Had he refused to make his confession, the execution would have been delayed until sunset, so determined are these merciful priests that the condemned man should have every chance of grace. So when the execution of one who was reputed to be a devout young man takes place on time, it may be assumed that he has made a full and free confession of his guilt.'

'And had he not confessed?'

'Then the case would have been altered,' said Holmes grimly. 'So a guilty man has been sent to his Maker. All that I wished to ensure was that this mountebank of a would-be detective should not be able by misuse of my reputation to send other, perhaps less guilty, men to their dooms. I believe there are at least two already languishing in jail as a result of his so-called deductions. I trust once our friend Chiari, and some of the other pressmen also, have their say, these will be released, and any other attempt by the count to interfere with justice will be greeted by indignation and derision!'

'Holmes, you are a marvel,' I said. 'And not the least marvellous thing is that we should be sitting on this train heading heaven knows where.'

'Why, where else should a man head at this time of year but home?' my friend replied. 'We shall travel non-stop across the face of Europe and not stop until we are safe in Baker Street. I have telegraphed Mrs Hudson that we are coming, so, though you may eat it late, you will not after all be deprived of her famous goose, which I know you value so much.'

'But, Holmes,' I said. 'Non-stop, you say? How may that be?'

'Because this is a Special,' he said.

'A Special? All the way to England? But that must be costing us a king's ransom!' I said alarmed.

'Possibly. Fortunately we have a king, or one who will be a king, to pay for it. It is not our Special but His Royal Highness, the Prince of Wales. You may recall I was able to do him a trifling foolish service some years ago, and he said if ever he could be of use to me, I had only to let him know. Hearing that he was at Ostia, and guessing that he would not disoblige Her Majesty, his mama, by spending the whole of Christmas out of the country, I telegraphed him via the embassy. He is not the man to forget a promise. So rouse yourself, Watson. We are to take lunch with the Prince in half an hour, and I hardly think you will want to appear looking like a municipal rat catcher! One thing you may neglect to take with you, however.'

'What's that?' I asked.

'That infernal notebook of yours. This part of the tale you will not be able to tell for a hundred years!'

The Game of Dog

It was Charley Field the landlord of the Punchbowl who started it.

Like his great namesake, Charley didn't much care for dogs or children. In fact, being a Yorkshire publican down to his tap-roots, Charley didn't much care for anything except brass, Geoff Boycott, and his own way.

But if the price of getting the brass out of his customers' pockets into his till was admitting their little companions into his pub, he bit the bullet and said that as long as they didn't yap, fight, defecate or smell too high, they were welcome in the rather draughty and uncomfortable rear bar.

That was the children. The dogs were allowed in the cosy front snug under the same very reasonable conditions.

One misty October evening, Charley peered through the snug hatch to make sure no one was sitting there with an empty glass and he saw a scene to warm a canophilist's cockles.

In one corner, a terrier sat with its bright eyes fixed on the face of its owner, who appeared to be dozing. Stretched out across the hearth in front of the glowing fire lay an aged bloodhound, looking as if it were carved out of bronze till the crinkling of cellophane brought its great head up to receive its tribute of barbecued beef flavour crisps. Beneath the window-nook table a Border collie and a miniature poodle were sharing an ashtrayful of beer while above them their owners enjoyed one of those measured Yorkshire conversations that make Pinteresque dialogue sound like a Gilbert and Sullivan patter song. At the table by the door, a small mongrel by dint of crawling around in ever-decreasing circles was contriving to bind the leg of its blissfully unaware owner to the leg of his chair.

This last was Detective Chief Inspector Peter Pascoe, the newest member of this canine club. The mongrel was Tig and belonged to his young daughter. As the nights drew in, he didn't care to have her wandering the streets even with such a fiercely defensive companion, so he'd taken over the evening walk, whose turning point was the Punchbowl. Observing the bloodhound drooping in behind its owner one damp night, he'd followed suit and over the past couple of weeks had become almost a regular, though he never stayed long enough to exchange more than a polite good evening with the others nor to identify them beyond their dogs.

'Bugger me!' said Charley Field after drinking in the scene for a few moments. 'You lot and your bloody dogs. You'd think you'd given birth to 'em! I bet if there were a fire and you'd only got time to rescue one human being or your dog, you lot would have to think twice!'

'Nay, Charley,' said the poodle. 'If it were thee, I'd not have to think once!'

Before Charley could respond to this sally he was summoned to the bar, leaving the poodle to enjoy the approving chuckles of his fellow drinkers.

As they died away the Border collie suddenly said, 'Hitler.'

'Eh?'

'I'd rescue Floss here afore I'd rescue Hitler, no question.'

The others considered. There was no dissent.

'Joe Stalin,' said the poodle.

'The Yorkshire Ripper,' said the bloodhound.

Both went through on the nod.

The collie looked towards the terrier, who still seemed to be dozing, then turned his gaze on Pascoe. He thought of explaining to them that as a policeman he was duty bound to regard all human life as sacred. Then he thought of trying to explain this to his daughter when he returned home with an incinerated Tig. Then he thought, lighten up, Pascoe. It's only pub talk!

'Maggie Thatcher?' he said tentatively.

This gave them pause.

'Nay,' said the bloodhound. 'She had her bad side, agreed, but she did some good things too. I don't think we can let her burn.'

'I bloody could. Aye, and throw coals on the fire if I could find any to throw,' growled the poodle. 'She closed my pit and threw me and most of my mates on the slag heap, the cow.'

The bloodhound looked ready to join issue, but the collie said, 'Nay, we need to agree one hundred per cent on something like this.'

And the terrier defused the situation entirely by suddenly sitting up straight, opening his eyes, and saying, 'My mother-in-law!'

Over the next few weeks the game took shape, without formal rules but with rules that its participants instinctively understood, and their choice of candidates for the fire gave Pascoe more information about his fellow players than he was likely to get from general enquiry. In a Yorkshire pub a man's private life is a man's private life. You can ask a direct question, but only if you can take a direct answer. Pascoe on one occasion, finding himself alone with the bloodhound, had enquired casually what the man did for a living.

'I'm by way of being an expert,' replied the bloodhound.

'Oh yes. An expert in what?'

'An expert in minding my own bloody business.'

Which was reasonable enough, he decided, and had the upside of meaning he didn't have to tell them he was a policeman.

The one topic on which they all spoke freely was their dogs, and Pascoe, by listening and by observation, was soon familiar with all their little ways. Fred, the ancient bloodhound, had three times been pronounced dead by the vet and three times given him the lie. He loved barbecue beef crisps and howled in derision if offered any other flavour. Floss, the collie, was a rescue dog, having been kicked off a farm when the farmer realized she was frightened of sheep. She was in love with Puff the poodle, who shared her beer but showed no sign of wanting to share anything else, which was why his non-PC owner had changed his name from Percy. Tommy, the terrier, was a genius. He could die for England, stand on his hind legs and offer left or right paw as requested. His *pièce de résistance*, when given the command *Light!*, was to go to the fireplace, extract one of the wooden spills from a container standing on the grate, insert it in the flame and bring it back to light its master's cigarette. Tig always watched this performance with a sort of sneering yawn. The human race, apart from Rosie Pascoe whom he adored, was there to serve dogs, not the other way around. He didn't want any dog's nose up his behind that had already been up a human's.

The one thing the dogs had in common was that their owners could all find someone, indeed several someones, whom they asserted they would put beneath their pets on a rescue priority list, and the game soon became a regular part of their evening encounter, its rules established by intuitive agreement rather than formal debate.

It was always initiated by someone saying, 'Hitler!' Thereafter the others spoke as the spirit moved them. Approval of a nomination was signified by an aye or a nod, and if unanimous, the game moved on. In the event of objection, the proposer was given a fair hearing, after which objectors either stated their case or admitted themselves persuaded. Unless the vote was unanimous the nominee was declared saved. And the game was usually closed by the terrier declaring, 'My mother-in-law!' though it was possible for someone else to close it by calling out, '*His* mother-in-law!'

Pascoe, after his initial failure with Mrs Thatcher, restricted himself to historical characters. Nero was given a universal thumbs-down and he successfully argued the case for leaving Richard the Third to the flames, but when he ventured closer to living memory and suggested Field Marshal Haig, who commanded the British Forces in the First World War, he met surprising resistance and failed to carry the field. On the other hand it was only his unyielding opposition which pulled the fingers of the Hand of God, Diego Maradona, out of the fire.

When he explained the game to his wife, Ellie, she wrinkled her nose in distaste and said, '*Men!*'

'Hang about,' he protested. 'It's only a bit of fun. Anyway, you tell me, you've got the choice between saving Tig and saving George Bush, who do you grab?'

'That's what I mean,' she said. 'This stuff's too serious to make a game out of.'

To which he replied, '*Women!*'

One December evening when the frost was so sharp that even Tig's normal indifference to sub-zero temperatures was sorely tested, the pair of them burst into the snug like a pair of Arctic explorers discovering a Little Chef at the Pole.

They got as close as they could to the roaring fire without standing on the bloodhound and gave themselves over to the delicious agony of defrosting. It wasn't till the process was sufficiently advanced to make him admit the wisdom of stepping back a foot or so that Pascoe became aware that the atmosphere in the room, though physically warm, was distinctly depressed. His greeting had been answered by a series of non-committal grunts, and even the dogs looked subdued.

He went to the hatch and attracted Charley Field's attention.

'I'll have a Scotch tonight, Charley,' he said. Then, lowering his voice, he asked, 'What's up with this lot? I've seen livelier wakes.'

'You're not so far wrong,' said Charley. 'You've not heard about Lenny then?'

So used was he to thinking about the others only in terms of their dogs, it took Pascoe a moment to work out that Lenny was Tommy the terrier's owner, who was absent tonight.

'No. What?'

'There was a fire at his house last night.'

'Oh God. Is he all right?'

'He's fine.'

'And Tommy?'

'He's fine too.'

Pascoe thought for a second and didn't like where his thoughts were taking him.

'Was anyone hurt?' he asked.

'Aye,' said Charley Field. 'His mother-in-law. Burnt to a cinder.'

The following morning Detective Superintendent Andy Dalziel sat listening to Peter Pascoe with growing disbelief.

When he'd finished, the Fat Man said, 'I had a dream the other night. Wieldy came to see me to say he were getting married to Prince Charles and it was going to be a white wedding and he wanted my advice on whether he should sell the photo rights to *Hello!* or *OK!*.'

'And which did you go for?'

'I went downstairs for a stiff drink. But thinking about it, I reckon my dream made more sense than what you've just told me.'

He looked at the local paper spread out on his desk. Its headline was the hero of Hartsop Avenue over a photo of a man with a terrier in his arms and a blanket around his shoulders being comforted by a fireman outside a smouldering house. The legend below read:

Mr Leonard Gold (38) returned from a meeting at the Liberal Club to find his house in Hartsop Avenue ablaze. Knowing that his mother-in-law, Mrs Brunnhilde Smith (62), was still in the building, despite all efforts to stop him, he rushed inside in an attempt to rescue her. Unhappily his courageous act was in vain, the fire was too far advanced for him to reach the upstairs room from which Mrs Smith's body was later recovered, and it was only the arrival of the fire brigade that enabled Mr Gold himself to make his escape.

'Let me get this straight,' said Dalziel. 'This guy's a hero, nearly gets burnt to death trying to rescue his ma-in-law, ends up in hospital being treated for second-degree burns, and because of some daft game some dog fanciers play in a pub, you want to investigate him for choosing to get his dog out and leaving the old girl to fry? Have I got the gist?'

'That's about it,' said Pascoe.

'And have you got any evidence to support this, apart from this dog game you play?'

'No,' said Pascoe. 'But I haven't looked into it yet. I only heard about the fire last night and I wanted to run it past you first.'

'I think you need to run a lot bloody faster,' said Dalziel. 'Preferably out of my sight. Have you got nowt better to do, like for instance your job? Best keep your hobbies for your own time.'

'In actual fact,' said Pascoe prissily, 'this is my own time. I've got the day off, remember? But in any case, I always thought the investigation of suspicious death was a large part of my job.'

'Suspicious? Has anyone from the fire department been in touch with us to say there's something dodgy about the fire? Or anyone from the path lab to say they've got worries about the way the old girl died?'

'No. But it's not that kind of suspicion.'

'So what kind of suspicion is it, Pete? I mean, even supposing what you say is true, where's the sodding crime?'

'I'm sure there's got to be something,' said Pascoe. 'I'll ring up the CPS and talk to a lawyer, shall I?'

'If you must,' sighed Dalziel. 'And while you're at it, ask 'em which they'd go for, *Hello!* or *OK!*.'

It wasn't often that the CPS and Andy Dalziel were in accord but this seemed to be one of those occasions.

The lawyer he spoke to was a young woman called, appropriately, Portia Silk, who had what might have been in other circumstances an infectious laugh, which he heard as she quoted at him, 'Thou shalt not kill but need'st not strive / Officiously to keep alive.'

'But surely if you let someone die when you could have saved them . . .' he protested, whereupon she interrupted with, 'Only if you have a professional relationship as in doctor/patient, or a duty of care as in teacher/pupil. But if you're walking along the canal bank and you see someone struggling in the water, it may be regarded by some people as reprehensible of you not to dive in and try to save them, but it's not a criminal act. Even if it were, in the circumstances you cite, proving deliberate choice of dog over woman would be very difficult.'

Pascoe had not survived and prospered under the despotic rule of Andy Dalziel by being easily deterred from a chosen path, and after his disappointing talk with Ms Silk, he immediately dialled the fire station and had a chat with Keith Little, the officer who'd been given the job of looking at the Hartsop Avenue blaze.

'No, nothing suspicious else we'd have been on to you. Fire started downstairs in the living room. Dead woman was a chain-smoker by all accounts. From the look of things, it started in an old sofa, fag end down between the cushions, which predated the fire-retardant regulations, and eventually you'd get a nice little blaze going which once it burnt through to the stuffing would really explode. After that, well, it's an old house, wooden floors, wooden beams, even wood panelling on some of the walls. Some of them old places are bonfires just waiting for someone to toss a match on to them. Why are you asking, by the way? You got a sniff of something iffy?'

'No,' replied Pascoe honestly. 'Just curiosity. It was in my neck of the woods and I know Mr Gold slightly. You've spoken to him?'

'Yeah. He's still in hospital. Hero they're calling him. Right idiot in my book. Two of our lads had to go in there to get him out. Found him crouched down in the shower room, half-unconscious from smoke inhalation. Could have cost them their lives too if things had gone wrong.'

'Did they get the dog out as well? The one he's holding in the *Evening News* picture.'

'No. I gather it were waiting for him when our boys brought him out. They remarked what a fuss it made of him. The paramedics had to let it in the ambulance with him. If you want to be loved, get a dog, eh?'

'Wasn't there a window in the shower room?'

'Aye, but far too small for a grown man.'

'Where did they find the dead woman?'

'Her room was right above the sitting room. Seems her favourite hobby was lying on her bed with a bottle of vodka and listening to music full blast. She'd not have heard anything. In fact it's likely, if she'd drunk enough, she'd have died in her sleep afore the fire erupted through the floorboards. Let's hope so. No way our lads could get to her. They did well to get our sodding hero out.'

When a further call to the pathology lab confirmed that Mrs Smith had indeed been asphyxiated by smoke inhalation before the flames got to work on her, it seemed to Pascoe he'd reached the end of the road. Ellie hadn't been all that pleased when he'd announced that morning that despite having the day off there was something he had to check out at work, so now he made his exit before the Fat Man found him something to do.

Hartsop Avenue was a mile and a half the far side of the Punchbowl from where Pascoe lived, and there was no reason for him to go anywhere near it on his way home. Nevertheless, somehow or other he found himself parked outside the burnt-out shell of the Gold house thirty minutes later.

He got out of his car and stood looking at the wrecked building. Two women walked by him, carrying shopping bags. As they passed, one said to the other in a deliberately loud voice, 'I think it's disgusting the way some people make an entertainment out of other folks' disasters.'

She then turned into the gateway of the house next door while her companion went on her way.

Pascoe hurried towards the neighbour, pulling his warrant card out of his pocket.

'Excuse me,' he called.

She turned an unfriendly face towards him, but when she saw the card her manner became conciliatory.

'I'm sorry what I said just now,' she apologized. 'I thought you were just one of them sightseers. We had a lot of them yesterday, just walking or driving by to take a look. Ghouls, I call them.'

'I agree,' said Pascoe. 'But it's human nature, I'm afraid. You know the Golds well, do you?'

'Oh yes. Greta, that's Mrs Gold, is staying with us till they get something sorted out. Poor woman, she's devastated.'

'I gather she was away when it happened.'

'Down in London, visiting an old school friend and doing some Christmas shopping. *She* wanted to go too, but I think Greta's friend made it quite clear the invitation was for Greta only.'

She Pascoe took to refer to Brunnhilde Smith.

'So you get on well with the Golds then?'

'Oh yes. Lovely couple. Very quiet. At least they were till *she* came to live with them. But I shan't speak ill of the dead.'

Pascoe's long experience recognized this as the precursor of ill-speaking in the same way as a wassailer in a Danish mead-hall knew that *Hwæt!* signalled the start of *Beowulf*.

Two minutes later he was seated in Mrs Woolley's kitchen drinking tea and listening to an account of Lenny Gold's mother-in-law which put her on a par with Grendel's mother.

Mrs Woolley was a friend and confidante of Greta Gold and had got the family background from her. It seemed her mother,

Brunnhilde Hotter, a native of Hanover, had married a British soldier in the sixties and on his demob they'd settled in London, where Greta was born. She'd married Lenny Gold in 1985 and they made the error of setting up home only ten minutes' drive from Greta's family home in Kilburn. By 1990, Lenny had had enough. Despite being a Londoner born and bred, he started looking for a job as far away from the capital as he could get, which in the event turned out to be mid-Yorkshire.

'Everything was fine,' said Mrs Woolley. 'She came visiting occasionally, but you can put up with a short visit, can't you? So long as you can see an end. And Mr Smith never liked to be away from home too long. Then five years ago he died. Naturally Greta made her mother come and stay with her for a while to help her come to terms with things. Couple of weeks, she thought. Month at the most. Well, the way Greta put it, there was never a time when they actually asked her to live with them permanently, but somehow it just happened. Hilda – that's what she was known as; Brunnhilde's too much of a mouthful – Hilda had a bad leg. Circulatory problem she said. Fat problem I said. Human limbs weren't made for that kind of load-bearing. She was a big woman, must have cost a fortune to feed. I've seen her sitting where you are now, Mr Pascoe, and watched her eat the whole of one of my Victoria sponges, four slices and it was gone. Plus I had to get my husband to strengthen the chair she sat on, she left it so wobbly.'

As well as her dietary excesses, there were plenty of other strikes against the Widow Smith, according to Mrs Woolley. She was a chain-smoker, she dominated conversations, she often said things in German to her daughter which were clearly comments on others present too rude to be spoken in English, she liked to lie on her bed and play her favourite records very loud ('Wagner, it was,' said Mrs Woolley. 'I know because George, that's my husband, he likes that kind of stuff, but he listens through his headphones, knowing I can't put up with all that screeching and howling.') And she complained bitterly to any who couldn't avoid listening that it was a tragedy her Greta had married such a useless idle man as Lenny. ('One time she said to me,' said Mrs Woolley, 'she said, "Don't you think that's a Jew name, Lenny Gold? All right, they got married in a church but I have seen him coming out of the shower and his thing was like a skinned rabbit." I told her live and let live, she should be ashamed saying such things but she just laughed and tapped her nose.') Above all she hated Tommy, saying the dog was unhygienic, and she was allergic, and it ought to be put down. ('Such a nice little dog,' concluded Mrs Woolley. 'And so clever. I bet if it was one of those things like wolves they had at Colditz, she'd have been a bit fonder of it!')

With the woman's permission Pascoe wandered out into the garden and looked up at the burnt-out shell next door. The garage was on this side, its sloping roof joining the main house wall just below a small square window which was closed, though its glass was cracked, presumably by the heat of the fire.

'Right mess, isn't it?' said a cheerful voice.

He turned to see a round bald man who introduced himself as George Woolley.

'That window,' said Pascoe. 'Is that the shower room where they found Lenny?'

Woolley confirmed that it was.

'Like a door it was to that dog,' he went on. 'Lenny used to leave it open for Tommy so he could get out to do his business when he was shut in the house by himself. A bloody marvel, that dog. Many's the time I've seen him hop out, run down the garage roof, jump down on to the rain barrel there, do the job, then head back in the same way.'

'But the window's closed,' said Pascoe. 'Presumably Lenny didn't bother to open it last night because he wasn't leaving Tommy shut in the house by himself. Mrs Smith was there.'

'*Her*,' said Woolley with the same intonation as his wife. 'She'd not have bothered to let him out even if she'd noticed he wanted to go. In fact she'd rather he messed up in the house so that she'd have something else to complain about.'

'You don't seem to have liked her much,' said Pascoe.

'Sorry, I know she's dead, but I'm not going to lie. She was a pain and I doubt if even Greta will mind very much that she's gone, not once she gets over the first shock. No, if Lenny had been killed trying to save her, that would have been the real tragedy. I couldn't believe it when he set off into the house.'

'You were there?' said Pascoe.

'Oh yes. I'd been at the Liberal Club with him. Not that we're Liberals. Who is, these days? But it's a good pint and not too pricey.'

'But he didn't take Tommy?'

'No. No dogs in the club, that's the rule.' He grinned and added, 'And no women either, except on Ladies' Night. Oh yes, it's a grand place.'

'It sounds it. So where did he leave Tommy? He can't have been in the house, can he?'

'I suppose not. He's got a kennel in the garden, sometimes he stays out there when the weather's fine.'

'I see. And you came back together from the club . . .' prompted Pascoe.

'That's right. In my car. We turned into the Avenue and I said, "Hello! What's going off?" We could see one or two people standing around and it's usually dead quiet. Then Lenny said, "Oh my God, it's my house!" Well, the ground floor was already well alight. I knew that Hilda must still be in there,

there was a light on in her bedroom and you could hear her hi-fi system belting out Wagner. Lenny jumped out of the car, I've never seen him so agitated. He didn't seem to know what to do with himself. I asked someone if they'd rung the brigade and they said yes. Lenny ran up the side of the house, I presume to see if he could get in the back, then he appeared at the front again. I got hold of him and said, "It's no use, Lenny, we can't do anything, the fire brigade will be here any minute." But he broke loose and before I could do anything he was up the path and going in the front door. I went after him, but the heat was too much for me. I could hear the sirens in the distance and knew that help wouldn't be long, but I really did fear the worst. And what made it worse was Tommy came running around the side of the house, barking and agitated, like he knew Lenny was in there. I've never been so relieved in my life as I was when the firemen brought him out, and I thought Tommy was going to have a fit, he was so happy. He's at the hospital too, you know. Against all the rules, but there was no separating the two of them.'

'Yes, they really worship each other, don't they?'

'That's right. Hey, does that mean you know Lenny and Tommy?'

'Yes. In fact I meet them sometimes when I'm out with my dog.'

'That explains it,' said Woolley, smiling. 'I was wondering what a cop was doing looking around after the fire. So it's just personal interest, is it?'

'Oh yes. I live quite close and I thought, knowing Lenny, that I'd take a look,' said Pascoe, feeling rather guilty as he uttered the lie.

'Understandable,' said Woolley. 'You're not thinking of visiting him in hospital by any chance, are you?'

161

'I suppose I might, some time,' said Pascoe vaguely.

'It's just that I'd told my wife I'd take her in at lunchtime and we'd bring Greta home and make sure she got a bite of lunch. That's why I'm back here now, but to tell the truth it hasn't gone down too well at work, there's a meeting I should be at in half an hour's time, and there's no way I'd be able to make it . . . but if you were going to the hospital to see Lenny . . .'

Why not? thought Pascoe. His morning was knackered anyway, and his suspicions, which had been looking more and more stupid over the past half-hour, had left him feeling very guilty.

He said, 'Yes, I could do that.'

'Great! You're a star! I'll just tell my good lady.'

As they went back into the house, Woolley suddenly laughed and said, 'I know I shouldn't but I had to smile when I thought about it later . . .'

'What?'

'Do you know your Wagner, Mr Pascoe?'

'A bit.'

'Well, when we got out of the car and saw the house burning, the music blasting out of the upstairs window was *Götterdämmerung*. It was that bit right at the end when they've lit Siegfried's funeral pyre. Brunnhilde gets on her horse and sends him plunging into the heart of the flames. Ironic, eh?'

'Always good for a laugh, old Wagner,' said Peter Pascoe.

At the hospital, they found Lenny Gold fast asleep in a small private room. His wife was with him and so was Tommy, who greeted Pascoe like an old friend.

Greta Gold, a slender, pale-faced woman with more of the Rhine maiden about her than the Valkyrie, said, 'They let me bring him but I have to take him away with me. He doesn't mind. I think he understands he can come back.'

'I'm sure he does,' said Pascoe. 'He's a very clever dog. I know how fond Lenny is of him.'

'Yes, he is,' said Greta, smiling at the terrier. 'Sometimes I'd tell him I thought he loved the dog more than me.'

'Nonsense,' said Mrs Woolley. 'Lenny adores you.'

'I know he does. I was only joking. But Tommy means such a lot to him. Sometimes, if we were out for a long time, he would even ring home, just so Tommy could hear his voice on the answer machine and be reassured. I'm so glad we didn't lose him too, that would have been too much to bear . . .'

Her eyes filled with tears. Mrs Woolley put her arm around her shoulder and led her aside.

Pascoe stood awkwardly by the bed, looking down at the sleeping figure. Lenny's hands were encased in plastic bags to protect the dressings and his face and head had been scorched too. All this suffered in his brave attempt to save a woman he had every cause to hate, thought Pascoe, his guilt returning with interest.

Mrs Woolley said, 'I'm just taking Greta down to the waiting room for a cup of tea, Mr Pascoe. We won't be long.'

'Yes. That will be fine.'

The two women left. Tommy showed signs of wanting to accompany them but Pascoe called, 'Tommy, come. Down. Stay.'

The dog trotted back, lay down under the bed, and looked up at him, eyes bright, ears pricked waiting for the next command.

Pascoe thought of Tig's likely reaction to such an instruction. He might obey in the end but it would involve a lot of thought and a great deal of yawning. Much as he loved the little mongrel, it must be nice to have a pet who didn't regard you as inferior, to whom your every word was like the voice of God . . .

God, which is dog backwards . . . the Game of Dog . . . the Game of God . . .

Into his mind came an image of Tommy lying in his basket in front of the fire in the Golds' parlour. The phone rings. After a while the answer machine switches on. The voice of God says, 'Tommy.' His ears prick. He sits up. The voice of God says, 'Light!' He goes to the fireplace, picks up a spill of wood left there, sticks it through the bars of the guard, and when it catches, he takes it to . . . where? To, say, the sofa, where a cigarette has been left stuck between two cushions. He lights the cigarette, drops the spill, gets back into his basket. And the cigarette burns, and the spill burns, and the cushion . . . Perhaps a small section of the cushion had had something rubbed into it, one of those cleaning solutions, for instance, which the instructions warn are highly inflammable . . .

The fire starts. The dog becomes aware of it. After a while he realizes this is something it would be a good idea to distance himself from. He wanders up the stairs to his usual exit, the shower room window.

But it is closed.

Brunnhilde, either because she thinks there's a draught, or out of sheer malice and in the hope that Lenny will be confronted by a dog mess on his return, has closed it. As the smoke drifts up the stairs, Tommy starts barking. But his warning cries are drowned by *The Twilight of the Gods* at full belt, and Brunnhilde on her bed is too deep into her vodka bottle and too immersed in Wagner's Germanic flames to be aware of this puny Anglo-Saxon fire building up beneath her.

Lenny comes home. He expects to be greeted by Tommy. When the dog doesn't appear, he rushes down the side of the house and sees that the shower room window has been closed.

And now in panic he returns to the front. The fire roars, the heat is intense. But Tommy is in there. He breaks free from his friend's grasp and rushes into the flames. He knows where Tommy will be. He opens the window, urges the dog out.

And then because he fears, probably foolishly, that the dog's love may match his own, he pulls the window shut again in case Tommy tries to get back in to be by his side. And he sinks to the floor and prepares to die.

A story of great ingenuity . . .

A story of great villainy . . .

A story of great courage . . .

A story of such absurdity that Pascoe shuddered at the thought of Andy Dalziel even suspecting that his right-hand man had let it pollute his mind.

Such ludicrous fantasies belonged, if anywhere, to the world of fairy tales, of escapist movies, of childish parlour games.

Like the Game of Dog.

He mouthed a silent *sorry* at the poor burnt hero who lay before him.

Lenny's eyes opened.

He looked up, focused, and recognition dawned.

He tried to say something.

Tommy, aware his master was conscious, put his front paws on the bed and raised his head to the level of the pillow, his tail wagging furiously.

Lenny reached out one of his bagged hands, touched the terrier's head and winced.

Then he looked at Pascoe and smiled and winked, and tried to speak again.

'What?' said Pascoe, stooping closer.

'Hitler!' said Lenny.

The Man Who Defenestrated His Sister

'Certainly, when I threw her from the garret window to the stony pavement below, I did not anticipate that she would fall so far without injury to life or limb.'

Inspector Bunfit glanced at his constabular scribe to make sure he was recording this incriminating admission. Under the weight of that benign gaze, a pencil point snapped, but the man had two more in reserve. It was a foolish officer who appeared unprepared in the service of Bunfit of the Yard.

Satisfied, the inspector returned his attention to the young man seated at the other side of the table. Slightly built, with thin, sensitive features, he had eyes of cerulean blue which met Bunfit's scrutiny with unblinking candour.

'So what you mean to say, Mr Arlecdon, is that it was your intention to kill her?'

'What?' The sky-blue clouded with shock. 'Of course it wasn't! Kill Alice? It would be like killing myself. She is my twin, Inspector, the other half of me. The better half. As children we seemed to have but one mind, one spirit. It was only as we left that innocent age that she started to draw a curtain between us.'

'A curtain? You mean like you shared a room?'

'No! I speak figuratively,' cried the young man. 'What we shared were thoughts and feelings. I felt this as a gift from heaven, a source of indescribable joy. But Alice, alas, as we grew older clearly came to find it an intolerable burden.'

The scribing constable was beginning to look lost.

Bunfit said, 'Yes, sir, I understand, sir. But you see my difficulty. It is my experience, born of more 'n thirty years observing the – saving your presence – criminal classes, that when a young man throws a young woman out of a fourth-floor window, his intention is generally homicidal.'

'I've explained all this. I was in a fury, a blind rage. I called her names. Foul names, God forgive me. She ran to me, trying to calm my anger, begging me to hear her defence. But I was beyond reason and I flung her from me with all the force I could muster.'

'Yes. I see. You flung her through the window.'

'Not intentionally, I swear. It was a warm night, the casement was open, the sill low. One moment she was there. The next, gone.'

He buried his face in his hands as if to shut out that dreadful vacuity.

Bunfit shifted his comfortable frame in his uncomfortable chair. It was late, and he would be lucky if he got to bed while it was still early, but he didn't mind. Soon he was to retire and a desert of uninterrupted nights stretched ahead of him. It was more than twenty years since he had risen to his present eminence on the back of his not inconsiderable part in solving the famous Eustace Diamonds case, and broken nights had always seemed a small part to pay for that tremor of respect and fear when Bunfit of the Yard appeared on the scene of a crime.

It occurred to him that this might well be his very last case. It would be nice if it turned out a good 'un.

'You all right, Mr Arlecdon?' he enquired with unfeigned solicitude. A sick suspect is to a detective policeman what a dead mouse is to a cat. You can poke it and prod it, but if you can't make it run, all the fun's gone out of the game.

The young man took a deep breath.

'Yes, yes. I'm sorry.'

'Good. Then why don't you carry on a-telling me what happened next?'

'Next?'

'That's right. You'd just been a-telling me how the unfortunate young lady tripped over the sill and fell through the window. What did you do then?'

'I don't know. I honestly can't remember. In fact I can remember very little from the moment Alice disappeared till the moment when your sergeant came to the Settlement and . . . arrested me. Am I arrested, Inspector?'

'Helping with inquiries,' said Bunfit cautiously.

'Then of course I'm very glad to help. And perhaps in return you can help me. To remember, I mean. How did it come about that you were able to find me so quickly at the Settlement?'

The Settlement was the bricks-and-mortar manifestation of a noble project whereby young men with a university education were enabled to exercise, and exorcise, their missionary zeal without the inconvenience of long sea journeys and tropical disease. The East End of London offering the nearest home-grown equivalent to a tribe of untutored savages, it was here the good work began. Once lured into contact by gifts of food and shelter, the benighted natives were given access to such revelations of culture and religion as the worthy young settlers were equipped to make.

Arlecdon's more material contribution was in the field of medicine. Still a student, he was devoting his summer vacation to this good work and making sufficient of a mark for his name to be remembered when other more ethereal settlers remained in airy anonymity.

But Bunfit was not yet ready to reveal all the cards in his hand.

'As to that, we'll get there just now, sir,' he said. 'But perhaps this will help jog your memory.'

He plucked a sheet of paper from the tabletop and went on, 'This here's an account given by one of our officers, Constable Cox, of his part in these strange happenings in Brawling Alley. I should like you to listen carefully, sir.'

He coughed behind his hand; then, adopting the tone and manner which made even eminent defence counsel hesitate to hint a doubt of such a self-evident Custodian of Truth, began to read.

'On Saturday twenty-eighth of July eighteen eighty-eight, at approximately fifteen minutes before midnight, I was proceeding down Brick Lane in a southerly direction at the end of my shift when I became aware of a hullaballoo, and shortly afterwards I observed a party of female persons come out of Brawling Alley. When I got up alongside of them, I realized as how several of these female persons were known to me, in my professional capacity, as common prostitutes. I also realized they had drink taken, and when I admonished them as to their hullaballoo, they became abusive and began to threaten me with assault. Upon which, I played my rattle, and Sergeant Gager who happened to be proceeding up Brick Lane in a northerly direction in company of my relief, Constable Vector, came running to join me. With their assistance I quelled the disorder and set about putting the women under arrest. Upon which, one of the prisoners, Mary Ann Nicholls, commonly called Polly, protested, "What's your game, fish face? Stopping a few working girls having a bit of a birthday party when there's corpses lying in the street!" I asked her what she meant, and she pointed into Brawling Alley and said, "Look there if'n you don't believe me." Upon which Sergeant Gager and I proceeded along Brawling Alley in a westerly direction, and in the light of my bull lamp, we observed a body lying on the pavement.'

Bunfit paused and examined Arlecdon keenly. The young man had the rapt expression of a child listening to a favourite bedtime story. Or a pet mouse anticipating cheese.

'Go on, Inspector,' he urged.

Bunfit laid the statement on the table and, never taking his eyes off Arlecdon's face, he said, 'This body was lying precisely where it might have been anticipated your sister, Miss Alice, would be lying after her fall from the garret window.'

'Yes. Yes.'

'The only thing is, sir. This body as Constable Cox and Sergeant Gager discovered. It was not the body of a young woman, sir. It was the body of a young man.'

Arlecdon's blue eyes opened wide, not in surprise but in recognition.

'Ah. Of course. Purey!'

'That's right, sir,' said Bunfit, rather disappointed to find his mouse so cooperative. 'George Addison Lestrange Purey, Esquire. You know— knew him, sir?'

'Yes. At Cambridge. God forgive me, it was through me that the swine met my sister.'

'He knew Miss Alice as well then?'

'Knew her? Do you understand nothing? He was her seducer! It was in order to meet him that she went to that dreadful place last night.'

'Ah, I'm with you now, sir,' said Bunfit. 'You surprised them, is that it? So tell me, sir; did you throw Mr Purey out of the window before or after the defenestration of your sister?'

He produced the word modestly. Promotion had made him conscious of certain educational deficiencies and he had surreptitiously followed a programme of self-improvement at the Institute. His historical studies of the origins of the Thirty Years War had introduced him to the concept of defenestration, but hitherto he had had no occasion for the actual use of the word.

Arlecdon was now regarding him in amazement, but it was not at his vocabulary.

'What are you suggesting?' he demanded. 'I don't deny I would have gladly taken a horsewhip to the rogue, but I certainly never threw him out of any window.'

'Then how do you account for his presence on the pavement, sir?' demanded Bunfit.

'Because God is not mocked,' cried the young man, his eyes purpurescent with religious fervour. 'And sometimes He reminds us of His immutable laws with a most savage irony. How else may we explain that Purey, coming late to his evil assignation, should have been occupying precisely that spot necessary to break Alice's fall and thus preserve her life?'

Inspector Bunfit rose. It was an old maxim of his that when God appeared on the scene, a wise detective left. Though clearly responsible for much, the Deity was not indictable under Common Law.

'If you'll excuse me for a moment, sir, I'll see about some refreshment.'

'Good idea,' said Arlecdon. 'It must be nearly time for breakfast. We rise early at the Settlement, you know. Too early for me, if truth be told. I don't have much of an appetite till luncheon, so don't fuss. Couple of lightly poached eggs and a devilled kidney will do.'

Out in the corridor, Bunfit proceeded in a sou'-sou'-westerly direction (Cox's style was catching) till he reached a door marked DETECTIVE DEPARTMENT – *Knock and Wait*.

He went straight in. A fresh-faced man some ten years his junior, with his feet on a desk and a half-eaten ham sandwich in his hand, greeted him with a grin.

'What ho, guv. Popped out for breakfast?'

Sergeant Gager had risen on the same tide as Bunfit, but had not felt the same need for self-improvement. He was still as indiscriminate with his aspirates as in his Angel infancy, and his head was still glossy with the same oil he had used to dazzle the youthful beauties of Islington in his minority. In contrast to Bunfit's clerical grey suit, he wore a hacking jacket of amber and ochre maculae, and his Doric neck was garlanded with a celluloid collar white enough and a floral necktie bright enough to make the rash gazer wipe his eye.

Bunfit sighed a reproof of his subordinate's posture, language and tailor, but he had learned from long experience that against the incorrigible, even a corrective sigh is wasted breath.

'Don't talk to me of breakfast,' he said. 'Lightly poached egg and devilled kidney His Lordship fancies. Some hope!'

'So what's his yarn?'

'He says as how he followed his sister to that crib in Brawling Alley, had a row with her about her fancy man, accidentally threw her out of the window into the alleyway where her fall happened to be broke by this here Purey, hotfooting it below on his way to meet the lady. Did you ever hear the like?'

Gager laughed, not allowing a mouthful of sandwich to inhibit him.

'More 'n 'otfooting it, I'd say. Seems he wasn't going to hang about saying 'owdidoo when he met her. He was all unbuttoned and his John Thomas was sticking out! Mind you, might 'ave been them there tarts when they found 'im.'

'For heaven's sake, Sergeant,' said Bunfit with distaste. 'Not even them debased creatures would stoop to abusing a dead man.'

'Dying, not dead, remember? He 'ad enough strength to say "Arlecdon". But I don't mean they was playing with his parts, just 'aving a looksee if 'e were wearing a money belt. There weren't a penny piece in his pockets, so there's no prize for guessing where the poor sod's geldt went.'

'Bloody vultures. You'll be a-charging them with theft then?'

'Not I,' grinned Gager. 'I know a thing worth twice that. Once charged, them gals will clam up tighter 'n a flea's fanny. It's knowing as 'ow they *can* be charged that'll keep 'em cooperative.'

'You'll go too far one of these fine days, Gager,' said Bunfit gloomily. 'Any word from the sawbones yet?'

'Cause of death, fractured skull, is all. Details to follow.'

'You have a word with him, Sergeant. Tell him to keep a sharp eye open for any sign Mr Purey might have been hit by a large falling object. Not that but I'm thinking he'll need a very sharp eye indeed.'

'You ain't hinclined to believe our Mr Arlecdon then?' said Gager mildly.

'If there's plain and if there's fancy, it's my experience you don't go far wrong by sticking to plain,' intoned Bunfit. Then something in Gager's expression alerted him.

'You got any reason to think different, young Gager, you just spit it out,' he said sternly.

'Well, guv, now as you comes to mention it, there may be a couple of reasons you should hang back from calling the young gent a liar to 'is face,' said Gager, tossing the remains of his sandwich on to the desk and swinging his feet on to the floor. From a drawer he plucked a battered volume of Burke's *Peerage and Baronetage*.

'It was 'im being a medical student as rang a bell,' he went on. 'I reckon he ain't just any old Mr Arlecdon, but the son and heir of Sir Ambrose Vasey Arlecdon who just 'appens to be the private and very personal physician of his Royal 'Ighness, the Prince of Wales. That being so, then our Mr Arlecdon, if the gen'lemen of the press 'ave got it right, is a boyhood chum of young Eddie, the Prince's eldest.'

He's enjoying this, thought Bunfit. He resents me taking the case off of him, so he thinks to embarrass me. Right, lad, you need to get up very early in the morning to embarrass Bunfit of the Yard!

He said, 'I don't care who he may be, Sergeant. You shouldn't need reminding that it's our job to administer the law without fear or favour.'

'Which I takes to mean there's not much fear we won't do them as deserves it a favour. Just my joke.'

'Not funny. You said there was two reasons?'

'That's right. The other is Polly Nicholls. She weren't so pissed as the rest or she 'olds it better, and I've got a sort of statement from 'er.'

'A sort of statement? I've told you, I want no doxies' gossip. What sort of statement's a sort of statement?'

'The sort where I've made notes but she ain't signed anything, not till I'm sure she's saying what we want her to say. Here, take a look.'

'Just give me the gist,' said Bunfit.

'The gist is this,' said Gager, openly enjoying himself now. 'The gals were 'aving their birthday party in the room one of 'em has in Brawling Alley. Balling Alley they should call it, it's a real whore's nest, that place. Anyway, they runs out of booze, and one of 'em says she's got a flask of mother's ruin in her crib at the top of Brick Lane, so they all tumble out into the alley, and there in the light from the door they see Purey's body. Only Nicholls now recalls as how there was someone else there, a woman in white sort of kneeling over the body.'

'A woman in white?' said Bunfit sceptically. 'She been reading that whatsit Collins book or what?'

'Don't do much reading, our Polly,' said Gager.

'So why didn't she mention this woman in white before?'

'Says she forgot, but I reckon she thought as how she was another working girl and din't want to nark on her, less'n she had to.'

'Loyalty among whores? You'll make me cry,' sneered Bunfit. 'So what did she do, this woman in white?'

'When she saw the girls, she got up and ran off towards Commercial Street. Polly says she ran sort of funny. "Like she was 'urt?" I asks. And she says, "Yes, it could 'ave been that." So it all fits, don't it, guv?'

Bunfit looked down again at the entry in Burke's which confirmed that Lady Arlecdon had given birth to twins, Arthur Ambrose and Alice Victoria, in 1866. There was no getting away from it. It all fitted.

Gager said, 'How's he want his eggs, Inspector?'

'He'll get no eggs till I see things a bit clearer,' said Bunfit furiously. 'Howsoever you look at it, there's a man dead. And where's this woman in white got to, that's what I want to know. But I suppose, seeing as he is who he is –' he tapped Burke's accusingly, unhappy at having to make any concession in front of the sergeant '– we'd best send word to the major.'

The major was Sir James Sholto Mackintosh, head of Scotland Yard these past thirty years and with a title to show for it the past ten, but still known to his subordinates by his old military rank.

'Done,' said Gager complacently.

'Done?' echoed Bunfit.

'I knew as how that's what you'd want, and as I didn't like to interrupt you in the pulpit, I took the liberty.'

'Seems to me you take a lot of liberties, young Gager,' growled Bunfit.

He returned to the interview room feeling he'd lost another round in his long battle with Gager. Though the sergeant was now well in his middle years, in Bunfit's eyes he was still a young upstart whose flash must one day die out in the pan.

But the inspector gave credit where it was due, at least in the privacy of his own thoughts, and though he'd not hesitated to take over what seemed like a promising case, he had to admit it was Gager who'd made all the running so far.

It had been the sergeant who responded to Cox's rattle, the sergeant who heard Purey's last word, the sergeant who sensed a reaction when he repeated the name to the riotous whores.

As Gager put it, getting information from drunk women was like drawing teeth, but by the use of God knows what threats he'd learned that some of them, attracted by curiosity and the promise of a good meal, had tried the University Settlement. The moral diet they'd found less tasty, and after a few days they'd drifted away. But they'd remembered a handsome young doctor who'd shown a lively interest in their occupational ailments and offered not preaching but practical advice and medication.

The Settlement was at the bottom end of Commercial Street. Bunfit, despite his asseverations on the high impartiality of the Law, knew he himself would probably have been much more circumspect in pursuing this line of inquiry. Behind the Settlement project there were powerful, influential people who didn't like the even tenor of their days, and still less of their nights, disturbed.

But Gager hadn't hesitated. He'd hurried down Commercial Street and hammered at the Settlement door till an irate porter opened up.

The main door, he learned, was locked at nine-thirty, after which hour presumably evil stalked the streets like a roaring lion. There was however a side door to which some of the young gentlemen, Mr Arlecdon among them, had keys.

Without more ado, Gager had brushed the porter aside and gone up to Arlecdon's room.

He had found the young gentleman fully dressed though somewhat dishevelled, and in a state of considerable agitation.

Gager had come straight to the point. Had Mr Arlecdon been out tonight? Yes, he had. Had Mr Arlecdon been in the vicinity of Brawling Alley? Yes, he had. In that case, would Mr Arlecdon do Sergeant Gager the favour of accompanying him to Scotland Yard?

It was the decision to have everyone and everything centred at the Yard rather than the local nick which had been Gager's downfall. Bunfit had found himself more and more reluctant to make for home as retirement approached. Tonight after his supper at a chop house in Villiers Street, he had returned to his office to deal with some unimportant business which could quite easily have waited till morning. His reward had been that he was on the spot, perfectly placed to pluck this ripe apple of a case out of his subordinate's hand.

Only now he was beginning to wonder if the wily Gager had not already begun to suspect the worm at the fruit's core and deliberately brought his prize back to the Yard in order that it might be claimed from him!

Perhaps the clever thing would be to follow this good example and put the lid on things till the major showed his face.

But Arlecdon himself forestalled this discreet course of action.

He rose to his feet as Bunfit re-entered the room, his thin face flushed with excitement, and said, 'It's coming back to me now, Inspector. After Alice fell from the window, I of course rushed to the casement and peered out. It was Stygian gloom out there and I could see nothing. I wanted to hurry straight downstairs and see what had become of her, but my legs were turned to lead. It was, I believed, some form of sympathetic paralysis, by which I mean a condition in which, without physical cause, the body responds to a strong mental stimulus and behaves as if a physical cause were present.'

He paused as if fascinated by the clinical details, then hurried on.

'How long I remained like this I cannot say. But finally I cast off these emotional fetters and ran down the stairs, terrified at the prospect of what I might find. Imagine then my amazement when, instead of the broken body of my beloved sister, I found the corpse of her seducer!'

'Not the corpse, sir,' corrected Bunfit. 'Mr Purey was mortally injured, true, but not yet totally gone from this life.'

'Not dead?' Arlecdon looked at him with consternation. 'If only I had realized . . .'

'So you could have finished him off, you mean?' said Bunfit in a sudden fit of rashness.

'How can you say so? True, he was of all men the one I had least cause to love, but I am training to be a doctor, Inspector, and to men of our profession, all life is sacred.'

He spoke so earnestly Bunfit felt abashed.

'So, thinking as how he was dead, sir, what did you do then?'

'Naturally I cast around for sign of Alice. You can imagine my relief when I found none. For her to have vanished so quickly meant that she must have been uninjured, or only very slightly hurt. My heart sang, believe me, Inspector.'

'I can understand that, sir. What did you do next?'

Arlecdon's face screwed up in the effort of memory.

'I must have gone back to the Settlement,' he said.

'Indeed, sir? It didn't cross your mind that the proper thing to do, the civic thing, was to report this matter to the authorities?'

'I believe I did consider that. But how could I? Think of what it would have meant revealing about my dear sister.'

'I can see as how that might have weighed heavy against it, sir,' agreed Bunfit. 'But in that case, how was it you didn't go a-searching of the lady? I mean, there she was . . . there she may still be a-running around in an hysterical condition, and you don't go a-looking for her!'

Arlecdon subsided into his chair.

'I feel your reproof strongly, Inspector. I was in a state of panic. Like a wounded beast, all I wanted was to get back to my lair. But very quickly a consciousness of poor Alice's plight reasserted itself and I was on the point of going in search of her when your sergeant arrived at my door. You never explained how he got there so quickly, Inspector.'

'Mr Purey spoke your name before he died,' said Bunfit, seeing no reason to withhold this information now. 'Some female persons who first came across him had been clients of yours at the Settlement, it appears, and the name rang a bell.'

'Indeed. How fortunate.'

'Fortunate, sir?' said Bunfit, suspecting an irony.

'Because it enabled you to find me so quickly. I would of course have come forward voluntarily once my rationality had returned, but by that time rumours of this sad business might have been bruited far abroad.'

Bunfit was getting his drift. He said, 'I fear, sir, that when it comes to sudden death, there's no keeping quiet about such things.'

'I understand. But there is surely no need to drag an innocent woman's name into the public gaze? A man found dead in an East End alleyway can hardly be so remarkable?'

'Perhaps not, but the coroner will have to be informed, sir.'

'Old Ferdie Sackloe? Then there's no problem. He's a particular friend of my father's.'

It was hard not to respond to the young man's pleasure in a problem solved, and hardly worth not responding, thought Bunfit gloomily. He could see no way this wasn't going to be settled by a typical upper-crust job. So much for his hopes of one last big case to make his exit on.

'Breakfast on its way, is it?' enquired Arlecdon.

'I'll just check, sir,' said Bunfit. It was an act of surrender, no less humiliating for being symbolic.

The Yard did not run to devilled kidneys, but he was promised boiled eggs and toast. At least Gager was no longer around to see his superior's capitulation. As Arlecdon tucked into his breakfast, Bunfit took the scribing constable to prepare the young man's statement. Hushed up the business might be, but he would make sure there was something on the official record.

He was on his way back to the interview room with the document ready for signature when his name was called. He turned to see Major Mackintosh hurrying towards him in the company of a stout, florid man of middling years whose expensively cut clothes looked as if they had been rather hastily thrown on.

'Mr Bunfit,' said the major. 'This is Sir Ambrose Arlecdon.'

'How do you do, sir?' said Bunfit. 'I hope as how Miss Alice has returned safely.'

'You do, do you? Then you're a fool, sir,' said Sir Ambrose. 'Where's my son? In here? Right.'

And without further ado he went into the interview room, slamming the door behind him.

Bunfit turned indignantly to the major, but Mackintosh merely compounded the eminent physician's rudeness by snatching the statement out of the inspector's hand and glancing quickly through it before crumpling it into his pocket.

'Shan't be needing this,' he said. 'Where's Sergeant Gager?'

'He's around somewhere, sir,' said Bunfit, struggling with difficulty to repress his personal outrage. 'He's been a-questioning of the ladies as found Mr Purey.'

'The prostitutes, you mean? Call a spade a spade, man. Get him. I'll be in here.'

Bunfit watched the long, gaunt figure of his superior pass into the main office of the Detective Department. In the long years of his acquaintance with the major, he had never known the man treat his subordinates with anything but courtesy. Something must be troubling him deeply.

He made inquiry after Gager and discovered that the sergeant had been seen going down the stairs at the main entrance. As he descended the last flight, he saw Gager's glowing face rising towards him like the sun which in truth was already gilding the chimney pots of the sleeping city.

'There you are then,' said Bunfit. 'You're to come with me. The major's here and he's brought Sir Ambrose Arlecdon.'

'Yes, I know,' said Gager running lightly up the stairs. 'That's where I've been, to 'ave a chinwag with Sir Ambrose's coachman.'

'Why on earth should you want to do that?' grumbled Bunfit.

'Just you listen and you'll soon see,' said Gager. 'I've been a-talking to them girls, off and on, ever since we brought 'em in. Very friendly we got, specially after I promised 'em I'd see there were no charges—'

'You promised them what?' exclaimed Bunfit.

'No charges. Stands to reason. Case like this, the nobs ain't

going to risk some tart standing up in court and wafting a nice
scent of scandal up the news-hounds' noses. Right?'

Bunfit couldn't deny the logic.

'Anyway, I'd got all I could out of 'em with threats, so it made
sense to try gratitude.'

'And what did you get from these grateful whores?' demanded
Bunfit, urging the sergeant up the stairs.

'All sorts, and not just likorish either. Seems like this woman
in white, Miss Alice by her brother's account, 'as been around
Brawling Alley for a few weeks now. That 'ere garret is rented
out to her, not to Mr Purey, who incidentally is well known to
the gals as a young gent with a prodigious appetite for their
favours.'

'What are you saying, Gager? That this weren't no romantic
assignation, but a common pick-up? That Sir Ambrose Arlecdon's
daughter has set herself up as a common Whitechapel whore?'
said Bunfit, aghast.

'No, I hain't a-saying that.'

'I'm very glad to hear it.'

'What I'm a-saying is far stranger than that.'

'What?'

'Listen to this. Couple of these girls 'ave 'ad clients recently
who mentioned picking up a new girl, pretty young thing, only
when they got down to the job, turned out she weren't no girl
after all!'

'Good God. And what did they do, these clients?'

'One of 'em said things had gone too far for turning back,
and a change was good as a rest anyway, so he just went ahead
and wouldn't mind trying it again. Takes all sorts, don't it?
Another cut up rough, though, and wanted to give the "tart" a
good kicking, only before 'e can get fairly started, "she" hollos
out, "Eddie!" and some fellow, must've been her ponce, comes

running up, waving a pistol. All the gals 'ave been talking about it. They thought as 'ow it was a good laugh. I mean, they don't reckon a fellow playing charades is going to be any competition, do they?'

'Are you trying to tell me . . . what is it makes you think that . . .?'

'That the woman in white and our Mr Arlecdon might be one and the same? Well, the gals all reckon from what their clients said that this 'ere lady works out of Brawling Alley. And it'd explain 'ow no one saw Arlecdon, only the woman in the alley, wouldn't it? It makes sense, guv, don't it? "She" picks Purey up. Perhaps "she" don't recognize him, or perhaps "she" do and thinks it a bit of a joke. They gets up to the garret, "she" unbuttons Purey – which 'ud explain how we found him all ready primed – 'e sticks 'is 'and up her skirt, and he gets the shock of his life! But what really turns out fatal for 'im is that the shock triggers the memory of his old college chum. He says, "You're Arlecdon!" And that does it. Perhaps Eddie the ponce is 'iding in a cupboard and lends a hand. Whatever, next thing Purey finds 'isself flying through the window. Our "girl" runs downstairs to make sure she's done a good job, gets interrupted by the other tarts and takes off. Remember how Polly Nicholls thought she ran awkward because she was 'urt? I think she ran awkward because she was running like a man!'

They were at the door marked DETECTIVE DEPARTMENT, and Bunfit had about five seconds to decide how much of this nonsense to trouble the major with.

He said, 'If'n I was you, Gager, I'd be very careful as to your tongue. Flights of fancy is all very well between colleagues, but if once you go shouting your mouth off without evidence . . .'

'Evidence you want, guv?' said Gager, stung. ''Ow about this? I spotted the major coming up the stairs with Sir Ambrose so, like I said, I went down to have a chat with Sir Ambrose's coachman. Very casual, I mentioned Miss Alice and wondered if she were at home just now. 'E laughed sort of 'ollow, and said Miss Alice was always at 'ome in one manner of speaking and never at 'ome in another. Naturally I asked 'im what 'e meant. Seems that ten years back Alice and 'er brother were playing out on Sir Ambrose's estate in Leicestershire, and they got too near one of 'em new-fangled mechanical threshing machines, and there was an accident and the little girl fell in.'

'Good God,' said Bunfit. 'Are you saying she's dead?'

'Might as well be. She got mangled to bits in front of her brother. By the time they put her together again, she was short a pair of legs and half an arm, not to mention her marbles. She's never spoken a word since and the only time she leaves the house is when they carry her out for a ride around the estate. So I don't think there's much chance she's been plying her wares in Brawling Alley!'

Before Bunfit could properly digest this, the door was flung open.

'What's this, Bunfit? Gossiping out here like a tea-wife when I told you to fetch the sergeant as quickly as possible?' cried the major.

This repetition of the major's unaccustomed rudeness made up Bunfit's mind. He held nothing back, but with scarcely concealed relish, dumped the whole unpleasant mess into his superior's lap. Gager, mistakenly interpreting the inspector's prolixity as an attempt to gather all the kudos unto himself, chipped in with comments and qualifications underlining his own sharpness in coming to grips with the case.

The major listened in attentive silence but with a gloomy expression which did not prognosticate the reward of praise, and finally the detectives' flow of words faltered to a trickle.

The major spoke.

'What do you have in writing? Statements? Notes?'

He already had Arlecdon's unsigned statement in his pocket and he sat at the Detective Department desk till Cox's report, the notes of record made in the interview room, and every jotting made by Bunfit and Gager themselves, lay on the desk before him.

'This is all?' he asked.

They looked at each other and nodded.

The major began to read, only speaking when he needed some obscurity interpreted.

'This, Sergeant, what is this?'

Gager looked and said, 'Oh yes, sir. This fellow, Eddie, the ponce. Some of the girls reckoned they'd seen him with the woman in white. Tall, good-looking fellow with wavy hair and an elegant moustache, not one of 'em soup strainers. They said as 'ow he reminded them of . . .'

'Of whom, Sergeant?' asked the major quietly.

There was a pause. Gager's wily instincts were reasserting themselves after his earlier competitive garrulity.

'Of some chap runs a boozer in Cheapside,' he said vaguely. 'They didn't know 'is name.'

'No? But I see here they were quite certain on reflection that the woman in white had a look of Mr Arlecdon from the Settlement.'

'Yes, sir. Could be I put that idea in their minds. Very suggestible, them gals.'

'Suggestible, you say? To a policeman? How might they be to a newspaperman with a thick wallet?'

Gager didn't reply and the major returned to his reading.

As he finished the door was thrust open and Sir Ambrose's head appeared.

'Mackintosh, a word.'

The major went out into the corridor.

Bunfit said, 'Gager, my lad, these are deep waters. You and me had best keep a hold of each other, else we may drown.'

'Is that right, Inspector? What price without fear or favour now?'

'Listen, my boy. You want my job, you'd best follow my example. Show me a copper who don't know when to turn a blind eye and I'll show you a bad copper. There's bound to come times when least said, soonest mended, and no real harm done.'

'There's a young fellow lying on a slab might give you an argument there, guv,' said Gager.

Before Bunfit could reply, Major Mackintosh came back into the room and began gathering up the papers.

'Well, that seems taken care of,' he said. 'Sir Ambrose is taking his son home. He says we had no authority to bring him here in the first place and I'm afraid I must agree. However, they are both willing to acknowledge honest error and let the matter drop.'

'But there's the body, sir,' protested Gager, ignoring Bunfit's warning glance.

'Ah yes. Mr Purey. A young man, I gather, of regrettably lax morals. It is sad that there are still corners of this great city which a stranger enters at his own peril after dark, but reasonable men know this and direct their steps accordingly. I regret Mr Purey should have been waylaid and robbed, and I will try to keep from his family the true nature of these dark excursions.'

'Waylaid and robbed!' exclaimed Gager.

'Your own notes suggest he was robbed,' said the major mildly. 'Therefore it follows, or rather precedes, that he was waylaid. There are, of course, no witnesses—'

'No witnesses? Why, there's the . . .' Gager's voice tailed away.

'Ladies of the night, you were going to say? Yes, but in fact, what did they see? What can they say that isn't speculation? And, in their condition, both physical and moral, who would believe them?'

The questions came across as real rather than rhetorical.

Gager said, 'You're dead right, sir. Who's going to take notice of trash like that?'

He and the major locked glances, the sergeant's defiant, his superior's doubtful.

Bunfit, suddenly eager for that retirement which earlier in the night he had anticipated with such little enthusiasm, said, 'I'll order their release then, the prostitutes, if that's all right.'

'Yes,' said the major. 'That's all right.'

'I'll do it,' said Gager, making for the door.

'We have, I suppose, a list of their names, just for the records?' said the major. 'Only I don't see such a list here.'

Bunfit looked urgently at Gager who stood with his hand on the door handle.

'You got that list you showed me, Sergeant?' he said. 'You put it in your inside pocket, I seem to recall.'

Slowly Gager reached into his gaudy jacket and withdrew the list.

'Don't see no point in keeping it,' he said. 'Not if there's no charges.'

'That *is* the point,' said Bunfit, plucking the paper from his fingers. 'We've kept these girls here all this time without charge. Prozzies they may be, but they've got their rights, same as anybody else. So let's keep the record straight, then if any of them should put in a claim for compensation, we can make sure as how they're properly taken care of. Isn't that the way of it, sir.'

The major took the list from him and ran his eyes down the six names.

Martha Turner
Mary Ann (Polly) Nicholls
Annie Chapman
Elizabeth (Long Liz) Stride
Catherine Eddowes
Mary Kelly

Gager at the door was standing like a man at the foot of the gallows.

'I am right, sir,' urged Bunfit. 'It's so they can be taken care of?'

'Oh yes, Inspector,' said Major Mackintosh wearily. 'You may rest assured of that. They will all be taken care of.'

Behind Gager the door slammed shut like a trap.

Editor's footnote: *Between August and November 1888, the prostitutes of Whitechapel were terrorized by the killer known as Jack the Ripper.*

His certain victims were named: Turner: Nicholls: Chapman: Stride: Eddowes: Kelly.

He was never caught.

Urban Legend

This is Anne Hardcastle's story and it's a true story, not one of those urban-legend things which, according to her, never really happened to anybody. This really happened to Anne. Definitely. I'd stake my life on it. We were very close at the time.

How she knew so much about these legends was she'd spend eighteen months doing research on them so she'd get an MA or something. She had this notebook full of stories. A lot of them I heard before, like the one where this chap accidentally leaves his wife in a lay-by in her nightie, or the one where this chap's granny dies on a touring holiday and the car gets stolen. Though I think my favourite's the one about the young married couple next door who like playing Spider-Man.

Anyway, Anne had finished her research and come to stay at this old inn at Ludlow to write it up, and one lunchtime she was sitting in the bar when this girl at the next table started telling a story, and Anne's ears pricked because she guessed from the way the girl started that it was going to be one of these urban legends.

'It happened up near Church Stretton on Sunday,' said the

girl. 'I heard it last night from my cousin Jenny, who works in the tourist office in Shrewsbury – and her boyfriend works in the same accountancy firm as Colin.'

'Who's Colin?' asked someone.

'Shut up and I'll tell you. There was this christening party, see, and when they went to church someone had to stay behind to see to the smoked salmon and champers, and Avril, the youngest daughter, volunteered. She was a bit of a reb, evidently – worked in London and disapproved of christenings, so she didn't mind missing church. Now this Colin had always fancied her, only she couldn't stand him, so she wasn't too pleased when he said he'd stay, too. In fact, she told her sister that any funny stuff and she'd be off back to London like a shot.

'According to Colin, fifteen minutes after the christening party left, this chap appeared saying he was a cop and there'd been an accident and Avril's parents were on their way to hospital in Shrewsbury. Naturally Avril jumped straight in her car, but the cop made her move over, saying she was in such a state he'd better drive. And Colin got in, too, though he said the cop didn't seem too keen.

'Off they went. It's a maze of little roads around there, but suddenly Colin realized they weren't even on one of these but belting along a rutted cart-track. He asked where the hell they were and the cop said a shortcut, but next thing they ran into this stream across the track where there was a ford for cattle – only the car didn't make it, but stalled in the middle.

'They couldn't get it started and Avril was getting really upset, so the cop suggested Colin go for help while he dried the plugs. Downstream, they could just glimpse the parapet of a humpback bridge and Colin set off along the bank. It was hard going, all overgrown with brambles and willows, and after a while he paused and glanced back. The cop was under the bonnet and

Avril was walking along the bank upstream. Colin could see a clearing there, and right at the water's edge was this old oak stump all overgrown with ivy – like an altar cloth, he said. On the stump someone had stood this sledgehammer with its long shiny shaft sticking straight up in the air – like Excalibur, he said. And as he watched, Avril sat down on the stump with her head between her hands.

'Finally Colin reached the bridge, only to find the road wasn't much better than the track. He scrambled onto the parapet to try to spot a house but couldn't see anything but woodland. Then suddenly this noise rang out, like a hammer driving a stake into the ground, echoing like thunder so he couldn't tell where it came from.

'Then he glanced down into the stream. And he saw that the water was running red.

'Without thinking, he jumped straight down and started scrambling back upstream like a mad thing. He'd hurt his ankle when he landed, and the willows seemed to be crowding even closer together, and long before he got there he realized the hammering had stopped and the water was running clear once more.

'When at last he reached the ford, the car was gone, *and* the policeman *and* Avril, and the sledgehammer had vanished from the stump.

'He doesn't know how he got back, but an hour later he came stumbling out of the coppice at the bottom of the garden. On the lawn the christening party were standing around with champagne glasses, but no one was drinking. They were all looking toward the patio, where two uniformed policemen were talking to Avril's parents. When Colin tried to join them, the other guests held him back and told him the police had come with dreadful news. Avril's car had run off the road this side of Worcester, flipped over down an embankment, and burnt with her inside.'

The girl paused for effect.

'My God!' said someone. 'But what did they do when Colin told his story?'

'Advised him to see his doctor. Everyone reckoned he'd tried it on with Avril, so she'd just taken off like she'd threatened, and Colin felt so guilty he'd say anything to shift the blame. Also, one of the policemen reckoned he'd heard the story before. But Colin was still telling it yesterday when Jenny's boyfriend rang to see why he'd stayed off work.'

At the next table, Anne was so excited she could hardly breathe. Evidently the impossible thing with these urban legends is to track them back to where they started. But with this one, it was different. You see, she reckoned she'd actually invented the original version of this christening-party legend and had been telling it around the Midlands for eighteen months! The idea was that if ever she heard it from someone else, she'd be able to backtrack it to herself with all its variations and if she could pull it off it would really make her name.

So, first stop was Shrewsbury!

To start with, it was easy. She boxed clever with Jenny in the tourist office, letting on she was a big mate of the cousin in Ludlow, and ten minutes later she was at the accountant's where Jenny's boyfriend George worked. This was where she expected the first hiccup, with George saying, 'Actually, it was this friend in another office it happened to.' But George took her by surprise. First he said he was rushed off his feet because he was having to do bloody Stark's work. Then he scribbled an address and handed it to her, saying, 'If you can get the silly sod to snap out of it and get back here, I'd be most grateful.'

'I don't follow,' said Anne. 'Whose address is this?'

'Stark's, of course. Colin Stark. Bye!'

Poor Anne was completely bewildered, but one thing she didn't lack was determination. The address was in Church Stretton. She got in her car and headed south.

It turned out to be a little cottage just outside the village, and as Anne approached she met an ambulance and a police car belting north. She could still hear their sirens fading as she knocked at Colin Stark's door.

And that was where we met for the first time. I came around the side of the cottage and stood watching her for quite a while before she spotted me. Then she jumped and said, all breathless, 'Mr Stark? Colin Stark?'

I said no, I wasn't, but why did she want to see Mr Stark? And she said private business, and who was I, anyway?

That's when I introduced myself.

'Detective Constable Brice, miss. Shropshire CID. So you don't actually know Mr Stark?'

'No. Why are you here?'

'There's been a bit of a tragedy, miss,' I said, watching her closely. 'You see, young Mr Stark's been found dead. Suicide, it looks like. He's hanged himself.'

For a moment I thought she was going to faint and I grabbed her arm. 'I'm sorry,' I said. 'I wouldn't have come out with it like that, only I thought as you didn't know him—'

'I'm all right,' she said. 'Oh God, this is terrible. Do you know why he—'

'Some girl he knew got killed in an accident and I gather he took it hard.'

That did it. It all came pouring out, all this stuff about urban legends and how she'd made this one up so it couldn't really have happened, and how she wasn't going to rest till she got to the bottom of it.

'Whoa!' I said finally. 'Look, miss, this all sounds so way out, I think you ought to talk to my inspector direct.'

'Fine,' she said. 'Let's go find him.'

She headed back to her car. I offered to drive as she was a bit upset, but she wasn't having that, so I got in the passenger seat. Off we went, with me giving directions and Anne still talking away ten to the dozen. I reckon I got a potted version of most of her research in the next ten minutes, but I still must have looked dubious for she dug out her notebook and handed it over, saying, 'It's at the back, under "The Christening Party". It starts: "It was a still, summer Sunday, somewhere in England. The champagne had just been put on ice when—"'

She was right. There it was, and it certainly had the general outline.

'See what I mean?' she said triumphantly. 'Either it's some crazy coincidence or some madman really did hammer a stake into that poor girl, then faked the car crash and fire.'

'Turn left here,' I interrupted.

She obeyed, still talking. 'And in that case, you really ought to be searching for this ford, there must be some traces— Where are we going?'

At last she'd noticed we were off the road and bumping down a green and rutted track.

'To see my inspector,' I reassured her. 'We've found the ford already and he's down here now, conducting a search.'

I don't think she was convinced, but you're ready to believe anything when the alternative's so unbelievable, aren't you? I think she knew when we reached the ford and I switched off the engine and the quiet came rushing in and there wasn't another soul in sight. But she didn't scream, not even when her head turned and she looked upstream into the clearing where the slanting sun fell like a spotlight on the old oak stump, all draped with ivy like an altar cloth, with the shaft of my sledgehammer rising from it like Excalibur.

I kept the notebook. I often thumb through it when I want a laugh. But I've never been convinced that Anne actually invented the christening-party legend. You see, I got the idea from this really genuine chap in Traffic who swears blind that it happened to this mate of his in Birmingham.

One thing I am sure of. Anne would have kept burrowing away till she got to the bottom of it.

Definitely.

I staked her life on it.

We were very close at the time.

Where are All the Naughty People?

A lot of kids are scared of graveyards.

Not me. I grew up in one.

My dad, Harry Cresswell, was verger at St Cyprian's on the north-east edge of Bradford. Once it had been a country parish but that was ages back. By the sixties it was all built up, a mix of council houses and owner-occupied semis, plus some older properties from the village days. We lived in one of them, Rose Cottage right up against the churchyard wall. We didn't have a proper garden, just a small cobbled yard out back, and out front a two-foot strip of earth where Mam tried to grow a few stunted roses to make sense of the name. A low retaining wall separated this from a narrow pavement that tracked the busy main road where traffic never stopped day or night.

Nearest park was a mile away. But right next door to us there were four acres of open land, lots of grass and trees, no buildings, no roads, no traffic.

St Cyprian's graveyard.

The wall in our back yard had a small door in it to make it easy for Dad to get to the church to do his duties. In the grave-

yard the door was screened by a bit of shrubbery. My mam liked
to tell anyone who cared to listen that she was a Longbottom
out of Murton near York, a farming family whose kids had
grown up breathing good fresh air and enjoying the sight and
smell of trees and grass. She wasn't about to deprive her own
child of the benefit just because of a few gravestones, so when
I was a baby, she'd take me through the door in our yard and
lay me on a rug to enjoy the sun while she got on with her
knitting. She was a great knitter. If her hands didn't have some
other essential task to occupy them, they were always occupied
by her needles. I've even seen her knitting on the move! And
I've never had to buy a scarf or a pullover in my life.

As I grew older and more mobile I began to explore a bit
further. Mam and Dad were a bit worried at first, but Father
Stamp said he'd rather see me enjoying myself there than running
around the street in the traffic, and in Mam's ears, Father Stamp's
voice was the voice of God.

I should say that though St Cyprian's was Church of England,
it was what they called High, lots of incense and hyssop and
such, and the vicar liked to be called Father. It used to confuse
me a bit as a kid, what with God the Father, and Father Stamp,
and Father Christmas, and my own dad, but I got used to it.

And folk got used to me using the graveyard as my playground. I think them as didn't like it were too scared of my
mam to risk a confrontation. She could be really scary when
she tried. For her part, she insisted I should always stay in the
area between our bit of the wall and the side of the church,
and not do anything naughty. 'Naughty' in Mam's vocabulary
covered a wide range of misbehaviour. She used to read the
News of the World and shake her head and say disapprovingly,
'There's a lot of naughty folk in this world. Well, they'll have
to pay for it in the next!' I assumed she meant bank robbers

and such. But in my own case, I didn't have to assume anything. I knew exactly what naughty meant – doing anything my mam told me not to do!

My designated playground area was the oldest section of the graveyard. All the headstones here dated back a hundred years or more, and no one ever came to tend the graves or lay flowers on them. There were quite a few trees here too and it was hard to get a mowing machine in, so the grass grew long and lush and on the rare occasions someone did come around this side, I could easily drop out of sight till they'd gone. Occasionally I'd see Father Stamp but I didn't hide from him because he'd always wave at me and smile, and sometimes he'd come and join me. Often he'd produce a bagful of mint humbugs and we'd sit next to each other on a tombstone, his arm around my shoulder, sucking away in companionable silence till suddenly he'd stand up, ruffle my hair and say he had to go and do something in the church.

Once I'd started at school, I soon realized the new activities I was enjoying, like playing football or cowboys and Indians, you couldn't do in a graveyard. Even Father Stamp wouldn't have cared to see a whole gang of kids rampaging around his church, cheering and yelling. So I spent less time there, but I still liked to wander around by myself sometimes, playing solitary make-believe games, or just lying in the grass looking up at the sky till Mam yelled my name and I had to go in for my tea.

Occasionally I'd have one or two of my special friends around at the house and to start with I took them through the door into my playground. I thought they'd be impressed I had all this space to roam around in, but instead they either said it was seriously weird, or they wanted to play daft games like pretending to be ghosts and jumping out on each other from behind the old gravestones. As well as being worried about the noise they were making, I found I was a bit put out that they weren't showing more respect. Father Stamp had told me that I should never forget there were dead people lying under the ground. No need to be scared of them, he said, but I should try and remember this was their place as well as mine. So after a while I stopped taking my friends there. I was still very young but already old enough to realize it mattered at school how your classmates regarded you. I didn't want to get known as daft Tommy Cresswell who likes to play with old bones in the graveyard.

I was what they called a slow learner, taking longer than a lot of the others to get into reading and writing, but suddenly one day when I was about seven it finally clicked and I took to it big. I read everything I could lay my hands on, so much so that Mam and Dad went from worrying about me not reading to worrying about me reading my brain into train oil, as Granny Longbottom used to say.

I don't know exactly when it was that I realized the graveyard was full of stuff to read! I'd seen there were words carved on the headstones, of course, but I never paid them much attention. I was more interested in the variety of shapes.

Some of the headstones were rounded, some were pointed, and some were squared off. Quite a lot had crosses on top of them, some of the older ones leaned to one side like they were drunk, and a few lay flat out. The ones I liked best were the ones with statues and these I gave names to in my private games. My favourite was an angel with a shattered nose that I called Rocky after Rocky Marciano who was my dad's great hero. Never got beaten, he'd say. I think he'd have called me Rocky rather than Tommy if Mam had let him.

It was Rocky the angel that got me looking at the words. I was lying in the grass one evening staring up at him when the words carved at his feet came into focus.

*Sacred to the memory of David Oscar
Winstanley taken in the 87th year of his life
loving husband devoted father in virtue spotless
in charity generous and a loyal servant of the
General Post Office for forty-nine years*

He was probably a pretty important GPO official, but I imagined him as an ordinary postman, trudging the streets with his sackful of letters well into his eighties, and I was really impressed that he'd been so highly regarded that they'd given him an angel to keep watch over his grave and a full-blown testimonial. This is what started me paying attention to the inscriptions on other headstones. A few were in a funny language I couldn't understand. Father Stamp told me it was Latin and sometimes he'd translate it for me. Mam was always telling me not to bother Father Stamp because he had so much to do in the parish. In the same breath she'd say I could learn a lot if I listened to him, he was such an educated man. When I wondered in my childish way how I could listen to him without bothering him, she told me not to be cheeky. Things have changed, but back then a wise kid quickly learned that in the adult world he was usually in the wrong!

I quite liked Father Stamp and I certainly liked his mint humbugs, but when it came to practical information about the graves, I turned to the men who dug them. There were two of them, Young Clem and Old Clem.

I don't know how old Old Clem was – certainly no older than my dad – but he 'had a back' and seemed to spend most of his time standing by the side of a new grave, smoking his pipe, while Young Clem laboured with his spade down below. Nowadays they have machines to do the hard work in less than half an hour. Back then it took Young Clem the best part of a morning to excavate and square off a grave to his dad's satisfaction. Occasionally Old Clem would seize the spade to demonstrate what ought to be done, but after he'd moved a couple of clods, he'd shake his head, rub his back, and return to his pipe. I heard Dad complaining to Mam more than once that Old Clem ought to be pensioned off, but he got no support from the vicar. Father Stamp just shook his head and said there was no question of getting rid of Old Clem. Mam said it showed what a true Christian gentleman Father Stamp was, and I should try to be less naughty and grow up like him. When I asked if that meant that Mam was naughty because she agreed with Dad that Old Clem should be sacked and Father Stamp didn't, she clipped my ear and said she didn't know where I got it from. I saw Dad grinning when she said that.

Young Clem was my special friend. Nine or ten years older than me, he was a big lad, more than twice my size, and he always had a fag in his mouth, though that was OK in them days. Dad smoked twenty a day and even Mam had the occasional puff.

Clem had been around all my life, helping his dad out when he were still a kid, then becoming his full-time assistant when he left school at sixteen. Like me he clearly thought of the grave-yard as his own personal play park. Wandering around in the dusk one spring evening I heard a noise I didn't recognize and dropped down in the long grass. After a bit, with the noise still going on, I reckoned I hadn't been spotted so I crawled forward and peered around a headstone. Young Clem was lying there in the grass with a girl. At eight, I already had some vague notion there were things older lads liked to do with girls but I'd no real idea what it was all about except that simultaneously it had something to do with courting, which was all right, and something to do with being naughty, which wasn't. We didn't have sex education in Yorkshire in them days. Whatever it was, Young Clem and his girl were clearly enjoying it. I watched till I got bored then I crawled away. I had enough sense to know that I ought to keep out of the way when my friend was doing his naughty courting so whenever I glimpsed Clem in the graveyard with a girl I made myself scarce.

But when there weren't any girls around to divert him, the years between us seemed to vanish. Young Clem just loved larking around. In his snap break, he was always up for a game of hide-and-seek, or tiggy-on-gravestones. Or if I had my cricket ball with me, he'd show me how to set my fingers around it so that I could bowl a googly. One day he was demonstrating how to do this up against the church wall when Father Stamp came around the corner and I thought we would be in real trouble. But Clem didn't seem bothered. He just lit a fag and blew smoke down at Father Stamp (Clem was a good six inches taller) till the vicar turned around and went back the way he'd come, like he'd forgotten something.

'He must like you too, Clem,' I said, impressed.

'You could say that,' said Clem. 'Doesn't mean I have to like him, does it?'

That struck me as odd even then. Under Mam's influence, I'd come to think everyone in the world must like and admire Father Stamp, so it was a shock to find that my mate Clem didn't agree.

I noticed after this that Clem often seemed to show up when I was with the vicar. I recall one occasion when I was around the back of the church where there was this funny old cross, very tall and thin with the actual cross piece set in a circle and not very big at all. Another odd thing was it didn't seem to mark a grave and I couldn't see any writing on it, just a lot of weird carvings.

Father Stamp came and stood beside me and started explaining what they all meant. I didn't understand a lot of what he said but I did take in that it had been there for hundreds of years, dating back to long before the present St Cyprian's had been built. He told me there'd always been some sort of church or chapel here right back to what he called the Dark Ages and this cross had been put up then and it was quite famous, and experts came from all over just to look at it. Then he lifted me right up on his shoulders so I could get a good look at the fancy carving on the topmost piece of the cross, and I was sitting there, clinging on to his hair, with his hands clasping the top of my legs really tight, when there was a cough behind us.

Father Stamp swung around so quick I almost fell off, and in fact I might as well have done, as when he saw it was Young Clem he dropped me to the ground so hard I was winded.

'Sorry to interrupt, Vicar,' said Young Clem, 'but Dad were wondering if you'd a moment to talk about tomorrow's funeral.'

It didn't sound to me all that important, but Father Stamp hurried away as if it was, and Young Clem said, 'Giving you a ride, was he?'

'He was showing me the carvings up on the cross,' I said.

'Is that right? Tell you what, Tommy. The vicar's a busy man. You want to play, you play with me. Or if you want to know about the carvings or anything, ask my dad.'

Even at that age, I couldn't imagine that Old Clem would know anything the vicar didn't but I followed Young Clem around the church to where his dad was sitting on a tombstone, puffing his pipe in the sun. There was no sign of Father Stamp so they must have finished their business quickly.

Young Clem said, 'Tommy here wants to know about the carvings on that old cross.'

Old Clem blew some smoke into the air reflectively then pronounced, 'Heathen, that's what they are. Nasty pagan stuff.

Don't know what summat like that is doing in a Christian churchyard.'

For all its shortness, I have to say I found this more intriguing than Father Stamp's more rambling account but when I mentioned it to Mam, she said, 'You don't want to listen to Old Clem. What's he know? No, you stick close to a clever man like Father Stamp and you never know what you'll learn. But don't you go bothering him!'

Mam didn't like Old Clem much. She wouldn't use the same words as Dad who said he was an idle old sod, but that's what she thought. And she really gave him a piece of her mind once when she found me searching through the long grass in the graveyard and I told her Old Clem had lost his rubber spade and asked me to help him find it. But she liked Young Clem. She said he had a nice smile and I noticed she used to pat her hair and sound a bit different when she was talking to him. She even knit him a scarf that he said was the best scarf he'd ever had though I never saw him wear it.

So what with the Clems and Father Stamp, I had plenty of company in the graveyard if I wanted it. But most of the time all the company I wanted was my own and that of my friends in the ground. I had no fear of them. Why should I? They were all such good people; I could tell that by what I read on their headstones. I found it a really comfortable idea that after you were dead, folk would come and read what had been carved about you, just like I was doing, and they'd think what a great guy you must have been!

Sometimes I'd lie in the grass by Rocky, looking up at the sky and inventing things they might one day put on my own stone.

Here lies Tommy Cresswell, loving son, and the best striker ever to play for Bradford City and England

The more I thought of it, though, the more I was forced to admit that it wasn't all that likely as Bradford were holding up the bottom division of the league back then, and anyway I was crap at football. But anyone could be a hero, I reasoned. It was just a question of opportunity. So in the end I settled for this:

> *Sacred to the memory of Tommy Cresswell,*
> *beloved by all who knew him, who lost*
> *his life while bravely rescuing 56 children*
> *from their burning orphanage.*

> *'He died that they might live.'*

I got that last bit from the stone of some soldier who'd been wounded in the Great War and then come home to die.

The graveyard was full of such inspiring and upbeat messages. Those who reached old age had enjoyed such useful and productive lives it was no wonder they were sadly missed by their loving friends and families, while those who died young were so precociously marvellous that the angels couldn't wait for them to get old before claiming them.

But eventually after I'd done a tour of the whole graveyard, a problem began to present itself. I went all the way around again just to be sure, and it was still there.

I thought of applying to Mam and Dad for help, but I didn't really want them to know how much time I was still spending in the graveyard.

Father Stamp would certainly be able to answer my question. After all he was in charge of everything at St Cyprian's. But he didn't seem quite so keen on talking to me as he'd once been. If we did meet and sit down for a chat, after a while he'd get restless and jump up and say he had to be off somewhere else, even if Young Clem didn't interrupt him.

Then one Monday in early October on my way home from school still pondering my problem, I spotted the Clems digging a grave and it came to me that if anyone would know the answer, they would.

It was the usual set-up, with Young Clem up to his knees in the grave, digging, and Old Clem leaning on his spade, proffering advice.

I said, 'Who's this for?'

'Old George Parkin,' said Old Clem. 'They'll not be putting him in the hole till Wednesday, but we thought we'd get a start while this good weather holds. Poor old George. He'll be sadly missed. He were a grand lad. One of the best.'

That was my cue.

I said, 'Clem –' letting them decide which one I was addressing – 'I know you bury the good folk in the churchyard. But where do you put all the naughty ones?'

Old Clem stopped puffing, and Young Clem stopped digging, and they both said, 'Eh?'

I saw that I needed to make myself a bit clearer.

I said, 'You only bury the good people in the churchyard. I can tell that from reading what it says about them on the headstones. But the naughty ones must die as well. So where are all the naughty people? What do you do with *their* bodies?'

There was a long silence while they looked at each other.

Old Clem put his pipe back into his mouth and took it out again twice.

And finally he said solemnly, 'Can you keep a secret, Tommy?'

'Oh yes. Cross my heart and hope to die,' I said eagerly.

'Right then,' said Old Clem. 'We puts them in the crypt.'

Young Clem said, 'Dad!' like he was protesting because his father was talking out of turn.

Old Clem said, 'The lad asked and he deserves to know. The crypt, young Tommy. That's where we dump all the bad 'uns. Pack 'em in, twenty or thirty deep till their flesh rots down to mulch. Then they grind the bones to bone meal and it all gets spread on the fields. But you're not to tell anyone else, OK? This is between you and me. Promise?'

I repeated, 'Cross my heart, Clem,' and went away, leaving father and son having what sounded like a fierce discussion behind me.

This explained a lot! I knew there was this sort of big cellar under the church that they called the crypt. And I knew that there'd been bones and stuff down there because a couple of years earlier there'd been some worry about the church floor sinking and I'd heard Dad talking about clearing out the crypt and setting some props to support the ceiling which was of course the church floor. So all the naughty people's remains must have been cleared out to spread on the fields then. That thought made me feel a bit queasy, but, after all, I told myself, if you were too naughty to be buried in the graveyard, what did it matter where you ended up?

I mean, who'd want a headstone saying, *Here lies John Smith who was really naughty and nobody misses him*?

I'd never been in the crypt, of course, though I knew where the door was in a hidden corner of the church porch. There was a notice on it saying, *Danger. Steep and crumbling steps. Do not enter*. Not that there was much chance of that as it was always kept locked.

But it had to be opened some time so that more naughty people could be put in there, that was obvious. And if, as Mam said, there were a lot of naughty people in this world, it was probably getting full up again after the last big clear-out.

Suddenly I was filled with a desperate need to see inside the crypt. I wasn't a particularly morbid child, but I recall one of my teachers writing on my report, *It's never enough to tell Tommy anything; if possible he's got to see for himself.*

So now I'd got the answer to my question, all I needed was for someone to open the crypt door for me and shine a torch in so that I could glimpse all the naughty people piled up there! Then I'd be satisfied.

But I was bright enough to know that this wasn't the kind of favour adults were likely to do for a kid. I was going to have to sort this out for myself.

The answer was as obvious as asking the Clems about the naughty people had been.

Dad could go anywhere in and around the church. Obviously he wasn't going to open the crypt door for me. But he did have a key. At least, I assumed he had a key. He certainly had a bunch of keys that opened up every other door.

And as I thought of this, I also realized that tonight being a Monday night was the perfect time to put my plan into operation. Not that I realized I had a plan till I thought of it! The thing was, Dad always went down the pub to play darts on Mondays and Mam curled up on the sofa with her knitting to watch *Sherlock Holmes*, her favourite TV series, and nothing was allowed to interrupt her.

So tonight was the night! It seemed like fate, but for a while it looked like fate had changed its mind. It turned out that Dad had been feeling a bit hot and snuffly all day and Mam was worried it was the Hong Kong flu virus that was just taking a grip around the country. But after tea, Dad said not to be stupid, it was just a sniffle that a couple of pints of John Smith's and a whisky chaser would soon sort. So off he went down the pub, and not long after I went up to bed without any of my usual arguments and lay there till I heard the swelling introductory music of Mam's programme.

It was part two of *The Hound of the Baskervilles*, I recall, and I was confident there was no way she'd move till it was finished. I had at least an hour.

I slipped out of bed. I didn't bother to get dressed. I was wearing tracksuit pyjamas and it was a warm autumn night, so warm in fact I was perspiring slightly and the thought of putting on more clothes was unpleasant. I tiptoed downstairs, carrying the torch I kept for reading under the bedclothes. The TV was going full belt, and I moved into the kitchen, plucked Dad's church keys from the hook by the back door and headed out into the night.

Our door into the churchyard was locked but I knew by touch alone which key I needed here.

As I passed through, I paused for a moment. The graveyard looked different in the dark, and the bulk of the church silhouetted against the stars seemed to have assumed cathedral-like proportions. But I switched on my torch and advanced till I spotted the comforting outline of Rocky, my broken-nosed angel keeping guard over David Oscar Winstanley, the virtuous old postman. The long grass beneath my bare feet was pleasantly cool, the balmy air caressed my skin, and I felt sure somehow that Rocky would be keeping an eye on me too.

The door to the crypt was in a corner of the church's broad entrance porch. I thought I might have to unlock the church door itself as, ever since the theft of some items of silver a couple of years earlier, the building had been firmly locked at dusk. Tonight, however, the door was open. I didn't consider the implications of this, just took it in my superhero mode as a demonstration that things were running my way.

Now all I had to do was find the right key for the crypt door.

It proved surprisingly easy. Close up, I saw it wasn't the ancient worm-eaten oak door I'd expected but a new door, stained to fit in with the rest of the porch, and instead of a large old-fashioned keyhole, there was a modern mortice lock.

That made the selection of the right key very easy and the door swung open with well-oiled ease and not the slightest suspicion of a horror film screech.

Now, however, the thin beam of my torch revealed that the bit about the steep and decaying steps hadn't been exaggerated. They plunged down almost vertically into the darkness where the naughty people lay.

Suddenly I felt less like a superhero and more like an eight-year-old boy who got scared watching *Doctor Who* with his mam!

It felt a lot colder in the church porch and there seemed to be a draught of still colder air coming up from the crypt that made my sweat-soaked pyjamas feel clammy. I could smell damp earth – that was an odour I was very familiar with from hanging around the Clems while they were digging a grave. But what wasn't there, which I'd half-expected, was any of that decaying meat smell I'd once got a whiff of as Young Clem's spade drove into an unexpected coffin.

Far from reassuring me, this only roused a fear that maybe the naughty people didn't decay like the ordinary good people, but somehow got preserved like the salted hams that hung in Granny Longbottom's kitchen. Maybe they even retained a bit of life?

In fact to my young mind, already well acquainted through the school playground with notions of zombies and vampires, it seemed very likely that the new door and its mortice lock hadn't been put there to keep the inquisitive public out, but to keep the still active naughty people in!

I could have shut the door and retreated and gone home to bed, and no one would ever have known of my cowardice. Except me, of course.

Daft, wasn't it? Just to prove to myself I wasn't scared, I began to descend that crumbling sandstone staircase. And all the time my teeth were chattering so hard I could hardly breathe!

What did I expect to find? Bodies hanging upside down from the ceiling? Coffins stacked six or seven deep? Heaps of bones? I don't know.

And I didn't know whether to be disappointed or relieved when all that the beam of my torch picked out was . . . emptiness! Except that is for seven or eight pillars of steel rising from metal plates set on the packed earth floor to give them firm grounding, and with metal beams running between them at ceiling level to support the sagging church floor.

And that was it. It dawned on me that Old Clem had been having me on again, like he did with looking for the rubber spade! I should have known. Making a fool of people is what passes for a joke in Yorkshire. I felt really stupid! Also, despite the chilly air down here, I felt very hot. I pulled off my pyjama top to cool down and used it to wipe off the streams of perspiration running down my face and body.

Suddenly I was desperate to be back in my bed and I turned to go.

Then I heard a noise.

And all my fears came rushing back full pelt!

It was a relief to realize the noise was coming from outside the crypt not inside.

Someone was at the top of the stairs.

I clicked my torch off and stood in the dark.

A voice demanded harshly, 'Who's down there?'

I almost answered but the thought of the trouble I'd be in at home – sneaking out after I'd gone to bed and stealing Dad's keys to get into the crypt – kept me quiet. Also, as I say, all my old fears were boiling up again. Maybe this was one of the wicked zombies returning from a stroll around the graveyard! I found myself praying to Rocky who'd never been beaten to come and help me.

Then a bigger fear erupted to push out all the others. Suppose whoever it was pulled the door shut behind him as he went away and left me locked in the crypt all night!

So I stuttered, 'It's me,' and began to move forward.

Then I stopped, blinded as a powerful torch beam hit me right in the eyes.

I heard footsteps on the stairs and a voice I now recognized said, 'Tommy! What on earth are you doing here?'

It was Father Stamp! I was so relieved I rushed forward up the steep steps and flung myself around him and hugged him close with my arms and legs. His arms went around my back and I felt his large strong hands cool against my hot skin. My tracksuit bottom was always a bit loose, and I think it had slipped down but I didn't care, I was just so relieved to be safe! I wanted to explain what I'd been doing but when I tried to speak, it came out as sobs, and he lifted me up and held me so close, I could hardly get my breath, and I tried to push myself free.

My memory of what happened after that is vague and confused. It was like my head was full of colours all forming weird shapes, constantly flying apart and changing into something else. And my body didn't feel as if it belonged to me, it was like a girl's rag doll that can be twisted into any shape you want, and I knew I would have fallen away or maybe even flown away if Father Stamp's strong hands hadn't been grasping my weak and nerveless flesh.

And then . . . I don't think I heard anything and I certainly didn't see anything, but I knew there was someone – or something – else on the steps. I just had time to think that maybe

Rocky had answered my earlier call when there was an explosion of noise and violent movement, and something crashed into Father Stamp and together we went tumbling down the steep steps.

That was pretty well the end for me. I must have hit the crypt floor with such a bang that all of the breath and most of the consciousness was knocked out of my body. I had a sense of being embraced again but not in the strong muscular way that Father Stamp had embraced me. Maybe, I thought, this was Rocky. Then I was raised by strong arms and carried up the steps, and my lolling head gave me a view down into the crypt lit by a moving light that I think must have come from Father Stamp's torch, rolling around where he'd dropped it as we went tumbling down together.

Finally I was outside in the balmy night air and the sky was full of stars and I didn't remember anything else for sure till the moment when I opened my eyes and found myself back in my own bedroom with sunlight streaming through the window.

Four days had passed, four days that I'd spent being very sick, and sweating buckets, and tossing and turning with such violence that Mam sometimes had to hold me down. The doctor said I'd had a particularly extreme dose of Hong Kong flu, not just me but Dad too. He'd come back from the pub in almost as bad a state as me. How I got back to my bed, I don't know. I had some vague notion that Rocky had carried me there. My waking mind was awash with fantastic images of my visit to the crypt and these turned into really terrible nightmares when I sank into sleep, so no wonder I was tossing and turning so violently. I were poorly for nearly a fortnight, much worse than Dad who was up and about again after a week. And it was another two weeks after I first got out of bed before I really started getting back to something like normal.

By this time my memories and my nightmares had become so confused I found it impossible to tell the difference between them. Looming large in all of them was Father Stamp. Remembering how Mam always sang his praises as a visitor of the sick, I lived in fear of seeing him by my bedside. Finally when Mam didn't mention him, I did.

'Father Stamp's gone,' she said shortly.

'Gone where?' I said.

'How should I know. Just gone. Not a trace,' she said. 'Now, are you going to take that medicine or do I have to pour it down you?'

I couldn't blame her for being short. Luckily for me and Dad, she'd somehow managed to remain untouched by the flu bug, but she must have been worked off her feet for the past few weeks taking care of the pair of us.

Also she'd had time to get used to Father Stamp's disappearance. When I was up and about again, I found out he'd been gone a long time. Exactly when no one was certain. It wasn't till he didn't turn up for old Mr Parkin's funeral on the Wednesday after my adventure in the crypt that folk started to get worried. He wasn't married and he lived alone in the vicarage, looked after by a local woman who came in every morning to clean the house and take care of his meals. That week she'd been down with the flu too, so there was a lot of vagueness about who'd actually seen him last and when.

Should I say something? Best not, I decided. When you're a kid, you learn it's usually a mistake to volunteer information that might get you in bother! Also, once I started sharing my memory-nightmare of that night, it would be hard to stop till I got to the bit where I was carried home by a marble angel with a broken nose, and I knew that sounded really loopy!

Yet for some reason that was the bit of my memories that I

clung on to hardest. Maybe by clinging to what had to be fantasy, I was shutting out what might be reality. Anyway, soon as I felt well enough, I went back into the graveyard to say thank you to Rocky.

Young Clem spotted me and came over for a chat.

'All right, Tommy?' he said, lighting the inevitable fag.

'Yes, thanks,' I said.

'Me and Dad were dead worried about you,' he said. 'Hong Kong flu it was, right?'

I really didn't want to talk about it, but I didn't want to offend Young Clem, especially not after Mam told me he'd called around nearly every day to ask after me when I was ill.

'That's right,' I said. 'Hong Kong flu.'

'Aye, it can be right nasty that. My Auntie Mary had it, just about sent her doolally, thought she were the Queen Mother for a bit, we have a grand laugh with her about that now she's right again. Owt like that happen to you, Tommy?'

'Just some bad dreams,' I said.

'But you're all right now?'

'Yes, thank you.'

'Grand!' he said, stubbing out his cigarette on Rocky's knee. 'Everyone has bad dreams. Thing is not to let them bother you when you wake up. See you around, Tommy.'

'Yes, Clem, see you around.'

Father Stamp's disappearance was old news now. It seemed one of the papers had dug up some stuff about him having trouble with his nerves when he was a curate down south, and his bishop moving him north for his health. So most folk reckoned he'd had what they called a nervous breakdown and he'd turn up some day. But he never did.

After a while St Cyprian's got a replacement. He was nowhere near as High as Father Stamp; he wanted everyone to call him

Jimmy, and he had all kinds of newfangled ideas. Dad and him didn't get on, and pretty soon there was a big falling out that ended with us leaving Rose Cottage and going to live with Granny Longbottom in Murton till Dad got taken on at Rowntree's chocolate factory and we found a place right on the edge of York.

So Mam got her wish and I was brought up breathing good fresh air, and eating a lot of chocolate, and enjoying the sight and smell of trees and grass with never a gravestone in sight. In fact after leaving St Cyprian's, Mam seemed to lose all interest in religion, and as I grew up I don't think I saw the inside of a church again, unless you count a visit to the Minster on a school trip. I'd only been inside a few minutes when I started to feel the whole place crowding in on me and I were glad to get out into the air. After that I didn't bother.

That was forty-odd years ago. I still live with my mam. Lot of folk think that's weird. Let them think. All I know is I never felt the need to get close to anyone else. I never were courting. I did try being naughty with a girl from time to time, and it were all right, I suppose, but I could never get really interested and I don't think they liked it that much, so in the end I stopped bothering.

Maybe I should have moved out. I know Dad thought I should. I brought it up one night after he'd gone out to the pub. Mam was sitting in front of the TV, busily knitting away as she always did. That click-click-clicking of the needles is such a familiar accompaniment that it sounds strange if ever I watch a programme without it! She smiled up at me when I broached the subject of moving out and said, 'This is your home, son. You'll always be welcome here.'

Next year, Dad got diagnosed with cancer. After that I think he was glad I was still around to help take some of the strain off Mam. She was the best nurse he could have asked for and she kept him at home far longer than many women would have done. But three years later he was dead, and since then the thought of leaving has never crossed my mind.

As for Father Stamp and St Cyprian's, they never got mentioned at home, not even while Dad were still living. Was that good or bad? There's a lot of folk say everything should be brought out in the open. Well, each to his own. I know what worked for me. That's not to say I never wondered how different my life might have been if the events of that October night hadn't occurred. We're all what our childhood makes us, the kid is father to the man, isn't that what they say?

Though I doubt if many people looking at a picture of me back then could see much connection between little Tommy Cresswell at eight and this fifty-year-old, a bit shabby, a bit broken down, unmarried, living at home with his widowed mam.

There is, though, maybe one traceable link between that kid in the graveyard and this middle-aged man.

I'm a postman.

How much that can be tracked back to David Oscar Winstanley and Rocky, the broken-nosed angel, I don't know. I certainly don't aspire to anything like his memorial, either in form or in words. In fact I've lowered my sights considerably from the fantasies of my boyhood. *He looked after his mam, and bothered nobody* would do me. I suppose I could rate as a loyal servant to the Post Office, if loyalty means doing your job efficiently. But if it entails devoting yourself wholeheartedly to your employer, then I don't qualify. I never had any ambition to rise up the career ladder. Delivering the mail's been enough for me.

Then the other day, my first on a new round, I knocked on a door to deliver a parcel, and when the door opened I found myself looking at Old Clem.

Except of course it was Young Clem forty-odd years on.

'Bugger me,' he said when I introduced myself. 'Tommy Cresswell! Come on in and have a beer.'

'More than my job's worth, Clem,' I said. 'But I'll have a cup of tea.'

Sitting in his kitchen, he filled me in on his life. He'd worked most of his life for the Bradford Parks and Gardens Service (though they call it something fancier nowadays), he'd been a widower for five years, and he'd recently retired because of his health. No need for details here. Most of his sentences were punctuated with a racking cough which didn't stop him from getting through three or four fags as we talked.

'Me daughter and her two kiddies live here in York,' he said. 'She wanted me to move in with them but I knew that 'ud never do. But I wanted to be a bit handier so I got myself this place. How about you, Tommy? You married?'

'Who'd have me?' I said, making a joke out of it. Then I told him about Dad dying and me living with Mam. And all the time he was sort of studying me through a cloud of smoke in a way that made me feel uneasy. So in the end I looked at my watch and said I ought to be getting on before folk started wondering what had happened to their mail.

But as I started to rise from my chair, he reached over the table and grasped my wrist and said, 'Afore you go, Tommy –' here he broke off to cough – 'or mebbe I mean, afore I go, there's something we need to talk about . . .'

I should just have left. I knew what he was going to tell me, and it had been a long time since Rocky was a barrier against the truth. But I stopped and listened and let him give form and flesh to what for so long I'd been desperate to pretend was nowt but an echo of one of my Hong Kong flu nightmares.

That night as usual I cleared up after supper and washed the dishes. Mam says it's no job for a man but she's been having a lot of trouble with her knees lately. There's been some talk of a replacement but she says she can't be bothered with that. So I do all I can to make life easy for her. Most nights after we've eaten, we sit together in front of the telly and I'll maybe watch a football match while she gets on with her knitting. Like I say, doesn't matter how noisy the crowd is at the game, if that click-click-clicking of her needles stops, I look around to see what she's doing.

Tonight when I came in from the kitchen with a mug of coffee for me and cup of tea for her, she was knitting as usual but I didn't switch the set on.

I said, 'Met an old friend today, Mam. Remember Young Clem? Him and his dad used to dig the graves at St Cyprian's? Well, he's living in York now. So he can be close to his daughter and grandkids.'

'Young Clem?' she said. 'So he has grandchildren? That's nice. Grandchildren are nice.'

'Aye,' I said. 'Sorry I never gave you any, Mam.'

'Maybe you didn't, but I never lost you, Tommy, and that's just as important,' she said, her needles clicking away. 'So what was the crack with Young Clem then?'

She looked at me brightly. Sometimes these days she could be a bit vague about things; others, like now, she was as bright as a button.

I sipped my coffee slowly while my mind tried to come to terms with what Young Clem had told me.

My problem had nothing to do with his powers of expression for he'd spoken in blunt Yorkshire terms.

He'd said, 'I'd taken this lass into graveyard, for a bang, tha knows, and we'd just done when I saw this figure moving between the headstones. I nigh on shit meself till I made out it were your mam. She didn't spot me, but something about the look of her weren't right, so I told my lass to shove off down the pub and I'd catch up with her there. Well, she weren't best pleased but I didn't wait to argue, I went after your mam, and I caught up with her by the church door. She jumped a mile when I spoke to her, then she asked if I'd seen you. Seems she'd been watching the telly and all of a sudden something made her get up and go upstairs. When she found you weren't in bed, she went out into the yard and saw the back gate into the graveyard standing open and she went through it to look for you.

'I could tell what a state she were in – she'd nowt on her feet but a pair of fluffy slippers and she were still carrying her knitting with her – so I tried to calm her down, saying that likely you were just larking about with some of your mates. But she'd spotted that the church door were ajar, and nowt would satisfy her but that we went inside to take a look.

'Well, we didn't get past the porch. There was a noise like someone sobbing and a bit of a light and it were coming up from the crypt. That was when I recalled what Dad had said to you when you asked where we put the naughty people. I'd told him he shouldn't joke about such things with you as you were only a lad, but I never thought you'd take it serious enough to do owt like this.

'I told your mam I'd go first as the steps were bad, and that's what I did, but she were right behind me and she saw clearly enough what I saw down below.

'That mucky bastard Stamp were all over you. He'd just about got you bollock naked. I knew straight off what were going on. I'd been there myself, except I was a couple of years older and a lot tougher and more streetwise than you. When he started his tricks on me, I belted him in the belly and I told him I were going to report him, and I would have done, only I weren't sure anyone would believe me. They'd already marked my card as a bit of a wild boy at school plus I'd been done for shoplifting by the cops. So I said nowt, but when they started talking about giving Dad the boot because of his back, I stood in front of Stamp and I let him know that the day Dad got his papers was the day he'd find himself *in* the papers. I'd been keeping an eye on him when I saw him getting interested in you, and I thought he'd got the message. But there's no changing them bastards!

'Now I were on him in a flash. He must have thought God had hit him with a thunderbolt, and that were no more than he deserved. The pair of you went tumbling down the steps. His torch went flying but it were one of them rubber ones and it didn't break. He was lying on his back, not moving. You were just about out of it. Your mam gathered you up and it was only then I reckon that it fully hit her what the bastard had been at. She put you into my arms and told me to take you up the steps.

'I said, "What about you, missus?" but she didn't answer, so I set off back up to the porch with you in my arms. Do you not remember any of this, Tommy? Nay, I see you do.'

And he was right. I was remembering it now when Mam brought me back to our living room by saying impatiently, 'Come on, Tommy. Cat got your tongue? I asked what you and Young Clem found to talk about?'

'Oh, nothing much,' I said. 'I told him about Dad, and he told me that Old Clem had passed on too, about ten years back, heart, it was. And we chatted about the old days at Cyprian's, that's all.'

'Well, I'm sorry to hear about Old Clem, though he was a bit of a devil,' said Mam. 'Remember that time he had you looking everywhere for his rubber spade? I gave him a piece of my mind for that!'

A pity you hadn't been around to give him a piece of your mind when he told me about the crypt, I thought. Maybe life could have been very different for me. Maybe I'd be sitting by my own fireside now with my own family around me. I thought of Young Clem, moving house so he could be handier for his grandchildren. He was clearly made of stronger stuff than me. He dealt with the crises in life by looking them straight in the face and getting on with the life not the crisis. He certainly gave no indication he blamed Old Clem and his daft lie for what happened to me in the crypt. It was just another Yorkshire joke, like sending a kid to look for a rubber spade!

Any road, the way it turned out, it wasn't strictly speaking a lie any more. Old Clem had told me that the crypt was where they put the naughty people. And the crypt of St Cyprian's was where Young Clem had buried Father Stamp's body.

It must have taken him a couple of hours or more to dig a grave in that hard-packed earth. I wonder how long the poor lass he'd sent off to the pub waited for him? Maybe she'd forgiven him, maybe she was even the one who'd become his wife. I should have asked.

But the question that bothered me was, just how naughty had Father Stamp really been? That he had problems was clear. That he'd been foolish enough to grope Young Clem I didn't doubt.

But it wasn't his fault that I'd flung myself almost naked into his arms. And it had been me who'd been desperate to cling on to him, at least to start with. For all I know his intention was simply to carry me out of the crypt and take me home. However it had looked to Young Clem and my mam, there'd been no time for him to actually *do* anything.

No, it wasn't a memory of childhood sexual abuse that had dictated the pattern of my life. It was quite another memory, one that I'd only been able to bear because I could pretend to myself that it might after all just be the product of a sick child's fevered imagination.

My half-hour listening to Young Clem had removed that fragile barrier for ever.

I don't know how long Mam and me have before us living like this. Granny Longbottom lasted into her nineties so there could be a good few years yet.

There it is then. Night after night, month after month, year after year, I'm going to be sitting here in this room, still able to hear the click-click-clicking of her knitting no matter how loud the telly.

And every time I glance across at her to share a smile, I'm going to see her as I saw her from Clem's arms in the fitful light of the torch rolling around the crypt floor. I'm going to see her kneeling astride the recumbent body of Father Stamp with those same click-click-clicking needles raised high, one in either hand, before she drives them down with all the strength of a mother's love, a mother's hate, into his despairing, uncomprehending, and vainly pleading eyes.

The Difference

A good day for a funeral. Dark clouds, sagging like black drapes. Atmosphere chill and damp, a gusting breeze tugging at hair and clothes like a child's fingers. The others move away, leaving me alone by the grave. Death is a time for doubt, a time to review missed opportunities, unspoken words. I had the opportunity to speak, and I didn't take it. Was I right or wrong? Would it have made any difference? The funeral's over which suggests it hardly matters.

Man that is born of a woman is of few days and full of trouble. He cometh forth like a flower and is cut down.

We live, we die. Some in the fullness of years and some in the springtide of life, and we've precious little control over the When, Where or the How, else why do so many people end up places they don't want to be? Like me and Jamie Montegreen for instance.

I never really wanted to be a prison officer. I don't suppose Jamie spent much of his young life planning to be hanged by the neck until he was dead. But fate sent us both down the unavoidable path that led to our meeting in Parkley Prison.

Fate, in my case, took the form of my dad and his dad before him. They were both in the prison service and as I grew up I heard the words 'The Parkers have always been Prison Officers' so often that they rang in my ears like an eternal truth. Sometimes, lying in bed at night I did wonder how a mere two generations could add up to an 'always'. Occasionally, I even resolved to stand up to the precious tradition and tell them that yes, I was happy to embrace a career in the law, but I wanted to be someone who could make a difference. A barrister, keeping people out of prison, not a turnkey, making sure they stayed locked up.

The only person I mentioned my absurd ambition to was the so-called careers master at school. He didn't help. Disillusioned idealists rarely do.

He said, 'Forget it, Frank, nothing to do with ability. You need the background, but above all, you need the money. We all have our dreams. I thought everything would be different when we voted Labour in after the war but look what's happening now. Mark my words, the old gang will have their boot back on our necks before Christmas. Follow in your father's footsteps, boy, and make him proud of you.'

Sure enough, the 1951 election put Mr Churchill back in Downing Street. Fate, it seemed to me, had spoken. I accepted it with good grace. And that's how I came to be a Junior Prison Officer in Parkley when Jamie Montegreen was committed there to await execution. I had followed the trial in the papers so I already had some knowledge of the path that fate had plotted for him. Jamie and his sister Lucy had been at school in England when they heard that their parents, settlers in Kenya, had been victims of the Mau Mau uprising. Their only living relative, Henry Montegreen – their father's elder brother – became their guardian. Well, depending on which paper you read, it was a duty he embraced enthusiastically and performed with great generosity, or it was a task he undertook reluctantly and carried out with grumbling parsimony. Though what is certain is that when Jamie came of age in '57 his uncle revealed that after deductions for upkeep and education less than £100 remained of his father's estate. There was a furious row, that ended with Jamie storming out.

According to two independent witnesses his parting words were, 'I'll never set foot in this house again unless it's to end your miserable life.'

His sister Lucy had gone with him. Eighteen months his junior, she was still technically a minor, but her uncle didn't resist her departure. Two weeks after the quarrel, Henry Montegreen was found dead in his study with his brains blown out by his own shotgun, and his nephew was under arrest on suspicion of murder. Well, at first Jamie claimed to have been at home with his sister the evening of the murder. But the testimony of a neighbour who'd seen him coming out of his uncle's house put paid to that.

His new story was that he'd visited his uncle in hope of a reconciliation, found him dead, and left in panic. The defence counsel suggested that the true killer was a burglar who had been interrupted – pointing to the absence of Henry's wallet in support of this contention. Trouble was, that the wallet had been found in a nearby garden. No money had been removed and its smooth leather surface bore Jamie's thumbprint. Clearly, the prosecutor asserted, it had been taken in an attempt to make the murder look like a robbery that went wrong. According to the papers, Jamie sat through the early procedures looking bored to tears. It wasn't until the prosecutor tried to categorize him as a feckless young man that Jamie became agitated.

What was the point in trying to build a career in this decrepit old country, he demanded. All he'd ever wanted to do was to return to Africa as soon as he'd reached his majority and follow in his father's footsteps.

At this point, according to the *Daily Herald*, the prosecuting barrister had smiled thinly and said, 'So, Mr Montegreen, far from being feckless, you claim to be focused. Your sole ambition was to take up where your unfortunate father left off in Kenya, but you were thwarted in this by your uncle's alleged mismanagement of your father's estate. Am I right?'

Jamie had struck his fist against the edge of the dock and cried, 'Yes! The bastard robbed me!'

Well, that did it. In his summing up, the judge aligned the prosecution point that in the absence of a will, the Montegreen siblings would be heir to their uncle's substantial fortune. It took the jury only thirty minutes to find him guilty, and Jamie Montegreen was sent to Parkley Prison for his appointment with death. And with me.

A man in the death cell has to be watched over day and night in case he tries to save the hangman's fee by topping himself. Normally, a couple of hardened old warders are given the job. But our humanitarian governor felt the presence of someone his own age would be of comfort to the prisoner. So I was chosen. Jamie and I hit it off from the start. My fellow warder, a grizzled veteran called Dodd, who had seen everything and didn't make much of any of it, was more than happy to let me do what he called the 'socializing' while he snoozed over his racing paper. So Jamie and I played draughts and dominoes, and we talked.

After he'd got to know and trust me, his favourite topic was Lucy, his sister. He seemed far more worried about her than he was about himself. I asked why she never visited him, and he said she had an acute form of claustrophobia. I thought this was a poor excuse, until the day before the execution when she finally came to see him. As soon as I saw Lucy, I knew Jamie hadn't been exaggerating. Her limbs were shaking, her face was grey and beaded with sweat and her words verged on incoherency. She babbled on about the truth setting him free and he tried to soothe her and tell her it was all for the best and she had to accept her inheritance and live for both of them now. I could see this interview wasn't doing any good and fearing that Lucy might collapse completely I brought it to an end a couple of minutes early and practically hauled Jamie back to his cell. He flung himself on his bed and lay with his face to the wall for several hours, giving me plenty of time to think.

It was evening before he sat up. I asked him if he was all right.

He said, 'Yes,' and drank some water.

I drew my stool close to the bed and said in a low voice, 'Jamie? It wasn't you who killed your uncle, was it? It was Lucy.'

It was a bluff of course, I had no evidence. At first I thought he wasn't going to answer, but the story came pouring out. Henry had invited Lucy around to his house to discuss her brother's future. He told her he was willing to finance Jamie's return to Africa but there were conditions. Disgusting conditions. When she refused, he tried to force himself on her. The gun was standing in a corner of the study, Lucy seized it and took aim. He just laughed and kept on advancing. She pulled the trigger then she ran home and told Jamie, who ran straight around to his uncle's house and tried to cover her tracks. Even if it meant leaving tracks of his own.

When he fell silent I burst out, 'For God's sake, Jamie, you've got to tell them the truth! When they talk to Lucy they'll see it was self-defence.'

He said, 'No, it's too late for that! At best they'll charge her with perjury, at worst with being an accessory. You saw what she's like, she would be dead before it came to trial. As it is, this way at least she'll get Henry's fortune.'

I said, 'Jamie, if you don't tell them, I will. It's my duty.'

He said, 'For pity's sake, Frank, say nothing. You can't help me, but you can help Lucy. Go to see her after it's over, she has no one. I fear for her if she has to bear this alone. I beg you stay silent for her sake, and mine.'

Well, I didn't answer. It was all too much. I needed time to think, time to decide if I should speak out or hold my peace, and all I had was one night. It was enough. It had to be. I conveyed my decision to Jamie with a shake of the hand, just before they came for him. He conveyed his thanks with a nod and a ghost of a smile. Then I manacled his wrists behind his back and watched him walk away. Now, I walk away from the open grave, still debating the question: was I right, or wrong? Perhaps the answer lies in the elaborate memorial standing by the lichgate, ready to be erected as soon as the grave is filled. Justice in white marble blindfolded bearing her scales aloft, standing on a black granite pediment. I pause, to read the inscription.

Here rests Lucy, beloved wife of the Right Honourable Sir Francis Parker GBE QC LLD born May 1st 1938 died November 15th 2009.

And oh, the difference to me. Tad ostentatious, do you think? Even melodramatic? In fact, nothing but the simple truth. Legally, practically, and emotionally. Emotionally, I shall miss her deeply. We grew very close over the years. Practically, without her inherited fortune there's no way I could have followed the career path that led to my appointment as High Court judge. And legally, I smile as I recall the clinching argument in my proposal to her all those years ago. I said, 'Lucy, you do know that the law of England does not permit a husband to give evidence against his wife?'

On the Psychiatrist's Couch

I hate these things.

You come in with angst, you go out with backache. Aversion therapy. That'll be fifty guineas.

What's it stuffed with anyway? Rocks? Or electronic equipment? Perhaps it's really the couch that's listening to me, you're just a cut-out. Could be I'd get more sense out of it. Sorry, I don't really mean that.

Funny if it could talk, though. What tales it could tell! There must be more dirt spilled here than in a prozzie's pit.

Did I see you twitch there? One minute into the session and the patient makes first aggressive sexual reference to women. Worth a note, I'd say.

Please yourself.

I just want you to know that I've been here before. I know what's going on as much as you do. More. Think about it. You lot are all dying to find out what made me a serial killer.

Well, I know already.

So who's in control, eh?

OK, where shall I start? That's your cue for saying, where do you want to start, Jamie? So let's take that as read, and I'll say, the very beginning. My father, God rest his soul, had a heart attack while he was on the job. Fatal. But his last shot was a bull's eye. Me.

Must have been a bit of a shock for my dear mother, realizing that she'd screwed the poor sod to death. Probably a lot bigger shock when she found she was pregnant. Still, no problem those days. Back in the swinging sixties, you travelled fast and you travelled light and the next stop could always be the terminus.

But it wasn't. She had me. Don't ask me why. Clearly she didn't want me. How do I know that? Well, she gave a pretty strong hint by buggering off soon as she could stagger and leaving me high and dry. Or, knowing the way babies are, probably high and wet.

I didn't know this at the time, of course. I must have been three or so when I first asked why I didn't have a mum. Your mother died giving birth to you, I was told. Bit baffling for a three-year-old! What did I know about birth or death?

But at least the motive for this lie was probably kindness, you say.

No way!

More chance of a hand-job from the *Venus de Milo*, coming as it did from my paternal grandmother.

No, I suspect it was just wishful thinking. When it came to penal policy, she and her husband were Old Testament throwbacks. The way they saw it, my mother dying having me might just have evened things up for their son dying having her.

It was them that raised me till I was five. Not a labour of love, believe me. Love was pretty short in that household, but it fairly creaked with Victorian values, prime among which was spare the rod and spoil the child. *He* wasn't too bad, more of a tokenist than the real thing. The disgrace of a beating was the true punishment, he reckoned. Not *her*, though. *Whatsoever thy hand findeth to do* was her favourite text, and she did it with all her might. Across the knuckles just to keep you honest; back of the legs for minor offences; bare bum for the big ones.

This hurts me more than it hurts you, she once said. Oh, how I hoped it did, but I didn't really believe it.

You must have read all this stuff already. I'm not exactly the best advert for patient confidentiality you wankers have ever had!

Never mind. I don't mind going over it all again.

So how did I feel about her?

I hated her, of course. How else was I supposed to feel?

Even a guileless child soon gets the message when he's told every day he ought to consider himself a very lucky little boy and this wasn't how she'd envisaged spending the years of her prime and if I knew what was good for me I'd sit there very quiet and not draw attention to myself as I was only there on sufferance and there were plenty of places where bad little boys were taken care of as they truly deserved.

Firm but fair, that was how she described her paediatric philosophy.

Strict and stark-staring bonkers was nearer the mark.

That bit of my life ended that last Christmas, not long before my fifth birthday. I'm a Capricorn, by the way. That any help? No, I didn't think so. Not scientific. You and your science. Lot of good it's done me.

My grandparents had always gone to hotels for Christmas. Their Old Testament attitudes didn't extend to depriving themselves of any of life's little luxuries. Also hotels saved them the bother of mucking up their own house with pine-needles and tinsel and mince-pie crumbs, though I can't imagine a lot of people beating a path to their door in search of seasonal cheer.

Perhaps that was another reason for hotels. Company without commitment, the desideratum of the self-righteous egotist since time began. No, not my phrase. Another of you lot. I've picked up quite a lot of the jargon as I've bounced from couch to couch.

Far from changing their festive arrangements, my arrival probably simply confirmed their wisdom. Hotels offering traditional Christmas breaks really cater for kids. Crèches, childminders, special entertainment – they could dump me on arrival and hardly see me again till it was time to go.

Funny that. Despite what's happened to me, which I think you'll agree has hardly been calculated to inspire religious fervour, I still get a warm glow whenever Christmas comes around. The few good memories I've got of my earliest years all centre on those three days spent in the care and company of strangers.

That last Christmas had a real bonus in that it was white. Snow everywhere. We had snowball fights and went sledging and built huge snowmen with coal eyes and carrot noses. I loved it so much I didn't want to leave, and when it got to the day after Boxing Day, I went into hiding. By the time they tracked me down it was late morning. My grandparents were surprisingly laid-back about it, on the surface anyway. Thing was, there were other people around who'd helped in the search and they'd all made a jolly game out of it, so what else could they do but join in the merriment at the comical antics of a lovable little scamp? But I saw the long teeth behind my grandmother's wide smile and I knew what to expect once we were alone.

We set off at midday. Before we got out of the hotel grounds, the tongue lashing had begun. Things weren't helped by the fact that it was starting to snow again. We should have been home by now, my grandmother told me. It was all my fault, I was a wicked ungrateful child who thought about nothing but my own pleasure, just like my slut of a mother who had clearly known what she was doing when she ran off and abandoned me at birth. This was the first time I got the revised, and as it turned out authorized, version of the story. My grandmother was the kind of woman who could use truth like a whip to draw blood.

The only good thing about the situation was that she was driving (she always drove; she wouldn't trust my grandfather to drive sheep, she would say) and keeping two hands on the wheel meant she had to stick to verbal punishment. But she made plenty of promises, and she was a woman of her word.

The main roads which had been cleared were beginning to whiten over again and traffic was heavy and slow. My fault, of course. She decided to turn off and go across country, despite my grandfather's weak protests. Perfectly safe, she said. The only danger in these conditions was from all those incompetent idiots who insisted on hogging the main road back there. Give her an empty highway and she could guarantee to negotiate any obstacle unscathed.

I enjoyed these few minutes of relief while she directed her venom at her husband, but it was a short respite. Soon I was the target again. The weather was worsening and as the snow came down harder and harder, so her abuse of me increased till suddenly I could bear it no longer. I had to get out. We'd slowed down a lot because of the conditions and I suppose the all-enveloping whiteness blurred my impression of movement, so I probably thought we were almost at a standstill. It was a two-door car and I was in the back so normally there was no way I could get out till one of the front seats was empty. But I couldn't wait for that.

Suddenly I clambered over my grandfather, heading for the passenger door. He shouted, my grandmother swung her left hand at me, either to grab or more likely, to hit me, I kicked out and caught her in the face, and next thing the car was spinning around like a duck landing on a frozen pond.

At first it was quite a pleasant sensation. Then we went through a fence and down a steep embankment, and it stopped being pleasant.

We rolled over two or three times, hit something hard and came to a halt upside down.

That was it. The situation as I discovered later was that we were upside down against a stone wall under a snowdrift with the doors so badly buckled they couldn't be opened. My grandfather was already dead. Heart failure. The same weakness that killed my father, I suppose, which could mean my grandmother's revulsion from the idea of sex for pleasure gave him a couple of decades of extra life. Some prezzies aren't worth the pain, are they?

As for my grandmother, she was badly injured. Nothing wrong with her tongue, though. It took her a day and a half to die, during which time she never ceased to heap accusations on me and catalogue my failings. The one thing which did change was her language. Normally so precise, measured and magisterial, now she demonstrated a command of obscene abuse terminology which might have amazed me, if I'd been in any condition to be amazed.

The funny thing was that I didn't really become afraid till she finally fell silent. I wasn't too badly injured, in fact just scratches and bruises it turned out, but I was firmly trapped between my grandfather's body underneath me, and my grandmother's above. In a way, I suppose that saved my life. Kept the cold off. Gave me something to . . . hang on to.

Anyway, it was another two days before they finally found us. The snow had covered the car and it wasn't till a beginning thaw revealed the gap in the fence that someone thought of looking down the embankment.

I was taken to hospital where I recovered. Physically anyway. And then, in the absence of any other known relatives, I was put into care.

Care!

There's a four-letter word for you to lecture on, Doc.

The shelter I got from the decomposing bodies of my grandfather and grandmother was the last protection I was to receive from any adult human for many a long year.

Am I boring you?

God, how many times have I seen that same steady, blank, compassionate, non-judgemental gaze! What it says is, I know all this, I'm way ahead of you, I understand why you did what you did, and I can help you confront it, understand it, and finally come to terms with it. Trust me.

Well, it's crap, you hear me? Crap!

You people want to trace everything back to those early years. Adolescence, childhood, in my case birth even! Like there's some burden I was born with and it's got bigger and bigger over the years as other stuff's got loaded on to it, till finally my mind and personality cracked under the weight.

Well, you're wrong. Not altogether wrong. You lot are clever buggers, I've never denied that. You understand things about the human mind I could never grasp. Where you fail is in being too self-important. In not acknowledging that some people can shed their burden without your help. And shed it completely. Not a trace left. A completely new start. A rebirth, if you like. *Tabula rasa*, a born-again personality. Like I say, I know the jargon.

There's another way you go wrong too. Not arrogance this time. Almost the opposite. But I'll get to that later.

The point I'm trying to make here is that whatever it was I was suffering from, I was cured before any of you couch-artists got within sniffing distance of me. I remember my first meeting with Mr Barnfather. You'll know his work, of course. Really high powered, with enough letters after his name to write a paper on me, which in fact he did.

Later we came to be good mates, at least that's how I saw it. That first time, he naturally wanted to hear everything, so I told him everything. But even with him that first time, when I got to this point, I caught on his face the same expression I think I've just detected on yours – a little flicker of impatience, like he'd made his mind up already that everything I'd done had to stem from those very early experiences and the rest of my sad story was just mere confirmation, so let's get a wiggle on and get to the killings.

He was probably right. You are probably right. Like I say, I know what clever buggers you lot are. But bear with me, I feel I've got to make sure you have the full story. But I will keep it as short as possible, knowing you can fill in the gaps yourself.

OK, where was I?

Oh yes. Care. I went into care.

Was I unlucky or was what I experienced just the norm? You'll probably have access to more statistics than are ever likely to come my way, so I'll let you be the judge. All I know is that I experienced three different children's homes over the next ten years and all they had in common was that there was someone in there waiting to fuck you up. Mentally, physically, emotionally, every which way.

I was fostered too. Three times. Generally speaking that was worse. At least in the homes it was sometimes someone else's turn.

Worst of all was the last time. *He* was away most of the time. *She* used to treat me as a servant. Then her mood would swing and I'd be 'her baby'. She used to give me baths. I was eleven. Then she started getting in with me. 'I've lost the soap, Jamie. See if you can find the soap, there's a love.' I wanted to push her big fat smiling face under the water and hold it there till the bubbles stopped coming up.

But I didn't. In fact I never harmed anyone I was closely connected with. I mean, that would have been like leaving an arrow pointing right at myself, wouldn't it?

That was sensible, you must agree. That was rational. That alone surely points to my underlying sanity.

You don't look convinced. You're thinking, but he killed four women! Point taken, I can see your problem. Let me make no bones about it, if you'll excuse the expression. I murdered four women. Only four, mind you. If you believed some of the tabloids, I must have been responsible for every unsolved prostitute death from Jack the Ripper on!

But even four is too many. Even tarts have a right to live. I acknowledge it freely. I was right out of order. I was wrong.

I should only have killed one.

The one who started it all.

The one who should have died when I was born.

Odd, isn't it? I finally came around to my grandmother's way of thinking. Justice would have been served if my uncaring, unloving, hard-hearted, self-centred, runaway mother had died having me.

So you see, if only I'd known before I started what I found out within a very short time of being caught, none of this would have happened.

Say what you will about the tabloids, when it comes to digging up the past, they leave Egyptian tomb robbers eating their dust.

Me, I'd often thought of looking for her, but I didn't know where to start. Nobody knew nothing, nothing they were going to tell me anyway. But within a few days of the fuzz releasing details of my arrest to the media, those Wapping weevils had burrowed into my past and come up with the truth about my mother's vanishing trick.

Simple really. She'd died.

When she walked out of the hospital leaving me to field all the crap that life was about to throw at me, she headed back up north to the little Lancashire town she'd been born in. Up there she'd kept them as ignorant of her life down south as she'd kept those down south of her origins up there.

So when she got killed in a drunken car crash, enough was known about her locally to get her buried without need of any wider inquiry.

All those years of festering ignorance. Of wild imaginings. Of cancerous resentment.

If only I'd known . . .

But I knew now, and the knowledge had set me free.

There's the irony of it, you see. Before any of you lot had got down to attempting a diagnosis of the causes of my dysfunction, I was already cured.

I tried to explain this to Mr Barnfather, of course, and he smiled and he nodded and made notes, but I could see I wasn't getting through. It didn't bother me, however. Please yourself, I thought. Makes no odds. That's how I saw things then.

You see, and this is further evidence of my return to sanity, I *knew* I'd done wrong. Even though the deaths of those women had been in the strict sense of the word *accidental*, this didn't absolve me from responsibility. I knew I had to face up to this and I was ready to pay my debt to society, eat my porridge, whatever phrase you like to use.

I worked out that with remission for good behaviour, I could be out in seven years, perhaps less. Even with the worst-case scenario in which they threw the book at me, I couldn't possibly do more than ten.

I was so taken up with this long-term planning for the rest of my post-prison *normal* life that I didn't pay enough attention at the trial. I was eager to cooperate, and determined to let them all see just how much I *was* cooperating. I was a little taken aback to hear myself being sentenced to a secure mental institution rather than jail, but my solicitor assured me I'd be much better off there than in some draughty old nick with four to a cell and slopping-out every morning.

I was a model inmate. Whatever they told me to do, I did. Read the records, it's all there. No black marks against my name. I was on the best of terms with all the officers and nurses. And when it turned out that Mr Barnfather was the head trick-cyclist there, all I thought was, here's a chap who's got all the background. We'd established a good relationship, even though I knew I hadn't been able in our few pre-trial sessions to overcome his natural caution. But now with so much time on our hands, he must eventually come around to admitting the truth of my mental condition.

We had weekly sessions. Nice and relaxed, me on the couch talking about my dreams, my hopes, my fears; him taking notes, asking the odd question, always very kind and sympathetic. I never mentioned getting out unless he brought up the outside world.

Like I say, I admitted my guilt, and was very willing to serve my time and wipe the slate clean.

But after seven years, I did feel entitled to bring the question of my release up.

He was very optimistic. Not just him, all the staff. They talked about necessary procedures, and safeguards, and reassuring the public and all that stuff. But always it was made clear to me that it was just a matter of form, of getting the bookkeeping right.

And time went on.

At the start of my tenth year, I began to be a little more assertive. Not aggressive, you understand. Assertive.

Mr Barnfather was very open with me. Yes, my release was under consideration. Decisions were taken by the Board of Managers, some such body, consisting of representatives of all professionally concerned parties plus some outside lay members. In a case like mine, there were two major aspects to consider. First, was it in my interest to be released? Second, was it in the public's interest?

As to the first, I assured him, the answer was obviously yes. I had plans. I wanted to get down to catching up with all the normal life I had lost through my own foolishness. As for the second, there was probably no one in the free world less likely to harm any of his fellow humans than me! I had known this from the moment I heard that my mother was dead. Mr Barnfather must surely have reached the same conclusion after our years of consultation. And with his great reputation, how could the Board fail to be convinced if he offered them a copper-bottomed assurance about my condition?

The day of the meeting arrived. I didn't expect to be summoned personally, not for examination anyway. But I held myself in readiness just in case they decided to give me the good news direct.

I waited.

And waited.

And waited.

Nothing.

I wasn't even told officially that I'd been turned down.

Naturally it was the first thing I brought up in my next session with Mr Barnfather.

He looked uncomfortable and said he couldn't talk about what had been said at the meeting, it was more than his job was worth. But I mustn't give up hope.

It was a short session, which was probably just as well. I was ready to explode but I knew that any outburst would just confirm the Board in its wisdom. I sat on my bed and worked out what had probably happened.

I had no doubt Mr Barnfather was on my side, and I knew how much of a favourite I was with both the nursing and the prison staff. So clearly it was the lay members of the Board who had decided in their ignorant fear, doubtless underpinned by a political agenda, to keep me locked up. I knew how such things worked. They'd be on the government's quango list, picking up all kinds of undemanding but lucrative little jobs. All they had to do was make sure they toed the official party line and above all never got involved with anything which could be potentially embarrassing.

Like releasing a prisoner who immediately reoffended.

There was only one way to prove to the world what a bunch of short-sighted idiots they were.

I escaped.

It was easy. Like I say, I was a model prisoner. I could have walked out of there via any one of a dozen routes any time over the last several years. There again, the fact that I didn't just goes to show how sane and balanced I am.

I had money in a building society account. It was mainly what had come to me from my grandparents who, happily for me, had died intestate. No one knew about the account except me, and my solicitor who had set it up for me during the pre-trial period. Even then, knowing I was going to plead guilty and face a long sentence, I was preparing for my release. Knowing from their work on my mother just how good the press hounds were, and not wanting them to have an easy scent to follow on my release, I had taken considerable precautions – a slight change of name, a branch in a town with which I had no connection – so I was able to get at my money without arousing any particular interest.

After that, it was easy. None of the old photos they had was in the least like the well-fed, healthy-looking chap I'd become, and a moustache soon removed even the last glimmer of resemblance. I took a room. I got casual work. I moved around a bit, each time taking with me another small piece of official evidence of my existence, till finally for the last six months, I settled down in one community, became a regular both in my local pub and my local church, played in the darts team, sang in the choir, and all in all established myself as a perfectly acceptable, indeed desirable, member of any community.

At the end of a year and a day, I went back to the Institution. While I knew the period had no official legal function, I felt that its historical standing gave it some weight. It took some time to persuade them I really was who I said I was, and when it finally got through, I really enjoyed seeing their jaws drop.

'Here I am,' I said. 'I've been free for a year and a day, and even under the difficulties of having no official existence, I have not only survived without breaking the law, I have become a useful and well-liked member of the community. Now let me hear how you justify my continued incarceration.'

How naive I was! All you do when you demonstrate to closed minds that they are wrong is to drive them to even greater extremes in their search for self-justification.

Instead of being received like the conquering hero I felt I was, I found myself kept from all contact with fellow inmates and pumped full of drugs till I didn't know what time of day it was, let alone what I'd been up to for the past year!

I begged to see Mr Barnfather and was further devastated

when they told me he had retired from the public service and was now back in private practice in London.

The new man was most unsympathetic, obviously in the pockets of the self-seeking quangoites. There was another meeting of the Board, this one (so the grapevine told me) in the full glare of media publicity.

And the decision?

They were unanimous that my irrational behaviour in first effecting my escape and then returning with my grandiose claims to being a pillar of the community merely confirmed my basic unsoundness of mind. What outlet my violent impulses might have found had not yet become apparent, but I'd had plenty of time, and the kind of woman I attacked was often not readily or quickly missed in society.

My reaction to this decision and also to their drugs kept me in bed for several weeks. As I slowly returned to health I began to see very clearly where I'd gone wrong. I should have used my time outside to gain the confidence and support of the government's political enemies, those who knew as well as I did the hidden agendas which warped so many decisions in public institutions. And I should have worked through the media also, and returned in a spotlight of publicity which would have prevented them dealing with me as they had done. Also it would have got the papers concentrating on my struggle to prove my sanity rather than rehashing with gory details all those old killings that had put me here in the first place.

Above all, once out, I should have offered myself for examination by an independent psychiatrist, far removed from all the pressures of a job within the system.

Gradually hope began to revive in me. What I had done once I could do again. Only this time I would set the rules of the game myself.

It wasn't so easy getting out this time. Once bitten, twice shy, and they were very much on the alert. But I'd learned a thing or two. I faked being in a much more depressed state than I really was. Injections I resisted with all my strength. Of course, they just used more and more force to start with, but eventually I wore them down, and besides, they realized the bruising necessarily involved didn't look so good, and in the end I was taking all medication by mouth. They watched very carefully to make sure I took this, but I was way ahead of them here. What they concentrated on was my mouth, watching me put the pills in and drink the water, then checking to make sure I'd swallowed. But from one of my fellow patients who was diabetic I'd stolen a bottle of sweeteners which in size, colour and shape resembled my tablets, and I'd made myself expert at palming the real pills and substituting these. Also I developed an allergy to light and took to lying in my bed during the day with the sheet pulled over my head.

So it was easy to slip out one afternoon at the change of shifts, leaving a bolster taken from an unoccupied bed under the sheets, help myself to some clothing from the nurses' locker room and make my way out of the building by a door most of those who worked there didn't know the existence of. Ten years of exploration and observation had made me probably the world's leading expert on the topography of that institution.

My idea was to lie low for a while. Even under the delusion of the certain success of my first plan, I had still (superstitiously rather than in belief I'd ever need it) hidden away a fair sum of cash before I gave myself up.

This I now collected, and headed into London where I reckon anyone can drop out of sight into the huge underground world of runaways and derelicts.

Next day I bought a paper and read all about myself. God,

it sounded like Rasputin and Attila the Hun had broken loose together! This was no more than I'd expected, but what did shock and surprise me was an alleged interview with Mr Barnfather, now in private practice in Knightsbridge, and thus, I would have hoped, able to speak frankly. Instead, according to the tabloid, he declared that during all our acquaintance he had never detected what he would call any real remorse, and he doubted whether a man with my powers of self-delusion would ever have been safe to release into the community!

This was so obviously the old party line that I was certain some hack had merely gone through his years-old notes and had a quick chat with Mr Barnfather on the phone in which he tricked him into saying something which could be interpreted as support for this garbage.

I didn't doubt that he would come forward with an indignant denial that he'd ever said these things, but by the time the Press Complaints people dealt with it, nobody would remember what it was all about. If on the other hand I could get to him while he was still angry, perhaps his indignation plus his natural sense of justice would persuade him to accompany me to a press conference and declare his belief in my sanity to the world.

What a coup this would be!

And so I set off to Knightsbridge with my hopes once more soaring high.

Alas, what another huge disappointment awaited me.

I bluffed my way into his consulting room quite easily. His reaction when he realized who I was I put down to natural surprise and I made sure I kept between him and his alarm button until he'd had time to adjust.

It was a wiser move than I realized. At first as I explained the purpose of my visit, he nodded and smiled and said, yes, of course, he'd be only too happy to go along with me and do all he could to persuade the world that I presented no danger to the public at large. But something about his eyes told me a different tale. I put on a vulnerable face and pressed him for reassurance that I was doing the right thing, giving the impression that I would let myself be advised by him. Slowly his manner changed as he felt himself back in control. He talked with the easy sympathy he had shown in the old days, but the message that came across was that the best thing for me was to return to the Institution in his company and once there we could settle down with everyone concerned and sort things out.

Oh, he was smooth, and soothing and convincing, but as I listened I realized the truth I'd been denying for these many years.

It wasn't just the self-interest of the lay members of the Board which had been preventing my release. This man whom I had trusted with sight of my naked soul had been speaking against me at their meetings! I had never had a cat in hell's chance of getting out!

What his agenda had been I didn't stay to ask. All I knew was that here where I had looked for my closest ally I had found my worst enemy.

But not for that did I give up hope. I had been stupid to seek an ally against an unjust system from within the system itself. But just because one of their number was self-seekingly unprofessional didn't mean that all practitioners in the independent sector were tarred with the same brush.

So I set out to find an honest, independent psychiatrist who would assess my case without fear or favour, and that's why I've come knocking on your door.

So what do you say? You've heard my story from start to finish. Do I come across as a maniac, a potential menace to civilized society and totally unfit to be released into the community? Or have you penetrated to the man within, more sinned against than sinning, who has paid his debt and now deserves, not special treatment, but simple natural justice?

To put it bluntly, as it might be put to you by journalists and lawyers, is this man you see before you sane? Answer yes or no.

You nod your head. Vigorously. I am encouraged.

But it is not *at* your head I wish to look, but *into* it.

I mean, through your eyes, the portals of the soul.

Oh, there I read another story.

You can stop nodding, Doctor. I quite understand. Any man in your position, lying on his own consulting couch, with his arms strapped and his mouth taped, would probably nod his head as vigorously as you.

But your eyes give a quite different answer.

Or rather, they ask a quite different question.

To wit, how many psychiatrists have I killed since Mr Barnfather?

You'll be the seventh.

On the First Day of Christmas

The three policemen arrived simultaneously at the hospital, though from different directions. But quick as they were, the press in the shape of the lean and hungry figure of Sammy Ruddlesdin of the *Evening News* was there first.

'Now I know it's Christmas,' he said. 'The Wise Men have arrived!'

'How come you got here so fast, Sammy?' asked Andy Dalziel.

'Here already,' said Ruddlesdin. 'Just another working day. Feelgood stuff from the Maternity Unit in the morning, party round the wards, then down to A&E to wait for post-lunch casualties to be wheeled in.'

'So you met the mother whose kid's gone missing.'

'Katie Pocock. Aye.'

'Anything to tell us?'

'As long as it's two-way traffic. Four Christmas kids, but Katie's was the first, a bouncing boy, at twelve-twenty a.m. So she's due the *News* welcome pack and top billing. Except she doesn't want to know.'

'Probably just hates pushy journalists,' said Dalziel. 'It's a big club.'

'Who knows? But don't forget, Andy, you owe me one.'

'I won't forget. Here's something for starters.'

'Yes?' said Ruddlesdin eagerly.

'I'd lose that red crêpe hat afore you start interviewing grieving relatives.'

The Fat Man strode into the hospital followed by DCI Peter Pascoe and DS Edgar Wield.

They were met in the foyer by a broad-beamed woman who shouldn't have been wearing a pillar-box red trouser suit, and a grey-haired man with the crinkled face and worried expression of a bloodhound who's got a cold in the nose.

'It's Superintendent Dalziel, isn't it?' said the woman, in the clipped authoritative tone of one used to imposing order on chaos. 'Tatiana Bradley, Head of Administration. This is Les Hardy, our security chief.'

'How do, Tat. How do, Les. You were job, weren't you? DS in Manchester?'

Dalziel knew just about everyone, and more about most than their confessors.

'That's right,' said Hardy.

'Then you'll know what's what. What have you done so far?'

'Got my men checking the hospital exits and the car park. But I'm a bit short staffed, it being Christmas Day.'

'Checked your CCTV?'

'Yes. Got a picture of the so-called nurse who took the kid.'

'Good. Pete, you get on to that, will you?'

Peter Pascoe and Les Hardy walked away together.

Ms Bradley said, 'I shouldn't place too much reliance on Hardy.'

'Oh aye? Why's that?'

'He runs a very sloppy ship,' she said grimly. 'His firm's on a three-year contract here. Runs out next month. It won't be renewed.'

'It's a hard world,' said Dalziel. 'You saying that it were sloppy security that's at fault here?'

'That's for you to decide.'

She filled them in as they made their way to the Maternity Unit, bright with decorations. 'Do They Know It's Christmas?' blasting out.

Just before one o'clock, Katie Pocock had been resting in her bed with her son by her side. A nurse came into the ward, said there were some routine procedures they needed to do and took the baby away. At ten to two, Katie's mother had rung. The ward sister had taken the phone to plug in at the bedside.

Katie had asked when she'd be getting her baby back. Sister, who knew no reason why the child had been taken away, said she'd check. She rapidly established no one knew anything about Baby Pocock's whereabouts and alerted Security.

Katie went into hysterics, so much so that she had to be sedated.

'Sedated or not, I'll need to talk to her,' said Dalziel.

'That will be a medical judgement,' said Ms Bradley. 'Sister will be able to tell you more.'

Sister was Sandy Balfour, a young blonde with a face made for merriment. She didn't look merry now. She added little to Ms Bradley's story except Katie Pocock had been moved to a private room. The sedative wasn't all that powerful but she seemed to have gone into a state of shock and was barely responding to questions.

'I'll give her a go,' said Dalziel. 'Wieldy, you do the ward. Tat, I'll likely need to look at the lass's admission and medical records, OK?'

'I'm really not sure . . .'

Dalziel gave her his persuasive smile. It was a bit like the Terminator offering you a choice of sides.

'I'll get them together in my office,' said Ms Bradley.

Sandy Balfour took the Fat Man into the private room. The woman had short black hair and the kind of face grief made even more beautiful.

'Katie,' said the sister. 'This is Detective Superintendent Dalziel.'

'Have you found my baby?'

'Not yet, luv. But we will.'

Normally an assurance from Dalziel would have people buying shares in the Channel Tunnel but Katie's only response was to bury her face in the pillow.

In the ward, Edgar Wield's problem was different. Everyone wanted to talk to him, visitors and inmates alike. He rapidly identified those who'd actually been there when the baby was taken. Not that this produced anything of much use.

'She was just a nurse,' said one visitor helplessly. 'You just see the uniform. Like with policemen.'

The woman in the next bed to Katie's was the only one who came close to a description.

'Tall, thin, long black hair,' she said. 'No, I hadn't seen her around.'

'What about visitors?' asked Wield.

'Not a soul. I think she came in as an emergency. She didn't sound like she was from these parts.'

But she must have told people because her mother rang, thought Wield. Someone would need to tell the older woman before the media got the story out. Preferably not him.

He opened the bedside locker. Katie's handbag was still in there. He took it with him as he left.

*

Peter Pascoe was looking at a fuzzy image of a nurse coming out of the maternity ward, carrying a baby. It was going to require advanced technology to get more out of this than that she was tallish and had long dark hair. And also, it seemed, the ability to vanish.

'Where is she?' he demanded. 'Aren't all the corridors covered?'

'Yes, but this corridor meets another at a T-junction and we've been having bother with the connections there,' said Hardy. 'One of them intermittent faults it's hard to track down. Sometimes the cameras work fine. Today was a bad day. Sod's Law, eh?'

'But we've got pictures from later cameras in both directions and she doesn't reappear. What rooms are there at the junction?'

'A store room to the left. Staff loo to the right.'

'Check them,' ordered Pascoe.

He went through the other footage again as Hardy called up one of his men and gave commands. Finished, the man said, 'Anything interesting?'

'Few possibles. I like this one best.'

He tracked a woman in a long raincoat and a headscarf down corridors to the main foyer. Her head down, it was impossible to get a sense of her face. Tinsel and ribbon trailed from her large carrier bag.

'Why her more than anyone else? Place is full of visitors lugging bagfuls of prezzies around.'

'Yes,' said Pascoe. 'But they don't take them home.'

In the car park now, the woman was moving fast. A car drew up alongside. It was a dark blue Volvo estate with tinted windows; the driver appeared as little more than an outline. The woman opened the rear door, placed her carrier bag carefully on the seat and climbed in after it. The car pulled away.

Pascoe was already on his phone.

'Vehicle check,' he said.

He gave the number. As he waited he said to Hardy, 'Not much point, I suspect. Looked a bit newer than a Y reg to me. Hello? Thank you.'

He switched off. 'That number belonged to a white Ford Transit van scrapped and deregistered last year. This has been carefully planned.'

'So, no good, eh? Tough,' said Hardy sympathetically.

'Never say die,' said Pascoe.

He was on his phone again. He identified himself and said, 'Listen, I want a check on all speed cameras within a radius of, let's say, twenty miles of the Central Hospital. Dark blue Volvo estate is what I'm looking for. Most urgent.'

Hardy said, 'You're really on to it now, aren't you?'

'Maybe. Empty roads on Christmas Day. Very tempting to hit the gas, especially if you're making a getaway with a kidnapped baby.'

Hardy's walkie-talkie squawked. He picked it up and listened.

'Found a nurse's uniform and a black wig stuffed into one of the cisterns in that loo,' he said.

'Good. Get your man out of there, lock the door. I'll get a forensic team in asap.'

His phone rang. Wield directed him to administration. Here he found the sergeant and Dalziel, the former going through a small stack of official forms, the latter looking at the contents of a handbag he'd tipped on to a desk. Quickly he told them what he had done.

'Good,' said the Fat Man. 'Now let's see what we have here apart from enough gunk to paint a house. Passport, name of Katherine Pocock, age twenty-six, born Brighton, next of kin Mrs Janet Pocock, Brighton address. French work permit which if my Frog's any good says she's OK to work as an entertainer at the Paris Iskander . . . what's that then? A nightclub?'

'Hotel,' said Pascoe. 'Expensive. Whole chain of them across Europe. Big one overlooking Hyde Park in London. Pop stars and jet-setters love them. That guy Kosros owns them. The one who keeps getting turned down for UK nationality.'

'The guy who's got cancer, son flew a jet into Mont Blanc in the summer, reckons the Home Secretary must have a heart of stone?'

'That's the one. Does it say what kind of entertainer?'

'No. Permit's due for renewal in January. Nowt else interesting except a business card, embossed, expensive. The Endersby Clinic, Little Mortipole, Cambridgeshire. Wieldy, what you got?'

'Admitted as an emergency day before yesterday. On train heading north for hols when she started, so she got off. First examination showed no cause for immediate concern. Baby born early this morning. Seven pounds two ounces. Mother and child both doing well. Everything perfectly normal, in fact nothing to suggest that, as she claimed, the baby was a couple of weeks premature.'

'Admission record?'

'Bare details. Her GP is given as a Dr Smith, Blue Street Surgery, Wimbledon, London. Next of kin Mrs Joan Smithson, sister, of Doncaster Road, Wimbledon.'

'Smith. Smithson. Not very convincing. But let's not jump to conclusions. Wieldy, you check 'em out. Pete, you can croak Frog, right? You give this Iskander Hotel a call, see what they've got to say. Don't mention you're a cop. I'll ring Mrs Pocock in Brighton to tell her the bad news. Better she hears it from me than on the telly.'

Pascoe wasn't totally persuaded of this but saw no point in arguing. The switchboard at the Paris Iskander put him through to the entertainment manager, who turned out to be an ebullient young woman in the middle of a very jolly luncheon party.

Five minutes later, slightly shell-shocked, he turned from his corner of the office to find the other two just finishing off too.

'What've we got?' asked Dalziel.

'Details she gave are a load of crap. No Blue Street practice, no Dr Smith or Mrs Smithson of Doncaster Road, Wimbledon,' Wield said.

'Right little fibber then. Her ma does live in Brighton, despite which she is a God-fearing woman who hasn't spoken to her daughter since she chose to lead a life of sin as an exotic dancer in gay Paree. She'd no idea Katie was back in the UK and certainly didn't ring her today. Pete.'

'The Paris Iskander as well as being a luxury hotel provides a hot nightclub for well-heeled patrons. Pocock was one of their top dancers. Normally getting yourself banged up would mean a choice between a quick termination of your pregnancy or quick termination of your career.

'Pocock however was, according to the rather tipsy woman I talked to, a doubly lucky girl. Koko Kosros, son and heir of Ekrem Kosros who owns the whole Iskander empire, was almost certainly the father.

'Her second bit of luck according to my girl was that just as Katie was about to have her abortion, Koko flew his executive jet into the Alps.'

'How the hell was that lucky?' demanded Dalziel.

'Ekrem was heartbroken. Only son dead, his own use-by date getting closer, end of the Kosros line. He got wind of Pocock's condition. Suddenly he saw a chance of a grandson . . . what was more, one who'd automatically have what he had never been able to obtain either for himself or Koko: British nationality.'

'Rule Britannia,' said Dalziel. 'Wieldy, you start chasing up this call that didn't come from Katie's mother. Pete, let's you and me go and talk to the lass.'

The woman didn't even raise her head this time. She opened one eye, recognized Dalziel, and closed it again. The Fat Man sat down by the bed and brought his great face to within a few inches of hers.

'You don't know what's best to do, luv. The bastards who took your kid have probably told you your best chance of seeing him again is to keep quiet. They're wrong. I'm your best chance. But I'm pushed for time. I know about you and Koko Kosros. But I need to know more.'

Nothing happened for a moment then slowly that lovely pale face turned to look up at Dalziel at first doubtfully, then assessingly, and finally hopefully.

'What do you want to know?' she whispered.

Dalziel said, 'Let's start at the beginning, first time Ekrem Kosros came to see you after Koko died.'

Katie Pocock began hesitantly but once she got going, it all came spilling out. At first all she'd seen in Ekrem was a man of great charm, grieving for his lost son, eager to offer all the help he could to the woman bearing his grandchild.

He moved her into a suite at the Paris Iskander and for the next few months she lived a life of luxury. When an ultrasound scan showed the child was a boy, Kosros had been ecstatic.

'He was over the top, really,' said Katie. 'That's what started to worry me. I used to chat with Joe Runciman who ran Ekrem's security. Not that I cared much for him but at least he was English, ex-cop I think. I asked Joe how his boss would have felt if the scan had shown I was carrying a girl. Joe just grinned. Then he did this.'

*

The woman raised her right hand and made a gesture as if pulling a lavatory chain.

'Sounds a right charmer,' growled Dalziel. 'Didn't have a Manchester accent, did he? I once knew a Joe Runciman who'd have thought that were funny.'

'He did sound sort of rough north,' said Katie. 'A bit like you. Sorry, but you all sound the same. But Joe did get me thinking that in old Ekrem's eyes, I wasn't much more than an incubator.

'One of the nurses told me he'd even been asking about prenatal paternity tests, and only stopped pressing when told that getting a sample of amniotic fluid could pose a risk to the foetus and didn't guarantee a result anyway. But no one had thought to consult me.

'I even got the impression he'd have preferred to have me somewhere a bit more remote, Turkey maybe, where he'd be able to call all the shots.'

'But he didn't try to move you east, did he?'

'No. I think someone told him that in order to be absolutely certain of my baby's nationality, it would be best for him to be born in England. So instead of heading east, as my time got close, I was moved back here.'

'To the Endersby Clinic?'

'That's right. How do you know?'

'We know a lot, luv. What made you decide to do a runner?'

'I got scared,' she said. 'It was the way Ekrem talked about his plans for his grandson. He had it all worked out, upbringing, education, everything. He'd even chosen his name, like I had no say in anything.'

'But you were in an English clinic, not some faraway country,' objected Pascoe.

She shook her head in irritation and said, 'You weren't there!

The staff at the Endersby danced around old Ekrem like he was some sort of god. That's what real money buys. Not luxuries, but fear. He certainly scared me.

'The more I saw of him the more I thought, this guy can do anything he likes. OK, I was in England but all the people I thought of as my friends were back in Paris.

'The only person I could have rung was my mother, and I knew that as soon as I mentioned I was pregnant, she'd have gone down on her knees to beg forgiveness. Not for me but for herself, for bringing a monster like me into the world!'

'Aye, I've spoken with her,' said Dalziel sympathetically. 'What was it you thought Kosros might do?'

'I don't know. All I knew was that on my back just having given birth, I wasn't going to be in much of a position to argue. I needed to be somewhere he wasn't.

'I decided to run. The clinic was out in the sticks. I shoved a few things into my biggest handbag, watched from my window till I saw a taxi arrive to drop someone, then slipped out, walked down the drive, flagged down the taxi as it headed for the gate and asked to be taken to the nearest mainline station. Turned out to be Peterborough, half an hour's drive away. I got on the first train leaving.

'It was heading north. I thought I'd go all the way up to Scotland but by the time I reached here I wasn't feeling too clever so I got off. I made it to the buffet and asked for a glass of water. They took one look at me in there and called an ambulance.

'When I got here I told them I wasn't due for another couple of weeks so it wouldn't look so odd. I thought I would be safe. But he found me . . . he found me . . . what's going to happen to my baby . . .?'

*

Her control up to now had been amazing. She must have incredible strength of will, thought Pascoe. But suddenly she'd reached a point where it was running out. Her features seemed to lose all shape and elasticity and suddenly she began to sob. Dalziel put his arm around her. 'He'll be fine. You did well, luv.'

Pascoe thought to himself, yes, she did; but she must have left a trail a mile wide.

'The phone call you had, that was from Kosros, was it?'

Katie Pocock took several deep breaths before she could answer.

'It was from a woman. "You mustn't panic, your baby is safe," she said. "Nothing will happen to him. He's going to have a lovely life. And if you're sensible, you'll see him again very soon and be part of it. A baby needs his mother. Just think about what to say when they start asking you questions."

'As she spoke, I was telling myself it was a sick joke and any minute they'd bring him back from the nursery or wherever he'd gone for his tests. When they couldn't find him, I completely lost it.

'In the end they stuck a needle in me. It knocked me out for a bit. But not for long. When I came round, that woman's words kept on going round in my head. If I didn't say anything about Kosros, I'd get to see my baby again soon. But if I did . . . And I've been lying here ever since wondering what's best to do . . . I don't know if this is right, talking to you . . . It is right, isn't it? Isn't it?'

She grasped Dalziel's hand and stared into his face, desperate for reassurance.

'Oh aye. It's right, lass,' said the Fat Man grimly.

There was a discreet tap at the door. Dalziel jerked his head at Pascoe who rose and went out into the corridor where the sergeant and DC Novello were waiting.

Wield said, 'Had Control on. They got a dark blue Volvo estate on a speed camera doing eighty heading out of town north. Must have dumped the false plates. We got a real result on the registration. Woman Nikki Parolle. Manchester address. I've alerted Manchester to send someone round to check it out.'

'You seem pretty confident this is our car, Wieldy. Anything else?'

'The phone call. Pay as you go mobile, no billing address. But when I rang the number, I got a personal answer recording. Woman's voice. "Hi, this is Nikki. Leave a message."'

'Gotcha!' said Pascoe.

The Fat Man came out of the room, talking on his mobile.

'Yes,' they heard him say. 'I know it's Christmas Day, but I'd really appreciate it. Really. Thanks, mate.'

He switched off and said, 'Right, update.'

Wield filled him in. His phone rang as he finished. He answered, listened, said, 'Hang on.'

To Dalziel he said, 'Manchester. No sign of life at Parolle's flat. A neighbour said she saw her driving off in the Volvo on Christmas Eve.'

'Who are you talking to?' asked Dalziel.

'DCI called Broadstairs.'

'Bomber Broadstairs? Give it here!'

He snatched the phone from the sergeant's hand and walked away with it down the corridor. His usually booming voice dropped to an inaudible murmur. From the other end of the corridor Les Hardy approached.

'Any luck with Katie Pocock?' he asked anxiously.

Pascoe shrugged.

'Nothing much,' he said.

*

You didn't share info with civilians; Hardy might be an ex-cop but he was a civilian now. His wisdom was confirmed as the Fat Man rejoined them.

'Les, owt new? No? Us neither. That poor lass is out of it. Shock. Not to worry. Looks simple enough to me. It'll be the usual, some poor cow who can't have kids of her own finally snapping and deciding to help herself.

'I've just been on the phone to Social Services. They're digging through their files for possibles to cross-check with ours. We'd best get back to the station to take a look.'

'Hope you're right,' said Hardy, looking slightly happier. 'There's a few more reporters out there now. Word's getting round.'

'Not surprising. Do me a favour, Les. I'd like to get a bit further forward before I talk to them. Why don't you fetch them in out of the cold, give 'em a glass of punch, tell them the bare outlines? It's your patch after all. Could do yourself a bit of good.'

'Sure, if that's what you want,' said Hardy.

Dalziel watched the security chief out of sight and then turned to DC Novello.

'Ivor,' he said. 'Listen in. You will be in charge here. Stay by Pocock's bed. She talks to no one except you, right?'

She said, 'Not even Mr Hardy?'

Dalziel sighed deeply. 'Into what bit of "no one" would Les Hardy fit? Anyone tries to see her, tell 'em she's sleeping. Anyone insists, arrest them. In fact, now I think of it, if you haven't heard from me in an hour, arrest Hardy anyway.'

It boded well for Novello's future that she showed not the slightest surprise.

'Yes, sir. Any particular charge?'

'Obstructing the police for starters. With a bit of luck we'll have it up to conspiracy to kidnap afore we're done. Right, Kingfisher Patrol. Let's get out of here.'

Andy Dalziel led his puzzled subordinates down a flight of stairs and through a door marked EMERGENCY EXIT ONLY, which brought them out in a corner of the staff car park from which they could see a small crowd of reporters following Hardy through the main doors of the hospital.

Then he strode toward his car, a station wagon so grimy even the snow seemed reluctant to touch it.

'In you get,' he barked at DCI Peter Pascoe. 'You drive.'

A dozen objections crowded Pascoe's mind, the main one being that given a choice between riding in the Fat Man's car and on a municipal dustcart, a sensitive man would need time to think.

But DS Edgar Wield was already sliding into the back, pushing aside a strew of maps and newspapers and used takeaway packs and God knows what else to make room. At least the driver's seat was comparatively hygienic.

'To the station, is it, sir?' said Pascoe starting the engine, which happily did not sound as neglected as the rest of the vehicle.

'Why the hell would I want to go there on my day off?' said Dalziel. 'Head north, young man. Lower Greendale, that's where we're going. We've got a date with Ms Nikki Parolle and you should never keep a lady waiting!'

Pascoe and Wield exchanged glances but said nothing. They both knew from long experience that when the Fat Man was in his Magical Mr Mistoffelees mood, the best road to explanation was silence.

And as the car moved through the quiet streets and out on to the open road, heading north, the old magician began to speak.

'It were funny how Manchester kept coming up. Les Hardy, Nikki Parolle and Kosros's security man, Joe Runciman. The

Runciman I knew were a hard bugger, DCI in Greater Manchester. Left about six years ago, started his own security company, I heard, but that was all I heard. Bomber Broadstairs filled me in. You don't want to hear why he were called Bomber?'

Their silence answered. 'Suit yourselves,' he said. 'Yes, Bomber told me, it was our Joe who was working for Kosros now. Seems his company did some work for the guy and he were so impressed he made Runciman an offer he couldn't refuse. Only for Joe, not his company.

'Joe jumped at it, leaving his company in the tender care of his second in command. You've guessed. Ex-Detective Sergeant Les Hardy!'

'Who just happens to be in charge of security at the hospital Katie Pocock ends up in?' said Pascoe incredulously.

'Aye. It's called coincidence, lad. Sometimes it works for the bad guys. Sometimes it works for us. Any road, from the sound of it, getting the Mid-Yorkshire Health Trust security contract was the last thing Joe negotiated before he joined Kosros. I'd guess the company's gone into a nosedive since Hardy took over. He's a natural second banana, useless in the top job. Worked with a lot of those in my time.'

He paused to see if the provocation took, then went on. 'But I prefer men I can trust to take over if I get shot down. Hardy was ripe to be used. He needs money and he was used to taking orders from Runciman. He probably supplied the nurse's uniform and fixed the security cameras.'

'Runciman had to work quick,' said Wield almost admiringly. 'He must have had less than twenty-four hours to set this up once he tracked Katie down.'

'Always quick on his feet was Joe,' said Dalziel. 'And he had another old friend handily placed to be called on.'

'Nikki Parolle.'

'Aye. I never met the lass – but I recall if you rang Manchester and Runciman wasn't available, someone like Bomber might say, "Likely he's out on Parolle," with a dirty laugh.

'I asked about her once. Started as a tom, worked her way to being a madam, eventually went upmarket into the escort business which was just about legitimate, specially with Joe to cover her back. They were close, looks like they still are, and in any case with Kosros bankrolling this operation, there'd be plenty of incentive for Nikki to take herself a little Christmas present.'

'Kosros must be crazy to think he could get away with it,' said Pascoe.

Daziel replied, 'Everything I ever read suggests that crazy is exactly what he is. Nothing to lose. He's dying of cancer. When his lad died, he seems to have gone crazier.

'He wants his grandson. Thought he'd got it all tied up, then Katie decides different. All right, he could try persuasion to get her back on board or bribery – but by running she's shown she's not likely to give in to that.

'Legally he's nowhere. Grandparents have precious few rights, and in any case he thinks the British establishment is out to get him. So, grab the kid, get him out of the country, deny any knowledge, and see how things go from there.'

Pascoe pondered these matters for a while then said, 'If that's what you think, sir, shouldn't we be checking airports and ferry services rather than heading out into rural Yorkshire which, incidentally, I believe is covered with snow?'

'Aye. A white Christmas. Nice,' said the Fat Man.

'So why are we doing it?' demanded Pascoe.

'Because Nikki's Volvo was heading north, not west to Manchester or south to Heathrow or east to Hull,' said Dalziel. 'And Bomber Broadstairs told me he'd heard Nikki had a hideaway across the Pennines in Lower Greendale which is on our patch.'

'So we're going there in the hope that's where she's taken the kid?' said Pascoe. 'Fair enough, though I don't see why it's taking three of us.'

'You to drive, me to direct, Wieldy to navigate. There's a two-and-half-inch OS back there, Wieldy.' There was a scrabbling noise behind them then the sergeant said, 'Got it. What's the address?'

'No address. Not yet,' said Dalziel. 'Bomber's going to try to dig it up for me.'

'And if he can't?' cried Pascoe. 'Greendale's a maze of unmarked roads and lanes, all of which will probably be filled with snow.'

'Nay, lad. It's Christmas. Likely God will send a sign.'

They drove on. They were getting into the snow-affected region now. The Council (bless them) had had the main roads cleared and gritted despite the fact that it was Christmas Day.

When they turned into the narrow B-road that wound up Greendale, however, they found the clearance had been minimal and they were following a narrow trackway barely wider than the car between banks of snow piled up against the hedgerows.

Dalziel's phone rang. He listened, said, 'Thanks, Bomber,' and disconnected. 'House is called the Stables. Fitting that. Newborn kid. Christmas. And I bet all Kosros's hotels are packed full!'

'Sir,' said Wield. 'I'll need more details than just the house name.'

'Sorry, lad. That's the best Bomber could do.'

'So what do we do?' demanded Pascoe.

'Keep driving, not too fast but.'

His phone rang again.

He answered it, listened, smiled broadly and said, 'I owe you!'

'Was that Broadstairs? Has he got directions?' demanded Pascoe.

'No, it weren't Bomber,' said Dalziel. 'It were God, and He's sending us a sign. Wieldy, you got us placed on the map?'

'Think so, sir.'

'Grand,' said Dalziel. 'So let's take a look, shall we?'

And to Pascoe's horrified amazement, he reached up, dragged open the sunshine roof and stood upright so that his head was out of the car and his shoulders wedged in the gap.

'Sir!' he cried, braking hard. 'What the hell are you doing? You'll get yourself killed.'

Dalziel's voice, slightly muffled but still loud enough to resonate, replied. '*And when they saw the star, they rejoiced with exceeding great joy!* And there it is. Pete, get this thing moving. Wieldy, we need a left, soon as you can.'

Sometimes, in fact rather frequent times if you worked for Andy Dalziel, there is nothing to do but obey.

Pascoe drove as Dalziel shouted directions which Wield translated into a route – but the going was rough now with the engine revving madly and the tyres fighting for grip on the snow-covered surfaces of these narrow roads and lanes.

From time to time through the windscreen he actually caught a glimpse of this moving star in the sky which his crazy leader was following. Did that make him crazy too? He didn't know, but when the Fat Man between instructions began to chant 'We Three Kings of Orient Are', he found himself joining in.

Finally the inevitable happened and the car spluttered and spun to a halt. But it didn't matter, for when he managed to force his way out of his door he saw the guiding star had stopped too – or rather they'd both stopped for there were two of them, one white, one red. And now a great column of light poured out beneath them, illuminating a long low house.

'*And lo, the star went before them till it came and stood over where the young child was,*' said Dalziel. 'Wieldy. Give us a pull, will you. I think I'm stuck.'

By the time the Fat Man and Wield joined Pascoe in the lane, he'd worked it out. 'It's Kosros's helicopter, right? You knew it was coming up here.'

'Lucky guess,' said the Fat Man airily. He had no problem ascribing to luck what he knew everyone else would put down to natural genius.

'I got a mate in the Smoke to check that he was at that fancy hotel of his down there. I thought he'd likely keep well out of the way till he heard everything had gone according to plan. Then soon as he got the thumbs-up, he'd be in his chopper and on his way to pick up the sprog and head off to foreign parts. That last call confirmed he was in the air. Come on, don't hang around.'

The helicopter was slowly descending. Landing at night on unknown terrain even with your own lights blazing and someone on the ground waving a torch can't be easy, thought Pascoe. There must be some huge Christmas bonuses on offer here, for the pilot, for Runciman, for Parolle, to get them involved with such a crazy plan.

Dalziel was taking the direct route, through a hedge and across a snow-covered field. The other two followed in his wake, like infantrymen advancing behind a tank. Without the Fat Man blazing the trail, it would have taken them twice as long, thought Pascoe. Even so, the chopper was on the ground and the passengers hurrying into the house before they clambered over a small wall and got onto a driveway. The pilot stayed in the machine with the main rotor lazily swishing around and the small tail rotor idling also.

'Don't think they're planning to hang about,' said Pascoe.

*

Andy Dalziel advanced on the cottage, closely followed by DCI Peter Pascoe and DS Edgar Wield. What the helicopter pilot must have thought as they passed before his gaze, Pascoe could only imagine. The Abominable Snowman and family come to pay a call? Or some late carol singers come a-wassailing?

The Fat Man gave the pilot a cheery wave then walked up to the front door of the long, grey house which to Pascoe looked like it had been converted from the stables that gave the place its name.

The door was open. Dalziel walked in, through a narrow hallway and into a brightly lit room with a huge fire blazing on the hearth. There were four adults in there, two men, two women. The older man had to be Kosros, though this emaciated, hollow-cheeked little man showed all the hallmarks of a man stricken by cancer and bore scant resemblance to the photograph of the confident entre-preneur which usually accompanied articles in the financial pages.

In his arms he cradled a baby.

'God bless the house,' said Dalziel. 'And a merry Christmas to you all. Joe Runciman, long time no see.'

The other man, a lanky, fit-looking forty-year-old, showed no surprise at the sight of the new arrivals. 'Andy Dalziel, by God! You look perished. Take your coat off, have a Scotch, get your-self warm.

'Nikki, this is my old mucker, Detective Superintendent Dalziel. Andy, meet Nikki. This is her pad where she's been good enough to entertain us all this Christmas.'

Parolle was also fortyish, a slim tall woman with short blonde hair. She looked slightly rumpled now but with a bit of work could probably pass for at least ten years younger. She nodded indifferently.

'And this is my boss, Ekrem Kosros, who's just arrived this minute with his partner, Jehane, and their new baby.'

He was good and quick, thought Pascoe. He'd given them all their story, which would hardly hold water but might buy them a little time if they stuck to it.

The second woman, Jehane, was in her twenties, olive-skinned and wearing a high-fashion version of a burnous. A nurse, he guessed. Or even a doctor. Ekrem might be willing to put himself at risk, but he was taking no chances with his grandson. Her blank expression gave no hint of how far she would be willing to pursue this charade.

But in the end it was the man himself who proved unready to try to bluff it out. He must have known there was very little mileage in it. Whereas, even now, if he could only get himself out of British airspace . . .

Kosros ran. Despite his debilitated condition, he displayed a power of acceleration worthy of an international fly-half, slipping through the narrow gap between Pascoe and Wield without either of them laying a hand on him.

They set off in pursuit, Pascoe slightly to the fore, reminding himself that a flying tackle from behind wasn't an option, not when your opponent was carrying a newborn baby. The helicopter pilot had the door open and was shouting encouragement.

Except it didn't sound like encouragement . . . More like a warning . . .

But Kosros didn't hear it. Or if he heard it, he didn't understand it.

Then suddenly he came to a halt as if he'd run into an invisible wall.

What in fact he'd run into was the almost invisible tail propeller.

Pascoe and Wield, only a few feet behind, both acted instinctively, flinging themselves forward, arms outstretched, eyes fixed on a small object tumbling through the air.

Both ended up full length in the snow. Both rolled over and lay on their backs, triumphantly holding up their catches.

Pascoe's kicked and yelled in its cocoon of blankets. Wield's kept very quiet, which was more than the sergeant did when he realized what his athletic leap had plucked out of the air.

Andy Dalziel looked down at him and said, 'Like I always say, Wieldy, two heads are better than one.'

Baby Pocock was unharmed by his ordeal. The woman, Jehane, who turned out to be Kosros's personal nurse, checked him out first and her assessment was confirmed by the paramedics who arrived simultaneously with the police backup.

An hour later, the conspirators were on their way to the cells to await interrogation, Ekrem Kosros was on his way to the morgue, and the baby was on his way back to his mother at the hospital.

The three wise men of Mid-Yorkshire sat in the Stables, drinking Nikki Parolle's whisky. On another occasion Pascoe might have questioned the ethics of this but tonight he raised no objection. Wield looked ready to empty a whole bottle by himself.

'Poor bastard,' said Dalziel.

'Kosros? Yes, it's sad, but the guy brought it on himself,' said Pascoe. 'At least if he made it to paradise, he'll have the satisfaction of knowing he's got a descendant with an indisputable claim to a British passport.'

'Doubt it,' said Dalziel.

'Why? Born in Yorkshire, English mother, how can there be a problem?'

'None for the baby. But if this paradise exists, what Kosros will know now is that when he died, the Kosros line died with him.'

It took Pascoe several sips at his whisky to work it out.

271

'You're saying Koko wasn't the father? And Katie knew this? Of course. That was the real reason she did a runner. She didn't want to be around after the birth when Kosros had the DNA tests done!'

'Aye, you're partway there, lad,' said the Fat Man complacently. 'But life's usually more complicated, and a lot murkier than in thy philosophy, Horace.'

Oh God. Hamlet dressed as Falstaff, thought Pascoe looking at the gross, unbuttoned figure lounging before him with half a pint of single malt at his blubbery lips. 'Enlighten me,' he said.

'Katie gets pregnant. Who's the dad? Not Koko, that's for sure. The guy had been screwing his way round the world ever since his teens, and despite the fact that he was set to inherit billions, there's never been a sniff of a paternity suit. I reckon he were probably firing blanks. Katie is set for a termination but she checks it out with the likely father first. Why? 'Cos she's a bit scared of him.'

'Joe Runciman,' said Wield.

'Back with us, are you?' said Dalziel. 'Well done, lad. Yes, I think Joe had been dipping his wick there too. Now I don't think Joe's the sentimental type and I'd guess he gave Katie the nod to go ahead with the termination, but then Koko got his termination in first. And suddenly Joe had this brilliant idea.'

'Let Kosros think his son had got Katie pregnant,' said Pascoe.

'Got it! The old boy was sick, knew he hadn't many years left, so he was desperate to believe the story. But he wasn't a fool. He got talked out of insisting on a paternity test on the unborn child, but the minute Katie dropped the nipper in the private clinic, he'd have had his own paid-up specialists on the spot to do the tests. Joe knew this.'

'So it was his idea for Katie to do a runner to the NHS hospital,' said Wield.

'Right. But he went further. He knew that she'd be missed very quickly. And he knew that Kosros, with his resources, would track her down in no time flat. He had to keep control of the game.'

'So it wasn't a coincidence that she ended up at the Mid-Yorkshire Central,' said Pascoe.

'Coincidence is rubbish,' said Dalziel. 'I could smell it a mile off. No, Joe's a long-term player. What he could see at the end of all this was him, through Katie and their kid, having control of the Kosros billions. All he had to do was put the old man in a position where he acknowledged publicly that Baby Pocock was his flesh and blood. Where better than in the dock at the Assizes?'

'You mean Runciman set up the whole thing with a view to being caught?' said Wield.

'That's it!' cried the Fat Man with delight. 'He had to leave a trail that we could follow but not leave it so obvious we'd be suspicious. Katie had to make sure she mentioned Joe's name and the fact that he'd been a cop. Les Hardy was the head of hospital security and Joe knew that he was so useless that he reckoned he could probably rely on Les to draw suspicion anyway. Then using Parolle's own car – Joe would never have done that. And letting her ring Katie from her own mobile.'

'But it might have taken us longer than it did,' said Pascoe.

'With the three wisest heads in Mid-Yorkshire on the case? No chance! But even if they had got the kid away, I'm sure Joe had a contingency plan which was even better.'

'Wouldn't take much to be better – one in which they all get caught and go to jail,' said Pascoe.

'Mebbe, mebbe not. I can just see Katie getting a sudden fit of family feeling. This is her child's poor old dying granddad who's done all this, just for love. It was wrong, yes, but she can't give evidence against him. Judge in tears, jury box flooded, learned counsel blowing their noses on their wigs, producers fighting for the film rights.

'Pete, lad, your trouble is you lack the common touch. Just 'cos you're not greedy or gullible yourself, you can't imagine just how greedy and gullible other folk can be.'

'I'll take that as a compliment, shall I?' said Pascoe.

'Take it any way you like. Anyone like a top-up? Nice drop of malt this, shame to waste it.'

The other two both shook their heads. Dalziel replenished his glass.

'Just as a matter of interest, sir,' said Pascoe. 'Can you prove any of this?'

'Not a jot, unless someone talks,' said Dalziel.

'So Runciman's plan can still work?'

'Could do. Bothers you, does it?'

'Of course it bothers me to think of all that money going to someone who's got no right to it.'

'And who has got a right to it, Pete?' asked the Fat Man. 'It's only filthy lucre, which usually ends up in the right place. With the lawyers. When it comes to sorting out Kosros's estate, they'll all be demanding DNA tests all round before they let a farthing go in Baby Pocock's direction.

'So, unless Joe fixes it, your justice will be done. We'll never know if that'll make things better or worse.

'Just think, if they'd had DNA testing a couple of thousand years ago, where might we be now?'

They thought. Then Pascoe said, 'Think I'll change my mind and have that top-up after all.'

Wield held out his glass too. The Fat Man filled them then raised his own glass. 'To the kid,' he said. 'He's the only innocent one in all this. Didn't them three Maggies bring him presents?'

'Magi,' corrected Pascoe, he suspected unnecessarily. 'Gold, and frankincense, and myrrh.'

'Kosros had gold, lots of it, and a lot of good it did him,' said Dalziel. 'Them other things, they're some kind of perfume, are they?'

'I think so,' said Pascoe.

'Bit like getting a bottle of aftershave in your stocking. I hate that,' said the Fat Man. 'No, I think we need an update. Prezzies for the twenty-first century. Wieldy?'

The sergeant thought, then said, 'Peace. And tolerance. That's what I'd give him.'

'Oh aye. Pete?'

'Courage. He'll need it.'

'Jesus! I can see that Christmas morning must be a bundle of fun at your houses!'

'All right, Andy, what about you?' demanded Pascoe.

The Fat Man smiled and raised his glass. 'A big box of Smarties for now and a lifelong ticket to a hospitality box at Twickenham for when he gets older. Here's to Baby Pocock!'

'Baby Pocock!' they echoed.

And drank.

Bibliography

'A Candle for Christmas'. First published: *Ellery Queen's Mystery Magazine* (January 2000)

'A Shameful Eating'. First published: *A Suit of Diamonds* (Collins, 1990)

'Brother's Keeper'. First published: *Brother's Keeper and Other Stories* (Eurographica, 1992)

'Silent Night'. *Hayakawa's Mystery Magazine* (January 1987)

'The Boy and Man Booker'. First published: *Men From Boys* (Random House, 2003)

'The Italian Sherlock Holmes'. First published: *Holmes for the Holidays* (Berkley Prime Crime, 1996)

'The Game of Dog'. First published: *Mysterious Pleasures* (Little, Brown, 2003)

'The Man Who Defenestrated His Sister'. First published: *The Man Who . . .* (Macmillan, 1992)

'Urban Legend'. First published: *Ellery Queen's Mystery Magazine* (March 1989)

'Where are All the Naughty People?'. First published: *Original Sins* (Severn House, 2010)

'The Difference'. Previously unpublished. First broadcast: *BBC Radio 4* (*Red Herrings*, episode 2, 29 April 2009)

'On the Psychiatrist's Couch'. First published: *Whydunit? Perfectly Criminal II* (Severn House, 1997)

'On the First Day of Christmas'. First published as 'The Strange Case of the Mum on the Run, the Hotel Tycoon and the Evil Plot to Steal a Baby', *Daily Express* (24, 27 and 28 December 2004)

Acknowledgements

HarperCollins would like to thank the Reginald Hill Estate for partnering with us to create this second volume of short stories by Reginald Hill, and Mick Herron for his insightful foreword. We would also like to thank Tony Medawar for selecting and compiling these short stories from their original sources. Thank you, to Mary Chamberlain for copyediting the collection, Charlotte Webb for proofreading it, and Ellie Game for the cover design. More thanks go to John Cooper, Shunichiro 'Suigan' Futono, Shunta Kakuyama and Alexander Zapryagaevm, and staff of the Howard Gotlieb Archival Research Center of Boston University. Finally, we would also like to thank Becky Percival from United Agents for working closely with us on this collection.

FOREWORD BY VAL McDERMID

Reginald Hill

DALZIEL *and* PASCOE
Hunt the CHRISTMAS
KILLER
& Other Stories

A vicar nailed to a tree in Yorkshire.
The theft of a priceless artefact during a fire.
A detective forced to tell the truth for 24 hours.
A body hidden in a basement.

From the restless streets of London to the wilds of
the Lake District, displaying all his trademark humour,
playfulness and clever plotting, this landmark collection
brings together the very best of Reginald Hill's short
stories for the first time, complete with a foreword
from Val McDermid.